L
wind
to the visions of midnight . . .

A severed arm tucked in a sinister workman's toolbox.

A spiderlike monster weaving a blood-drenched web of human prey.

A leather-clad Hollywood legend rising from the grave.

A vile earthbound spirit driven by a hungering evil.

Night Visions: Dead Image

A visionary collection too horrifying to miss.

Books & Things
132 W. Cedar Ave.
Gladwin, MI 48624
517-426-7732

Coming soon: Clive Barker, Ramsey Campbell, Dean R. Koontz, Robert McCammon, and Stephen King.

Edited by: Clive Barker, George R. R. Martin, Alan Ryan, and Douglas E. Winter.

Lock the door, bolt the
windows, and open your mind
to the visions of midnight...

◄NIGHT VISIONS►
DEAD IMAGE

ALL ORIGINAL STORIES BY
DAVID MORRELL
JOSEPH PAYNE BRENNAN
KARL EDWARD WAGNER

Edited by Charles L. Grant

Originally published as <u>NightVisions 2</u>

BERKLEY BOOKS, NEW YORK

This Berkley book contains the
text of the original hardcover edition.
It has been completely reset in a typeface
designed for easy reading and was printed
from new film.

NIGHT VISIONS: DEAD IMAGE

A Berkley Book/published by arrangement with
the author

PRINTING HISTORY
Dark Harvest edition published 1985
Berkley edition/September 1987

All rights reserved.
Dead Image Copyright © 1985 by Charles L. Grant.
Introduction Copyright © 1985 by Charles L. Grant.

"Black and White and Red All Over" Copyright © 1985
by David Morrell.
"Mumbo Jumbo" Copyright © 1985 by David Morrell.
"Dead Image" Copyright © 1985 by David Morrell.

"Wanderson's Waste" Copyright © 1985 by Joseph Payne Brennan.
"Pick-Up" Copyright © 1985 by Joseph Payne Brennan.
"Canavan Calling" Copyright © 1985 by Joseph Payne Brennan.
"Oasis of Abomination" Copyright © 1985 by Joseph Payne Brennan.
"Starlock Street" Copyright © 1985 by Joseph Payne Brennan.
"The Haunting at Juniper Hill" Copyright © 1985 by
Joseph Payne Brennan.

"Shrapnel" Copyright © 1985 by Karl Edward Wagner.
"Old Loves" Copyright © 1985 by Karl Edward Wagner.
"Blue Lady, Come Back" Copyright © 1985 by Karl Edward Wagner.

This book may not be reproduced in whole or in part,
by mimeograph or any other means, without permission.
For information address: The Berkley Publishing Group,
200 Madison Avenue, New York, New York 10016.

ISBN: 0-425-10182-7

Berkley Books are published by The Berkley Publishing Group,
200 Madison Avenue, New York, New York 10016.
The name "BERKLEY" and the "B" logo
are trademarks belonging to the Berkley Publishing Corporation.

PRINTED IN THE UNITED STATES OF AMERICA

10 9 8 7 6 5 4 3 2 1

The publishers would like to express their gratitude to the following people. Thank you: Paul Talwane, Dawn M. Austin, Stan Gurnick, Luis Trevino, Jesse Arias, Gregory Manchess, George R. R. Martin, Lisa Tuttle, Ramsey Campbell, and Clive Barker.

And, of course, special thanks go to the five most important people to this book. Without them it would not exist. David Morrell, Joseph Payne Brennan, Karl Edward Wagner, Charles L. Grant and Robert W. Lavoie.

CHARLES L. GRANT

DAVID MORRELL

JOSEPH PAYNE BRENNAN

KARL EDWARD WAGNER

Introduction

THE SOUND OF horror is not always a scream.

In a room dark or light, whether you're alone or not, it's the whispering in the corner where no one is waiting, a whispering so faint you can't make out the words, or even be sure they're words at all; it's a walk down the sidewalk or the crossing of a street and hearing the warning shriek of brakes building right behind you; it's standing in front of a mirror and seeing, just for an instant, a reflection next to yours, hearing the creak of a shoe, and turning to realize you're the only one in the room; it's listening to someone tell you a loved one is dead; it's the wind in the eaves, and the rush of dead leaves scratching across the tarmac, and a heel on tile in a long empty hall, and a door slamming shut in a building long deserted; the whistle of steam from a radiator at night, the bark of a dog, the howl of a cat, and all the unidentifiable sounds that hover overhead, just beyond the reach of the light, the reach of the moon, in the places where the sun should be shining, and isn't.

The sound of horror is not always a scream.

It's a voice, more than anything, of an author who takes

what you thought was perfectly safe and twists it into something you know isn't safe at all.

Yet it isn't the voice of a single story, a lone novel; it's the accumulation of styles and characters, and plot lines and endings that rise above the individual work to claim it as an author's own.

The voices, for example, of David Morrell.

In 1971, Morrell began with "The Dripping", in *Ellery Queen's Mystery Magazine*, an unpleasantly chilling piece of contemporary horror that was, in many ways, the forerunner not only of **First Blood,** but also of **The Totem.** The former, the hit film notwithstanding, is not an action book aimed at those hungry for bloodletting and speed, but the story of one man's descent into horror and another who is forced to follow him there, creating his own horrors as he goes, discovering things that, as the old films are wont to say, are best left to the machinations of God; the latter is direct dark fantasy, with none of the trappings of the conventional and more shadows than one would ever want to meet.

With a writing style not ornate but somewhat lean, Morrell generally looks to people and what makes them mad (in both senses) to explore what's dark about those parts of us we usually claim we've exorcised in our years of growing up. An odd occupation for a man who is, when you meet him, rather unassuming. He is, in fact, like Joseph Payne Brennan—the clichéd horror writer; he looks like he wouldn't even think of tearing the wing off a fly or maiming your mother or axing your spouse. He teaches English at the University of Iowa, in Iowa City, laughs quite a lot and gets red-faced when he does, and when he's tired you can hear a trace of his Canadian accent.

On the other hand, he does have his quirks.

One evening in his room, at the World Fantasy Convention out in Chicago, he spent more than an hour describing what he called the Ford, Chevy, and Cadillac of garrotes, complete with demonstrations as to their effectiveness, and the only effective means of counteracting the slipping of one of them over your head and around your neck (the results can be seen in his best-selling **Brotherhood of the Rose**). He also interrupted himself to explain how you can tell if your room is electronically bugged.

In Ottawa, in 1984, he took a liking to my wife's dinner one evening and proceeded to clean her plate—after he had taken care of his own meal. He did it again at breakfast.

In order to bring a certain degree of realism to **First Blood,** he took a survival course, to learn what it was like to have to live off the land and not get yourself killed in the process. But it just wasn't the mechanics of survival he was after, it was also, and more importantly, the emotional and psychological stresses and horrors that come with such deprivation.

His voice, then, is unlike any other you're likely to meet, and made clear here in the stories he's done for this volume. A young boy, a high school student, a grown man—Morrell in three voices which begin with the commonplace and shade into dark fantasy.

And dark fantasy is where you'll hear Joseph Payne Brennan.

Brennan began his career in the early '40s, writing poetry; a few years later he began doing westerns for the pulps. In short order, he expanded into fantasy of all types, with the creation of Kerza (for those who liked the touch of so-called sword-and-sorcery), and Lucius Leffing (who, while a private investigator unearthing more than his share of supernatural problems, doesn't look at all like Sherlock Holmes). It wasn't long before his was the work against which others were measured, and his career has

been of such length—and shows, thank heavens, no signs
of stopping—that it can be rightly said he has created more
than one classic in the field.

In a time when stories and novels are picking up the
tendency to sound more like television shows and music
videos—snappy, a punch line every five seconds, and a
break for commercials because the audience has an attention span shorter than a young boy's—Brennan continues
to refine the traditional voice he began with forty years
ago. Not old-fashioned; that implies a reluctance to change,
a deathless wedding to the archaic. Traditional—the use of
form, and language, and an exploration of fears we thought
we had left behind when our childhood nightmares ended.

The first time I met Joseph Payne Brennan was at Roger
Williams College, in Rhode Island, and after the first
introduction, I didn't have the nerve to speak to him again
until almost a year later. What do you say to someone like
that—"Gee, Mr. Brennan, I sure do like your stuff."? I
blather enough without having to blather to someone I've
admired for years. But eventually we did talk and, as
Morrell is nothing like Rambo, Brennan is nothing like
Leffing, certainly not like Kerza, nor even like Canavan
prowling his backyard. He's a librarian at Yale, and self-
effacing, and definitely not the sort of man who writes
about creatures that enjoy the occasional dismemberment
for fun.

As co-Guest of Honor at the World Fantasy Convention
in New Haven, he received the special convention award
for his life's work and devotion to fantasy. He couldn't
believe it. We, however, could, and could only say, "It's
about time."

The voices here, then, are typically and uniquely his—
from Lucius Leffing, to Kerza, to a special sequel to

"Canavan's Back Yard." Quiet voices, with sometimes more than a hint of delicious thunder.

And thunder, I suppose, is what you'll think of when you first meet Karl Edward Wagner.

By now, it's a tired description—"he looks like a Viking having a holiday in Carolina". Maybe he does. But he's not as big as he looks—he gives the illusion of size, carries the illusion of intimidation, but to hear him speak is to hear a quiet man who tends to consider his words before they're out, who knows the field, and who cares about it and the writers who are trying to make their marks before they're smothered by the competition.

He is the creator of Kane, my favorite barbarian because he is a barbarian and not a Lancelot (or worse, Gawain) in furs; and he is the author of not enough short fiction for any of his fans' tastes. He does not write fast. He does not, on the other hand, write slowly either. He writes deliberately. There are few who care about the language as much as Wagner does, fewer still who care, or even realize, that dark fantasy must deal first with people, and only then with whatever fantastic element is to be included in the piece. "Sticks", "In the Pines", and "The River of Night's Dreaming" are my personal favorites and, if anyone is so inclined, can be found in his recent collection **In A Lonely Place**. There is thunder, to be sure, and there is also a delicacy of touch and genuine emotion that is particularly, and specially, his.

He is now a full-time writer. He is also a psychiatrist, a connoisseur of sippin' whiskey (not to be confused with a shot of scotch or a gulp of bourbon), and a man when I last spoke with him about to face his first word processor. Morrell uses one; Brennan uses an Adler (and no prizes for those who remember what that thing looks like); Wagner will take the technology offered, and

I'm willing to bet he'll write no faster. In fact, as his wife, Barbara, puts his work on disks, he intends to continue with his current project—in longhand. It's frustrating—to have more of his work to read is something I want quite a lot; but if having more means having less, I'd just as soon he did it with a quill pen, and ink made from roots in his garden.

Wagner's voice is a combination of both Morrell and Brennan—the contemporary and the traditional, not to be confused with either but a fusion which few, if any, have been able to achieve.

And these three voices, then, make up **Dead Image**.

All the sounds of horror.

Including the screams.

Charles L. Grant
Newton, NJ 1985

DAVID
MORRELL

Black and White and Red All Over

YOU PROBABLY READ about me in the paper this morning. Fact is, if you live near the corner of Benton and Sunset, I'm the kid who normally delivers it to you. 'Course I couldn't bring it to you today, being in the hospital and all with my arm busted and my skull what the doctor says is fractured. My Dad took over for me. To tell the truth, I kinda miss doing the route. I've been delivering three years now, since I was nine, and it gets to be a habit, even if I do have to wake up at five-thirty, Christmas and New Year's and every day. But if you think I slept in this morning, you're wrong. The nurses wake you up early here just the same as if my Mom was nudging me to crawl out of bed and make sure I put on my longjohns before I take the papers 'cause its awful cold these snowy mornings. You have to walk the route instead of riding your bike, and that takes a half hour longer, especially with the sky staying dark so long, and sometimes you can't see the numbers on the houses when you're looking for where a new customer lives.

The way this works, the *Gazette* has this guy in a truck

come along and drop a bundle in front of my house, and my Dad goes out to get the bundle and fold the papers in my sack while I get dressed. A lot of times, there'll be this card with the name of a new customer or else the name of a customer who doesn't want the paper anymore, and then my Mom and I'll have to add or subtract the name from my list and figure out how much the customer owes me, especially if he's starting or stopping in the middle of the week. It's pretty complicated, but my Dad says it teaches me how to run a business, and the extra money comes in handy for buying records or playing video games, even if I do have to put a third of what I earn away in my bank account.

But I was telling you about my customers. You'd be surprised how close a kid can feel to the people he delivers the paper to. They wake up early and rush to get ready for work or whatever, and I figure the only fun they have is when they sit down at breakfast to read what happened while they were sleeping. It's sorta like catching up on gossip, I guess. They depend on me, and I've never been late delivering the papers, and the only times I've missed are when I was sick or like now from what happened yesterday morning. The bandages around my head feel itchy, and the cast on my arm's awful heavy. The nurses have written lots of jokes on it, though, so I'm looking forward to going back to school in two or three weeks the doctor says and showing it to all the kids.

You get to notice things about your customers, stuff a guy wouldn't think of unless he delivers papers. Like after a big football game you can't believe how many people are awake with all the lights on before I even get there, waiting for the paper so they can find out something new about the game they already heard or went to or watched on TV. Or like this house on Gilby Street where for a week or so I had to hold my breath when I came up the sidewalk past the shrubs because of the worst scuzzy smell like something really rotten. Even when I held my breath, it almost made me sick. Like the bad potatoes Mom found in the cellar last month. Nobody was picking up the papers I left. They just kept piling up beside the door, and after I told my Dad, he looked at my Mom kinda strange and said he'd better go over to see what was wrong. I could tell he figured maybe somebody was dead, and I guess I wondered that myself, but the way things turned out, those people were just on vacation which is why the papers kept piling up, and the smell was only from these plastic bags of garbage they'd forgotten to put out and some dogs had torn open at the side of the house. That smell really made me nervous for a while, though.

And then there's the Carrigans. He lost his job at the mill last summer, and his wife likes fancy clothes, and they're always yelling about money when I'm next door playing with Ralph or when I come around to collect or even at six in the morning when I bring them the paper. Imagine that, getting up 'way before dawn to argue. Or what about old Mr. Blanchard? His wife's old too, and she's sick with what my Mom says is bone cancer, and I have not seen Mrs. Blanchard in a couple months, but old Mr. Blanchard, he's up when I put the paper under his mat. I can see through his living room window where the light's on in the kitchen, and he's sitting at the table, hunched over, holding his head, and his shoulders are shaking. Even out front, I can hear him sobbing. It makes my throat tight. He always wears this gray old lumpy sweater. I'd feel sorry for him no matter what, but he cries like it's tearing his chest apart.

And then there's Mr. Lang. He's got this puffy face and a red-veined nose and squinty angry eyes. He's always

complaining about how much the paper costs and claims
I'm cheating him by coming around more often than I
should to collect, which of course I've never done. Two
months ago, he started swearing at me so I'm afraid to go
over there. My Dad says it's the whiskey makes him act
like that, and now my Dad collects from him. The last
time my Dad came back from there, he said Mr. Lang's
not bad if you get to know him and realize he doesn't like
his life, but I don't care. I want my Dad to keep collecting
from him.

I guess I was spooked by what you read about that
happened in Granite Falls two months ago when Mr. Lang
swore at me. That paper boy who disappeared. His parents
waited for him to come home from his Sunday morning
route, and after they got calls from customers wanting to
know where the paper was, his Dad went out looking and
found his sack full of papers a block away in an empty lot
behind some bushes. You remember how the police and
the neighbors went out searching, and the paper he worked
for put his picture on the front page and offered a reward if
anybody knew where he was, but they didn't find him.
The police said he might've run away, but that didn't
make any sense to me. It was too darn cold to run away,
and where would he go? My Dad says he read how the
police even seemed to think the parents might have done
something to him themselves and how the parents got so
mad they wanted to sue the police for saying that. One
man was cruel enough to phone the parents and pretend he
had the boy and ask for money, but the police traced the
calls, and the man didn't have him. Now the man says it
was just a joke, but I read where he's in lots of trouble.

Granite Falls. That's not too far from here. My Dad said
some nut from there could easily drive to other towns like
ours. I wasn't going to give up my route, though, just

because of what happened there. Like I said, I'm used to the money I make and going downtown on Saturdays to buy a new record. But I felt kinda fluttery in my stomach. I didn't want to disappear myself. I'm old enough to know about the creepy things perverts do to kids. So my Dad went with me the next few mornings on my route, and I took a flashlight when I started going alone again, and I delivered the papers fast, believe me. You can't guess what the wind scraping through bushes behind you in the dark can make you feel when it's early and there's nobody around to shout to for help. But after a month when nothing happened, I started feeling easier, ashamed of myself for getting scared like I was a little kid. I slipped back into my old routine, delivering the papers half-asleep, looking forward to the home-made Orange Julius my Mom always has waiting for me when I get back from the route. I read the comics in the *Gazette* before I catch an extra hour of sleep till it's time for school. After being out in the snow, those blankets feel great.

Three weeks ago, another paper boy disappeared, this time right here in Crowell, and you remember how the neighbors searched the same as in Granite Falls, and his picture was in the *Gazette,* and the parents offered a reward, but they didn't find him, only his sack of papers stuffed behind some bushes like the last time. The police said it looked like the same M.O. That's fancy police talk for "pattern". But heck, you don't have to go to police school to figure out that both kids disappeared the same way. And one kid might have run away, but not two of them, leastways not in the snow.

Oh, yeah, that's something I forgot to mention. Both mornings when the kids disappeared, it was snowing real hard, so there weren't any tracks except for the neighbors searching. No kid runs away in a blizzard, I'll tell you.

The rest of us paper boys nearly went on what my Dad calls a strike. Actually it was our parents wanted us to quit delivering. They demanded police protection for us, but the police said we were overreacting, we shouldn't panic, and anyway there weren't enough police to protect us all. The *Gazette* said if we stopped delivering, the paper would go out of business. They asked our parents to keep a close watch on us, and they made us sign a contract agreeing to give up seventy-five cents a month, so the paper could insure us in case something happened to us on the route.

Well, that made my Dad twice as mad. He told me to quit, and I almost did, but I couldn't stop thinking of all the money I like to spend on Saturdays. My Dad says I was born a capitalist and I'll probably grow up to vote Republican, whatever that means, but I told him I won a ribbon last year on the sixth-grade track team, and I could run faster than any pervert I bet. Well, he just laughed and shook his head and told me he'd go out with me every morning, but my Mom looked like she was going to cry. I guess Moms are like that, always worrying. Besides, I said, I only have to worry if it's snowing. That's the only time the kids disappeared. My Dad said that made sense, but all my Mom said was "We'll see" which is always bad news, like if you ask for a friend to stay overnight and your Mom says "We'll see," you figure she means "no".

But she didn't. The next morning, my Dad went with me on the route, and it was one of those sharp cold times when your boots squeak on the snow and the air's so clean you can hear a car start up three blocks away. I knew for sure I'd hear any pervert if he tried sneaking up on me, and anyway my Dad was with me, and all the other carriers had it as easy as I did. Still, every morning I got up praying it wasn't snowing, and often it had snowed in the night but stopped, and when I saw the house across from ours clear in the streetlight, I felt like somebody had taken a rope from around my chest.

So we went on like that, getting up at five-thirty and doing the papers, and once my Dad got the flu, so my Mom went with me. You can believe it, she was nervous, more than me I guess. You should have seen us rushing to finish the route all the time we were looking over our shoulders. Mr. Carrigan was yelling at his wife like always, and Mr. Blanchard was crying for his own wife, and Mr. Lang was drinking beer when he opened his door and scared me, getting his paper. I almost wet my pants, no fooling. He asked if I wanted to step in and get warm, and I backed off, saying, "No, Mr. Lang, no, thank you," holding up my hands and shaking my head. I forgot about his stairs behind me. I bet I'd have broken my arm even sooner than now if he'd shovelled them. But the snow made them soft, and when I tumbled to the bottom, I landed in a drift. He tried to help me, but I jumped up and ran away.

Then last Sunday I woke up, and even before I looked out, I knew from the shriek of the wind that it was snowing. My heart felt hard and small. I almost couldn't move. I tasted this sour stuff from my stomach. I couldn't see the house across the street. The snow was flying so thick and strong I couldn't even see the maple tree in our front yard. As warm as I'd been in bed, I shivered like I was outside and the wind was stinging through my pajamas. I didn't want to go, but I knew that'd be all the excuse my Mom'd need to make me quit, so I forced myself. I dressed real quick, long underwear and the rest, and put on my down-filled coat that almost doesn't fit me anymore and my mitts and ski mask, and it wasn't just my Mom or Dad who went with me that time, but both of them, and I could tell they felt as scared as I was.

Nothing happened, as far as we knew. We finished the
route and came home and made hot chocolate. All our
cheeks were red, and we went back to sleep, and when we
woke up, my Dad turned on the radio. I guess you know
what we heard. Another paper boy had disappeared, right
here in Crowell. That's an M.O. if I ever heard of one.
Three carriers gone, and two of them from town, and all
three when it was snowing.

The storm kept on, so this time there weren't even any
tracks from the police and the neighbors searching. They
couldn't find his sack of papers. A couple of people
helping out had to go to the hospital because of frostbite.
The missing boys didn't live on our side of town, but even
so, my Dad went over to help. With the streets so drifted,
he couldn't drive—he had to walk. When he came back
after dark with his parka all covered with snow, he said it
was horrible out there. He couldn't get warm. He just kept
sitting hunched in front of the fireplace, throwing logs on,
rubbing his raw-looking hands and shivering. My Mom
kept bringing him steaming drinks that she called hot
toddies, and after an hour, he slumped back snoring. Mom
and me had to help him up to bed. Then Mom took me
back downstairs and sat with me in the living room and
told me I had to quit.

I didn't argue. Crowell's got forty thousand people. If
you figure three-quarters of them get the paper and most of
the carriers have forty customers, that's seven hundred and
fifty paper boys. I worked that out on my Dad's pocket
calculator. Kinda surprising—that many paper boys—if
you're not a carrier yourself. But if you're on the streets at
five-thirty every morning like I am, then you see a lot of
us. There's a kid on almost every corner, walking up
somebody's driveway, leaving a paper in front of a door.
Not counting the kid in Granite Falls, that's two missing

carriers out of seven hundred and fifty. That might make the odds seem in my favor, but the way I figured it, and my Mom said it too, that many paper boys only gave the nut a lot of choice. I like to play video games and all, but the money I earned wasn't worth disappearing the way those other boys did with my sack of papers stuffed behind some bushes, which by the way is where they found the third kid's sack like the others, when the snow stopped. After we put my Dad to bed and my Mom looked out the living room window, she made a funny noise in her throat. I walked to her and saw the house across the street, all shimmery, covered with snow and glinting from the streetlight. Any other time, it would've looked peaceful, like a Christmas card. But I felt sick, like all that white had something ugly underneath. I was standing on a vent for the furnace, and I heard the gas burner turn on. Warm air rushed up my pajama leg. All the same, I shivered.

I quit I said. But my Dad says we've got something called a body clock inside us. It comes from being used to a regular routine, like when you know even if you don't have your watch on that it's time for your favorite TV program or you know you'd better get home 'cause your Mom'll have supper ready. I wasn't going to deliver papers, but I woke up at five-thirty the same as usual, even if Mom didn't wake me. For just a second, I told myself I'd better hurry. Then I remembered I wasn't going to deliver the papers anymore. I slumped back in bed and tried to go back to sleep, but I kept squinting at the digital clock Mom and Dad gave me last Christmas, and the numbers kept changing, getting later. Twenty to six. Then quarter to six. At last I couldn't stand feeling guilty, like I'd done something wrong even though I hadn't. I crawled from bed and opened my drapes and peered at the dark snow in our driveway. I could see the tire tracks on the street where the

guy from the *Gazette* had pulled up and thrown my bundle.
It was all by itself in the driveway, sunk in the snow. It
was wrapped in a garbage bag to keep it dry, this big black
shape with all this white around it.

I kept staring at it, and the *Gazette* office hadn't been
open the day before, on Sunday. Even on Monday, they're
not open till eight, so there wasn't any way for the paper
to know I'd quit. I kept thinking of my customers getting
up, looking forward to reading the paper at breakfast,
going to the door, not finding it. Then I thought of all the
calls we'd soon be getting, forty of them, wanting to know
where their paper was. The more I thought about it, the
more I felt worse, till I told myself what my Dad always
says: "There's only one way to do a job, and that's the
right way." I put on my longjohns, my jeans and sweater
and parka. I woke up my Dad, whose face looked old all
of a sudden, I guess from being out in the storm searching
the day before. I told him I had to deliver the papers, and
he just blinked at me, then nodded with his lips pursed like
he didn't agree but he understood.

My Mom made a fuss as you'd expect, but my Dad got
dressed and went with me. I wasn't sure if I was shaking
from the cold or from being scared. It wasn't snowing,
though, and even shivering I knew I'd be all right. We
hurried. We'd started a half hour late, but we got the
papers to every customer without seeing any tire tracks in
their driveway to tell us they'd left for work already. A
couple places, we met a customer shoveling drifts, puffing
frost from his mouth from the work, and every one of
them looked glad to see me, like they'd been sure they
weren't going to get a paper and here I'd been as dependable
as ever. They grinned and promised me a tip when I came
around next time to collect, and I guess I grinned as well.
It made me feel warm all of a sudden. Even Mr. Lang,

who's normally so hard to get along with, came out and patted me on the back the way the track coach sometimes does. My Dad and I did the route the fastest we ever had, and when we got home, my Mom had pancakes ready and syrup hot from the Radarange. I guess I'd never been so hungry. My Dad even gave me a little coffee in a glass. I sipped it, feeling its steam on my nose, actually liking the bitter taste. Then my Dad clicked his cup against my glass, and I felt like I'd grown in the night. My chest never felt so big, and even my Mom had to admit it, we'd done the right thing.

But that didn't change what had happened. At eight, just before I left for school, my Mom phoned the paper and told them I was quitting. When I went outside, I felt relieved, like something heavy had been taken off my back, but that didn't last long. A block from school, my stomach started getting hard, and I couldn't stop thinking I'd lost something or like the track season was over or I'd missed a movie I was looking forward to. It's funny how you get used to things, even a job which I know isn't suppose to be fun, that's why it's called a job, but I liked being a paper boy, earning money and all, and I could tell I was going to feel empty now from not doing it.

All morning, I couldn't concentrate on what the teacher said. She asked if I was sick, but I told her I was only tired, I was sorry, I'd be okay. I tried my best to act interested, and when I got home for lunch, my Mom said the paper had called to ask if they could send somebody over to talk to us around suppertime. She'd done her hardest to tell them no, but I guess they insisted, 'cause someone was coming anyhow, and I ate my hamburger fast from being curious and I'll admit excited from getting attention.

The afternoon was the longest I ever remember. After

school, I didn't care about hanging around with the guys. I just stayed at home and played video games and watched the clock on the TV recorder. My Dad came home from work a little after five. He was just opening a can of beer when the doorbell rang. I don't know why but my arm muscles hurt when he went to the door, and it was Sharon from the paper. She's the one who came to the house and explained how to do my route when I first got started. Lots of times, she stopped at the house to give me extra cards for figuring out how much my customers owed me. Once she brought me the fifty dollars worth of movie passes that I won from going around the neighborhood and convincing the most new customers than any other carrier in town to take the *Gazette* in the morning instead of or maybe as well as the *Chronicle* from Granite Falls, which is the evening paper, but you know that, I guess.

Sharon's younger than my Mom. She's got a pony tail and rosy cheeks, and she reminds me of the student teacher from the college here in town that's helping my regular teacher. Sharon always shows more interest in talking to me instead of my parents. She makes me feel special and grown-up, and she always smiles and tells me I'm the best carrier she's got. But last Monday she wasn't smiling. She looked like she hadn't slept all night, and her cheeks were pale. She said so many carriers had quit and no new carriers wanted to take their place that the paper was worried, like it might go out of business. She said her boss had told her to go around to all the carriers that had quit and tell them the paper would pay them three dollars extra a week if they stayed, but my Mom wouldn't let me answer for myself—my Mom said no. But it was like Sharon hadn't heard. She said the *Gazette* would agree that any morning it snowed the papers didn't have to be delivered, and I could see my Dad agreed it was a good idea, but my Mom kept shaking her head from side to side. Then Sharon rushed on and said at least let her have a few days to find a replacement for me, which was going to be hard because I was so dependable, and that made my heart beat funny. Please give her a week, she said. If she couldn't find somebody else by next Monday, then I could go ahead and quit and she wouldn't bother us again. But—I can't describe how her voice sounded thick and chokey—at least let her have the chance because her boss said if she couldn't find kids to do the routes he'd look for somebody else to do her job.

Her eyes looked moist, like she'd been out in the wind. All of a sudden I felt crummy, like I'd let her down. I wanted to make myself small. I couldn't face her. For the first time, she paid more attention to my parents than to me, blinking at my Mom, then my Dad, sorta pleading, and my Mom didn't seem to breathe. Then she did, a long deep breath like she felt real tired. She said my Dad and her would have to talk about it, so they went to the kitchen, and I tried not to look at Sharon while I heard them whispering, and when they came back, my Mom said okay, for a week, till Sharon could find a replacement but no longer. In the meantime, if it was snowing, I wasn't going to deliver the papers. Sharon almost cried then for being grateful, that's the word she used. She just kept saying thanks, and after she left, my Mom said she hoped we weren't making a mistake, but I knew I wasn't. I figured out what had been bothering me all day—not quitting, but doing it so fast, without making sure my customers would get their paper without the chance to explain to them and say goodbye. I knew I was going to miss them. Funny, how you get used to things.

The next morning, I didn't feel nervous as much as glad to have the route back, at least for a few more days. It was one of the last times I'd see my customers' houses that early, and I tried to memorize what it was like, taking the paper to the Carrigans who still kept arguing, and Mr. Blanchard crying for his wife, and Mr. Lang still drinking beer for breakfast. My Dad went with me that Tuesday, and you could see other parents helping their kids do the routes. I'd never seen so many people out so early, and in the cold, their whispers and their boots squeaking were as clear as the sharp reflection of the streetlights off the drifts. Nothing happened, though the police kept looking for the boys who'd disappeared. And Wednesday, nothing happened either. The fact is, by Saturday, everything had gone pretty much back to normal. It was never snowing in the morning, and my Dad says people have awful short memories, 'cause we heard how a lot of paper boys who'd quit had asked for their routes back and a lot of other kids had asked for the routes that needed a carrier. I know in my own case I'd stopped feeling scared. Pretty much the opposite. I kept thinking about Monday and how it was closer all the time and maybe I could convince my Mom to let me go on delivering.

Saturday was clear. When my Dad came in from the driveway, carrying the bundle of papers, he said it wasn't hardly cold at all out there. I looked through the kitchen window toward the thermometer on the side of the house, and the light from the kitchen reached it in the dark. The red line was almost at thirty-two. I wouldn't need my ski mask, though I made sure to take my mitts, and we packed the papers in my sack, and we went out. That early, the air smelled almost sweet from being warmer than usual, and under my longjohns, I started to sweat. We went down Benton, then over to Sunset, and started up Gilby. That's the hardest street because it's got this steep long hill. In summer, I'm always puffing when I ride my bike to the top, and even in winter, I feel like I have to stop a minute going up with my heavy boots and coat on. How we did it was my Dad took one side of the street and I took the other. We could see each other because of the streetlights, and by splitting the work, we'd do the route twice as fast. But we'd got a note about a new customer that morning, and my Dad couldn't find the house number. I kept delivering papers, going up the hill, and the next thing I knew, I'd reached the top. I looked back down, and my Dad was a shadow near the bottom.

It wasn't snowing, so I figured I'd do a few more papers. My next customer was over on Crossridge. If you went by car, you had to drive back down Gilby hill, then go a block over to Crossridge, then drive all the way up to the top of the other hill. But if you went on foot or bike, you could cut through this sidewalk that one of my customers has in his yard, connecting Gilby and Crossridge, so I went through there and left the paper.

And I suddenly felt frozen-scared 'cause snow began to fall. I'd been looking at the dark sky from time to time. There wasn't a moon, but the stars had been bright, twinkling real pretty. I looked up fast now, and I couldn't see the stars. All I saw were these thick black clouds. I swear even in the dark I could see them. They were twisting and heaving like something was inside rolling and straining to bust loose. I should've remembered from school. Thirty-two: that's the perfect temperature for getting snow. My legs felt limp. I wasn't walking right from being scared. I tried to run, but I lost my balance and almost fell in a drift. I couldn't see the clouds because of the snow. It was falling so thick I couldn't even see the houses across the street. A wind started, and then it got worse and screechy. My cheeks hurt like something was burning them, but it wasn't heat. It was cold. The air had been sweet and warm, but now it was freezing, and the wind stung, and the snow felt like tiny bits of ice-cold broken glass.

I swung around looking for my father, but I couldn't see the houses next to me. The snow kept pelting my face, and the wind bit so I kept blinking and tears filled my eyes. I wiped them with my mitts. That only made them blurry. Snow froze to my cheeks and hair. I moaned, wishing I'd worn my ski mask. The shriek of the wind was worse. I yelled for my Dad, and gusting snow pushed the words back into my mouth. It went down my throat, and I felt suffocated. Then I couldn't see the sidewalk. I couldn't see my mitts in front of my face. All I saw was a wall of moving white. As cold as I felt, deep in my bones, my stomach scalded me. The more it felt hot, the more I shook. I yelled once more for my Dad and in a panic stumbled to find him.

I didn't know I was off the sidewalk till I hit Mr. Carrington's fence. It's sharp and pointy, like metal spears. When I banged against it, one of the points jabbed my chest. I felt it gouge me even through the padding of my coat. It pushed all the air out of me. I fell back, straining to breathe. I sank in a drift where I felt like I was in quicksand, going deeper, scrambling to stand, but my heavy sack of papers held me down, and the snow kept piling on me. It went down my neck, like a cold hand on my back. It stung so hard I jumped up screaming, but the wind shrieked louder, and all I saw was the swirling snow around me in the dark.

I ran, but I must've got turned around 'cause nothing was where it should have been. Invisible bushes slashed my face. I smacked against a tree, and I guess that's how my nose got broken, but I didn't feel it, I was too scared. I just kept running, yelling for my Dad, and when I didn't bump into anything, I guessed I was in the street, but I know now it was the vacant lot next to Mr. Carrington. Somebody's digging a foundation for a new house, and it was like the ground disappeared. Blinded, all I knew was I was falling. It seemed like forever, and I landed so hard I bit my lip right through. You ought to see the stitches. My Dad says sometimes when something terrible happens to you, you don't feel it because of what he calls shock. He says your body has a limit to what it can stand, and then it shuts out the pain. That must've been what happened because my chest and my nose and my lip got numb, and all I wanted was to find my Dad and get back home. I wanted to see my Mom.

I crawled from the hole. Don't ask me how I knew there was someone close. I couldn't see anything but snow, and with my eyes so full of tears I could barely see even that. But then I saw this dark shape rushing at me, and I knew it was my Dad, except it wasn't. In the comics, when someone gets hit on the head, they always show stars. And that's what I saw, stars around me, bright in the snow, and I knew I'd been hit, but I didn't feel it. My Dad says shock can do that too. Something can happen to you that would normally slam you flat, but if you're scared, you somehow get the strength not to fall.

I almost did, though. Everything got blurry and began to spin, and this is the strange part. I got hit so hard I dropped my sack of papers. The sack fell open, and all of a sudden as clear as day I saw my papers in a drift, the black ink with white all around it, and just as sudden the papers were splattered with red. You know that old joke? What's black and white and read all over? A newspaper. Only this is spelled different. The red was the blood from my head. I turned to run, and that's when the shadow grabbed my arm.

But I kept turning, and even in the shriek of the wind, I

heard the crack as clear as if my Dad had taken a piece of kindling and snapped it across his knee for the fireplace, but the snap was from my arm, and I felt it twist at the elbow, pointing back toward my shoulder. I fell, and the snow stopped gusting long enough for me to gape at old Mr. Blanchard kneeling beside me, raising the claw end of his hammer.

I tilted my head as he brought it down, so the claws glanced past my scalp, tearing away some hair. I kicked, and this time the hammer whacked my collar bone. I screamed. The claws of the hammer plunged toward the spot between my eyes.

And another hand shot from the storm, grabbing Mr. Blanchard's arm. Before I passed out, I saw my Dad yank the hammer away from him and jerk him to his feet. My Dad shouted stuff at him I'd never heard before. I mean terrible words I don't want to remember and I won't repeat. Then my Dad was shaking Mr. Blanchard, and Mr. Blanchard's head was flopping back and forth, and the next thing I knew I was here in the hospital with the bandages around my head, and my nose and mouth swollen and my arm in this heavy cast.

My Dad tried to explain it to me. I think I understand, but I'm not sure. Mr. Blanchard's wife died three months ago. I thought she was still alive, but I was wrong. He and his wife, they never had any children, and my Dad says he felt so alone without her he wanted somebody around the house to take care of, like a son, so the first boy he took home was from Granite Falls that time two months ago when he went to visit his wife's sister. Then he wanted another son and another, so he took home those two boys from here, making sure it was snowing so he could hide his tracks, but then he wanted all the sons he could get. It makes me sick to think about it, how after he realized the boys were dead he took them out to his garage and stacked them under a sheet of canvas in the corner, "like cord wood" a reporter said. It's been cold enough that the bodies got hard and frozen and hadn't rotted much. Otherwise they would've smelled like that other house I told you about. I wonder now if all the times I saw Mr. Blanchard crying it was because of his wife being dead or because he realized his mind was fooling him and he knew he was doing wrong but he couldn't stop himself. A part of me feels sorry for him, but another part keeps thinking about those missing boys and how scared they must've been when Mr. Blanchard came at them in the storm, and what he looked like when he knelt beside me, raising that hammer. I have a feeling I'll remember that till I grow up. Earlier I said the nurses wake me early here the same as if my Mom had got me up to do my route. I guess I lied. The nurses didn't wake me. I woke myself, screaming, remembering the claws of the hammer and the blood on my papers. The nurses ran in, and someone's been sitting with me ever since. My Mom or Dad is always here, and they say my collar bone is broken too, but what hurts worst is my arm.

The *Gazette* sent Sharon over, though I know she'd have come on her own. She's writing down what I say, but I'm not sure why 'cause she's also got a tape recorder turned on. You ought to see her smiling when I talk about her. She says she's going to put my story in the paper, and her boss is going to pay me for it. I can sure use the money 'cause the doctor says I won't be delivering papers for quite a while. I guess even after everything that's happened I'll go back to my route. After all, we know why those boys disappeared, and there can't be that many crazy people like Mr. Blanchard, though my Dad says he's beginning to wonder. He just read about a girl carrier in

Ashville that had somebody try to pull her into a car. What's going on that even kids who deliver papers can't feel safe? My Dad says pretty soon nobody'll want to leave their homes.

Well, never mind. I told Sharon I've been talking for quite a while. I'm getting sleepy, and I don't believe the paper will print all this, but she says my story's what they call an exclusive, and maybe some other papers will pick it up. My Mom says she hopes I won't start acting temperamental, whatever that means, now that I'm famous, but I don't feel famous. I feel sore. I hope my customers enjoy reading what I said though because I like them, and I hope they remember what they promised about giving me a tip on account of there's a new video game I want to buy. My Dad came in and heard this last part. He said it again. I must've been born a businessman and I'll probably grow up to vote Republican, whatever that means. I've been thinking, though. Maybe if I go around to a few houses and show them the bandages around my head and the cast on my arm, they'll subscribe to the paper. There's a new contest on. The kid who finds the most new customers gets a year's free pass to the movies. Now if only they'd throw in the popcorn.

Mumbo Jumbo

THAT'S WHAT THEY called it: Mumbo Jumbo. You wouldn't think they could have kept it a secret all those years. But Coach Hayes made them promise, and he wasn't someone you crossed, so there weren't even any rumors. I didn't know the thing existed till my junior year in high school when I tried out for the football team.

I promised myself I'd be honest. Trying out wasn't my idea. It was Joey's. Sure, I liked to throw a football around as much as any other guy. But showing up for practice after classes every day?

"And don't forget the pain, Joey. You know what I'm talking about? Coach Hayes makes the team run two miles double time before each practice. That's not counting all the jumping jacks and pushups and situps and God knows how many other ups he makes them do. For starters. Before they get down to the rough stuff. Agony, Joey. That's what I'm talking about. You're sure you know what you want to get us in for?"

We were having cherry Cokes and fries down at the Chicken Nest near the school. A lot of good times. Of

course, the Nest's torn down now. Seven years ago, the
city made it a parking lot. But I remember Joey bracking
through a straw at the bottom of his empty Coke, squinting
at me across the table. "Joining the team would be something to do," he said. "If we make it, of course."

"Oh, that's no problem. We'd make it all right."

"I'm not so sure."

"Come on." I ate a fry with ketchup on it. "We're big
guys, and we're in shape."

"We're overweight. And Danny, we're not in shape.
This morning I had to pull in my gut to button my jeans.
Anyway, that's not the point. I told you, playing with the
team would be something to do. We can't just hang around
here or down in your rec room all the time."

"What's wrong with playing records and—?"

"Nothing. But it's not enough."

I stopped eating fries and frowned at him. "What are
you talking about?"

"Don't you get the feeling we're not going anywhere?"

I shook my head, confused. I'd never heard Joey talk
that way before.

"Left out," he said. "All the extra stuff they do at
school. The student council, the way they're always included in what's going on."

"That stuckup Bill Stedman. Ever since he got elected
president last year, he walks around like he owns the
goddamned school."

"And the plays the drama club puts on, and the debat-
ing team and—"

"All that's candy ass. What's with you? You want to be
an actor now?"

"I don't know what I want to be." Joey rubbed his
forehead. "But I want to be *something*. Those guys on the
football team. They look like . . ."

"What?"

"Like they enjoy being good at what they do. They look damned proud. You can tell they're glad to belong."

"But all that pain."

His eyes had been bright. They seemed to be looking at something far away. Then all at once they came back to normal. He gave me that sly grin of his. "But here's the payoff. All those football players date the sexiest girls in school. All those muscles give the cheerleaders the hots."

I grinned right back. "Why didn't you say so? Now I get it. Why hang around here when there's a chance to date Rebecca Henderson?"

"Or her girl friend, huh?"

We started laughing so hard that the waitress told us to shut up or leave, and that's how we came to try out for the football team, and how I learned about Mumbo Jumbo.

These days I've got a beer gut, and I puff if I walk up a couple flights of stairs, and my doctor says my cholesterol count's too high. Cholesterol. Back then you should have seen us, though. Sure, granted, what Joey had said was right. We were overweight and soft. But we soon changed all that. The conversation I just described took place the week before school started, and Joey had us lifting weights and running laps even before Coach Hayes announced the dates for try-outs. When we showed up on the football field behind the gym that first Saturday of the school term, asking to join the team, Coach Hayes took his cap off, scratched his head, and wondered if we were kidding.

"No, we mean it," Joey said. "We really want to join."

"But you guys know my rules. You can't be on the team unless your scholastic average is B."

"Then we'll study harder. We'll raise our grades."

"Or waste my time, not to mention the team's. Your record speaks for itself. I've got no patience with guys who don't commit themselves."

"We'll try. We promise," Joey said. "Please. It's important to us."

"But look at the flab on you two. Sure, you're tall enough."

"Six foot," Joey said. "Danny's a quarter inch taller."

"But how are you going to keep up with the other guys? Look at Welsh over there. He's been working out all summer."

I glanced at Welsh, who was running through the holes in a double row of tires laid out on the field. He made it easily. Me, I'd have been groaning on my way to the hospital.

"You'll give up as soon as things get tough," Coach Hayes said. "Why pretend different?"

"All we're asking for is a chance," Joey said.

Coach Hayes rubbed a big, tanned, callused hand across his mouth. "A chance? Okay, I'll give you one. The same chance the other boys have. Show me you can keep up with the training. Get in shape, and earn decent grades. We'll see."

"That's all we want. Coach, thanks."

"One hundred percent. Remember, I won't accept less. If you guys get on the team and then stop trying, you'll wish you hadn't asked to join."

"One hundred percent."

"And Danny, what about you? You haven't said anything."

I nodded, wondering what the hell I was doing there. "Yeah, right, one hundred percent."

It was more like two hundred percent—of torture. The weightlifting and sprints Joey and I had been doing were a joke compared to what Coach Hayes soon made us do. Even the guys who'd stayed in shape all summer had trouble keeping up with the routines. That two-mile double-time warmup nearly killed me. And the calisthenics—I threw up when I got home and smelled the meat loaf my Mom had cooked.

The next morning, Sunday, my knees felt so stiff I hobbled when I crawled out of bed. I groaned to Joey on the phone, "This isn't going to work. I'm telling you I can't make the tryout today. I feel like shit."

"Danny," my mother said from the kitchen. "Watch your language."

"You think you feel worse than me?" Joey asked. "All night I dreamed I was doing situps. My stomach's got rocks in it."

"Then let's not go."

"We're going. We promised. I won't break my word."

"But what's the point? Even a date with Rebecca Henderson isn't worth the agony we'll be going through."

"Rebecca Henderson? Who cares? The team," he said. "I want to make the team."

"But I thought—"

"I said that just to get you interested. Listen, Danny, we've got a chance to belong to something special, to be good at something, better than anybody else. I'm tired of being a fuckup."

On the phone in the background, I heard Joey's mother tell him to watch his language.

"But my back feels—"

"We've been friends a long time, right?"

"Since we started grade school."

"And we've done everything together, right? We went to the movies together, and we went swimming together, and we—"

"I get the idea. But—"

"So I'm asking you, let's do this together too. I don't want to lose your friendship, Danny. I don't want to do this by myself."

Inside I felt warm, knowing what he was trying to tell me. Sure, it was sappy, but I guess I loved him like a brother.

"Okay," I said. "If it means that much to you."

"It means that much."

When we showed up that afternoon behind the gym, Coach Hayes blinked. "Wonders never cease."

"We told you we're serious," Joey said.

"And sore?"

"You bet."

"Legs feel like they've been run over by a truck?"

"A steamroller."

Coach Hayes grinned. "Well, at least you're honest. Even the pros admit they hurt. The trick is to do the job no matter how much it hurts."

I silently cursed.

"We won't let you down," Joey said.

"We'll see. Danny, you sure don't say much. Everybody, let's get started. Double time around the track. After that, I've got a few new exercises for you."

Inwardly I groaned.

After the first mile, I nearly threw up again.

But it's funny. I guess you can get used to anything. Monday morning, I felt awful. I mean really wretched. There wasn't a part of me that didn't ache.

And Tuesday morning was worse. I don't want to remember Wednesday morning. Plus, we didn't hang around the Chicken Nest anymore or go down to my rec room, playing records. We didn't have time. And I felt so tired all I wanted to do was watch the tube.

But I had to hit the books. Every night after supper, Joey phoned to make sure I was studying. What I missed most were those cherry Cokes and fries, but Coach Hayes insisted we stay off them. We could eat spaghetti but no mashed potatoes, beef was okay but the next day had to be chicken or fish, as long as it wasn't red meat. My mother went crazy trying to figure out the menus. For the life of me, I didn't understand the diet. But along about Saturday, after a week of tryouts, I started feeling not too bad. Oh, I still ached, but it was a different kind of ache. Solid and tight, pulling me in. And my mind felt brighter, clearer.

The first quiz I took I got an A.

Two Sundays later, Coach Hayes lined us up after our workout. The bunch of us stood there facing him, breathing hard, sweating.

"Freddie," Coach Hayes told the kid beside me. "Sorry, you just don't have enough weight. The West High team'd mash you into the field. Maybe next year. For what it's worth, you're nimble enough to get on the tumbling team." He shifted his glance. "Pete, you'd make a good tackle. Harry, I like the way you block."

And so on. Down till only Joey and I were left.

Coach Hayes spread his legs, put his hands on his hips and scowled. "As for you two guys, I've never seen a more miserable pair of . . ."

Joey made a choking sound.

". . . But I guess you'll do."

Joey breathed out sharply.

I guess I cheered.

"We made it." Joey grinned with excitement. "I can't believe we're on the team!"

We stood on the corner where we always separated going home.

I laughed. "It's the first thing I ever really tried for."

"And got! We're on the team!"

". . . I owe you. I couldn't have done it without you."

"Same goes here."

"But I'd have quit if you hadn't . . ."

"Naw. I was close to quitting a couple of times myself."

I didn't think so. He'd wanted it more than I had.

"I'd better go. My Mom'll have supper ready," I said.

"Yeah, mine will, too. I'll meet you a half hour early tomorrow so we can study for that science quiz."

"You bet." I didn't add what I was thinking.

Joey added it for me. "Now comes the hard part."

He was right. What we'd been doing till then was only exercises and sloppy scrimmage. Now we really got down to business.

"I've diagrammed these plays for you to memorize." Coach Hayes aimed a pointer against a blackboard in the social studies room after Monday's final bell. "I'll soon give you plenty more. You'll have to learn about game psychology, how to fake out the other team. And you'll have to build team spirit. That's as important as anything else. I want you guys to hang around with each other, go to the movies together, eat lunch together. I want you all to understand each other till you can guess what Joey or Pete or Danny will do on the field. Anticipate each other. That's the secret."

But Coach Hayes had another secret. I didn't learn about it till our first game, and that was two weeks away. In the meantime, the pressure kept building. Harder longer exercise sessions. Practice games till my shoulder ached so bad I thought I'd dislocate it throwing the ball.

That's right. Throwing the ball. I guess Coach Hayes had been more impressed with us than he let on. After trying different guys in different positions, he'd actually picked me as a quarterback and Joey as a receiver.

"You two think alike. Let's see if you can make it work for you."

Sure, I was proud. But there were still grades to keep up and even more plays to memorize. I had no time to think about Rebecca Henderson. The school, the team, and winning were all Coach Hayes told us mattered.

Six-thirty Friday night, we showed up at the locker room and put on our uniforms. I felt shaky enough already. The other guys hardly spoke. Their faces were pale. Coach Hayes didn't help any when he started bitching about how good the other team was.

"Covington High's gonna stomp us. You guys aren't ready. You look like a bunch of losers. Eight winning seasons, and now I'm stuck being nursemaid to a bunch of sissies. I can't take the embarrassment of going out there with you. Pussies."

He went on like that, sounding meaner, more insulting as he went along till he had us so mad I wanted to shout at him to shut the fuck up. I knew what he was doing—using psychology to work us up, so we'd take out our anger on the other team—but all of us respected Coach Hayes so much and wanted him to like us so much that hearing him put us down made me feel like we'd been fools. You bastard, I thought.

Joey kept glancing from Coach Hayes to me, his face in pain.

At once the insults stopped. Coach Hayes glared and nodded. "All right." He walked to a wooden cabinet at the far end of the room.

It was always locked. I'd often wondered what was in there. Now he put a key in the lock and turned it, and behind me I heard a kid who'd been on last year's team whisper, "Mumbo Jumbo."

Next to me, Joey straightened. Those who'd been on last year's team started fidgeting, and somebody else whispered, "Mumbo Jumbo."

Coach Hayes opened the cabinet's door. I couldn't see what was in there because he stood in front of it, his back to us.

Then he slowly stepped away.

Several guys breathed in.

I was looking at a statue. It wasn't big, a foot tall if that. Maybe four inches thick. Pale brown, like the color of a cardboard box. It was made from some kind of stone, not shiny and smooth but dull and gritty-looking, like the stone was sand squeezed together. It had tiny holes here and there.

The statue was a man, distorted, creepy. He had a round bald head and huge bulging lips. His stomach was so swollen he looked pregnant. He sat with his legs crossed, his hands in his lap so they hid his dong. His navel was an upright slit. He reminded me of pictures I'd seen of Chinese idols. But he also reminded me of those weird statues on Easter Island (we'd studied some of this in history class) and those ugly ones in ruins in Mexico. You know, the Aztecs, the Mayans and all that.

The guys who'd been on last year's team didn't act surprised, but they sure looked spellbound. The rest of us didn't know what the hell was going on.

"Boys, I'd better explain. For our new members anyhow. This is . . . I don't know what you'd call him. Our mascot, I suppose. Or maybe better, our team's good luck charm."

"Mumbo Jumbo," a kid from last year murmured.

"For quite a few years now, we've gone through a little ritual before each game." Coach Hayes slid a table into the middle of the room. Its legs scraped on the concrete floor. "Just as we're going out to play, I set the statue on this table. We walk around it twice. We each put our right hand on the statue's head. Then we go out there, kick the other team's butt, and win."

What kind of shit is this? I thought.

Coach Hayes seemed to read my mind. "Oh, sure, I know it's silly. Childish." He grinned in embarrassment. "But I've been having the team do it so often now, and we've had so many winning seasons, I'm almost afraid to stop. Mind you, I don't think for a second that touching old Mumbo Jumbo's head does us any good. But, well, when you've got a good thing going, why change the pattern? It's not as if I'm superstitious. But maybe some of you guys are. Maybe stopping the ritual would throw off your timing. Why not leave well enough alone?"

He studied us, letting what he'd said sink in. Boy, I thought, he doesn't miss a trick. Anything to psych us up. For Christ's sake, a lucky statue.

"There's just one other thing. A few outsiders might not understand the odd things we sometimes have to do to gear ourselves up for a game. They might object to what they thought was . . . who knows what? . . . voodoo or something. So we've always had this rule. No one talks about Mumbo Jumbo outside this room. We don't give away our little secrets."

I understand now why I hadn't heard about the statue before, even from the guys who'd been on last year's team. In a way, Joey and I hadn't been officially on the team until tonight when we went out to play.

"I mean it," Coach Hayes said "If any of you guys

blab about this, I'll boot you off the team." He glared. "Do I have your word?"

A few guys mumbled, "Sure."

"I didn't hear you! Say it! Promise!"

We did what he said.

"Louder!"

We shouted it.

"All right." Coach Hayes took the statue from the cabinet and set it on the table. Up close, the thing looked even uglier.

We walked around it twice, put our right hand on its head (I felt stupid as hell), then ran onto the football field and—

This is what happened. I didn't believe it then. Now, through the haze of all these years, I try to convince myself that my memory's playing tricks. But it happened. That's the terrible part, deep down knowing the truth, but too late.

Five minutes into the game, no score, Coach Hayes sent me out as quarterback. In the huddle, I called a passing play, nothing fancy, just something basic to get the feel of being in the game. So we got set. I grabbed the ball, and all of a sudden it wasn't like in practice. This was the real thing, what all the pain and throwing up and weeks of work had been about, and Covington High's players looked like they wanted to kick in my teeth and make me swallow them. Our receivers ran out. Covington's interceptors stayed with them. My heart thundered. Frantic, I skipped back to get some room and gain some time, straining to see if anybody was in the open. Covington's blockers charged at me. It couldn't have taken five seconds, but it seemed even shorter, like a flash. A swirl of bodies lunged at me.

My hands felt sweaty on the ball. Slick. I had the terrible fear I was going to drop it.

Then I saw Joey. He'd managed to get in the open. He was sprinting toward Covington's goal line, on the left, glancing back across his shoulder, hands up, wanting the ball. I snapped back my arm and shot the ball forward, perfect, exactly the way Coach Hayes had taught me, one smooth powerful motion.

And pivoted sideways so I wouldn't get crushed by Covington's blockers, staring at the ball spinning through the air like a bullet, my heart in my throat, shouting to Joey.

And that's when I froze. I don't think I've ever felt that cold. My blood was like ice, my spine packed with snow. Because that end of the field, to the left, near Covington's goal line, was empty. Joey wasn't there. Nobody was.

But I'd seen him. I'd aimed the ball to him. I swear to God he'd been there. How the—?

Joey was over to the right, streaking away from Covington's men, suddenly in the open. To this day, I still don't know how he gained so much yardage so fast. In a rush, he was charging toward the left toward the goal line.

And the ball fell in his hands so easily, so neatly . . .

The fans assumed we'd planned it, a fakeout tactic, a brilliant play. Coach Hayes later said the same, or claimed he believed it. When Joey sprinted across the goal line, holding the ball up in triumph, the kids from our school broke out in a cheer so loud I didn't hear it as much as feel it, like a wall of sound shoving against me, pressing me.

I threw up my hands, yelling to get rid of my excitement. But I knew. It wasn't any fakeout play. It wasn't brilliant. It had almost been a massive screwup. But it had worked. Almost as if . . .

(I saw Joey there. I know it. On the left, near the goal line. Except he hadn't been there.)

. . . as if we'd intended it to happen. Or it had been meant to happen.

Or we'd been unbelievably lucky.

I started shaking then. I couldn't stop. I wasn't steady enough to play for the next ten minutes. Sitting on the bench, I kept seeing the play again in my mind, Joey in two spots at once.

Maybe I hoped so hard that I saw what I'd pray I see.

But it felt spooky.

Coach Hayes came over to where I hunched on the bench. "Something the matter?"

I clutched my helmet. "I guess I'm just not used to . . ." What? ". . . a real game instead of practice. I've never helped score a touchdown before."

"You'll help score plenty more."

I felt a tingle in my gut.

The game was full of miracles like that. Plays that shouldn't have worked but they did. Incredible timing. With five minutes to go in the game and the score 35 to nothing in our favor, Coach Hayes walked along our bench and murmured to the defensive squad, "The next time they're close to our goal line, let them score. Hold back, but don't make it obvious."

Joey and I frowned at each other.

"But—" somebody said.

"No buts. Do what you're told," Coach Hayes said. "It's demoralizing for them if they don't get at least a few points. We want to let them feel they had a chance. Good sportsmanship."

Nobody dared to argue with him. Our defensive squad sure looked troubled, though.

"And be convincing," Coach Hayes said.

And that's why Covington scored when our guys failed to stop an end run.

The school had an after-game dance in the gym. Everybody kept coming up to me and Joey and the rest of the team, congratulating us, slapping us on the back. Rebecca Henderson even agreed to dance with me. But she'd come with some girlfriends and wouldn't let me take her home. "Maybe next time," she said.

Believe it or not, I didn't mind. In fact, I was so preoccupied I didn't remember to ask her out for Saturday night. What I wanted to do was talk to Joey. By ourselves.

A little after midnight, we started home. A vague smell of autumn in the air. Smoke from somebody's fireplace. Far off, a dog barked, the only sound except for the scrape of our shoes as we walked along. I shoved my hands in the pockets of my green-and-gold varsity jacket and finally said what was on my mind. "Our first play? When I threw you the ball and you scored?"

Joey didn't answer right away. I almost repeated what I'd said.

"Yeah, what about it?" His voice was soft.

I told him what I thought I'd seen.

"The coach says we think alike." Joey shrugged. "What he calls anticipation. You guessed that's where I was headed."

"Sure. It's just . . ." I turned to him. "We won so easily."

"Hey, I've got bruises on my—"

"I don't mean we didn't work. But we were so damned lucky. Everything clicked together."

"That's why Coach Hayes kept drilling us. To play as a team. All the guys did what they'd been taught to do."

"Like clockwork. Yeah. Everybody in the right place at the right time."

"So what's bugging you? You thought you saw me in one place while I was in another? You're not the only one who thought he was seeing things. When we started that play, I saw you snap the ball toward that empty slot in the field, so I faked out the guy covering me and ran like hell to get there ahead of the ball. Know what? As I started running, I suddenly realized you hadn't even thrown the ball yet. You were still looking for an opening. I saw what you were going to do, not what you'd already done."

I felt a chill.

"Anticipation," Joey said. "No big deal. Hell, luck had nothing to do with it. Coach Hayes had us psyched up. The old adrenaline started burning. I ran to where I guessed you'd throw."

I tried to look convinced. "It must be I'm not used to all the excitement."

"Yeah, the excitement."

Even in the dark, his eyes glowed.

"There's a lot of room for improvement," Coach Hayes said at Saturday's game analysis. "We missed a chance for at least two interceptions. Our blocking's got to be quicker, harder."

He surprised me. The score had been so misbalanced, our plays so nearly perfect, I figured we'd done as well as we could.

He made the team practice Sunday afternoon and every day after school. "Just because we won our first game doesn't mean we can afford to slack off. Overconfidence makes losers."

We still had to stay on that crazy diet of his. In my fantasies, I dreamed of mountains of cherry Cokes and fries with ketchup. For sure, we had to keep our grades up. The end of the week, he went around to all our teachers and asked how we'd done on our quizzes. "Let your studies slide," he warned us, "and you don't play."

Friday night, we packed our equipment in the school bus and drove across town to meet West High. We used the girls' locker room in the gym, and after we'd dressed, Coach Hayes insulted us again. He set down a small wooden case (it had a big lock on it) in the middle of the room, opened it, and took out Mumbo Jumbo. The thing looked twice as ugly as before, scowling with those big bulging lips and that upright slit for a navel.

But we knew the routine and walked around it twice and put a hand on the statue's head (I still felt stupid). Then we went out and won forty-two to seven. That seven wouldn't have happened except that again Coach Hayes made us let them score a touchdown. And again that spooky thing happened. Coach Hayes let me play in the second quarter. I got the ball and looked for an opening. There was Joey, far down the field, ready to catch it. And there was Joey, twenty yards in front of where I saw him, trying to get away from a West High player.

My mouth hung open. My hands felt numb. I couldn't breathe. At once something snapped inside me, and the next thing I knew I'd thrown the ball.

Joey raced from where he'd been trying to dodge the West High player. He ran toward the other Joey who was in the open. The two Joeys came together. And of course he caught the ball.

Our fans went nuts, screaming, cheering.

Joey crossed the goal line and jumped up and down. Even halfway down the field, despite the noise, I heard him whoop. Our guys were slapping me on the ass. I tried to look as excited as they were.

The next time I walked to our bench, Coach Hayes said, "Nice pass."

We studied each other for a second. I couldn't tell if he knew how startled I'd been out there, and why.

"Well, Joey's the one who caught it," I said.

"That's right. Team spirit, Danny. Everybody's in this together. All the same, nice pass."

Beside him, close, its lock shut, was the box.

We played eight games that season. Sometimes I had nightmares about them—double images of Joey or other players, the images coming together. I felt as if everything happened twice, as if I could see what was going to happen before it did.

Impossible.

But that's how it seemed. One night I scared my Mom and Dad when I woke up screaming. I didn't tell them what the nightmare was about. I didn't talk to Joey about it, either. After the first time I'd tried to, I sensed that he didn't want to listen.

"We're winners. Jesus, it feels good," he said.

And the scores were always lopsided. We always let the other team score a few points when we were way in front.

Except one time. The sixth game, the one against Central High. Coach Hayes didn't call us names that night before the game. In the locker room, he sat in a corner, watching us put on our uniforms, and the guys started glancing at each other, nervous, sensing something was wrong.

"It's tonight," a kid from last year said, his voice tense.

I didn't understand.

Coach Hayes stood up. "Get out there, and give it your best."

Joey looked surprised. "But what about—?" He turned to the cabinet at the end of the locker room. "Mumbo—"

"Time to go." Coach Hayes sounded gruff. "Do what you're told. They're waiting."

"But—"

"What's the matter with you, Joey? Don't you want to play tonight?"

Joey's face turned an angry red. His jaw stood out. With a final look at the cabinet, he stalked from the locker room.

It could be you've already guessed. We didn't just lose that night. They trounced us. Hell, we never scored a point. Oh, we played hard. After all the training we'd been through, we knew what we were doing. But the other team played harder.

And it was the only game when I wasn't spooked, when I didn't see two images of Joey or what would happen before it actually did.

The after-game dance was a flop.

And Joey was mad as hell. Walking home with me, he kept slamming his fists together. "It's Coach Hayes's fault. He changed the routine. He got us used to him making us pissed at him before the game, calling us names and all that shit. We weren't prepared. We weren't worked up enough to go out there and win."

I tried to calm him down. "Hey, it's just one loss. We're still the winning team in the league."

He spun so fast he scared me. "He didn't even bring out that dumb-ass statue! He wanted us to look like fools out there! He wanted us to lose!"

"I can't believe that."

"Maybe you like being a loser! I don't!"

He surged ahead of me. When I reached the corner where

we always talked for a bit before splitting up, he was already heading down his street.

"Joey!" I wasn't sure what I wanted to say to him. It didn't matter. He didn't shout back.

And maybe you guessed the rest of it too. The next game, everything was back to normal. Or abnormal, depending on how you look at it. Coach Hayes cussed us out before the game. He set Mumbo Jumbo in the middle of the locker room.

"Why didn't you do it the last time?" Joey demanded. "We could've won!"

"You think so?" Coach Hayes squinted. "Maybe you'd have won. Then again maybe not."

"You know we could've! You wanted us to lose!"

"Joey, it seems to me you've got things turned around. You're supposed to get mad at the other team, not me. I'm on your side, remember."

"Not last time you weren't."

Coach Hayes stood awful straight then, his eyes blazing. "I'll forget you said that. Listen, I'll explain this only once. Last time I broke the routine to make a point. It doesn't matter what tricks I use in the locker room to prepare you for a game. What counts is how you play. And last time you guys didn't give your best. It's your fault you didn't win, not mine. You got that?"

Joey glared.

"Besides, it's good for you to lose once in a while."

"Bullshit!"

"Don't try my patience. It's good for you to lose because it makes you try harder next time. It makes you hungrier. It makes you appreciate how sweet it is to be a winner. Don't say another word. Believe me, if you want to play tonight, don't say another word."

We walked around Mumbo Jumbo, touched him, and started the game. Of course, I saw things again. And of course we won, finally letting the other team score.

One more week, the final game. And after touching Mumbo Jumbo, we won that too. City High's ninth winning season. Yet another gleaming trophy stood in the glass case in the lobby near the principal's office.

A lot had happened. My parents couldn't get over my B's and A's. They raised my allowance. They let me borrow the family car more often. Rebecca Henderson and I had started going steady.

And Joey and I continued drifting apart. He was obsessed with being a star, with having attention directed at him all the time. So when football season was over, he couldn't get used to being treated the same as everybody else. He tried out for the basketball team—Mr. Emery, the science teacher, coached it—but he didn't make the squad. "So what?" he said, but you could tell how disappointed he was. "They lose more games than they win. Who wants to be a loser?" He hated how everybody crowded around the new student council president. He finally decided to try out for the drama club—it figured, I thought, being on stage, everybody looking at you—and he made it. He didn't get the starring role in the big production they always put on in December, but he did have a half-decent part. He had to fake a German accent and play a maniac doctor called Einstein in a murder comedy called *Arsenic and Old Lace*. I took Rebecca to it, and I have to say he did okay, not great but pretty good. I mean at least he made me laugh at the jokes, and I hoped that now he'd be satisfied, though I heard later on how he was always grumbling in rehearsals about not being on stage enough and wanting more lines.

* * *

I'll skip to all the trouble—the following year, our last
one at City High. Our grades had put Joey and me on the
junior honor roll. He and I stayed in shape all summer.
Rebecca and I were spending even more time together.
Maybe she was the reason I tried out for the football team
again, even though I hated the prospect of seeing that ugly
statue again, not to mention getting spooked seeing that
other stuff on the field. But I knew we wouldn't have got
together if I hadn't been a football player, and I didn't
want things to change between us, so I tried out again and
made the team.

Joey did too, and his reasons were obvious—getting attention, being a star.

Coach Hayes did everything the same. I dragged myself
home after practice each day. I heard the same old speeches
about grades and diet. I listened to him cuss us out before
the starting game (but he didn't make me mad anymore),
and watched him bring out Mumbo Jumbo. "Our mascot," he explained, swearing us to secrecy, the same
routine (but that squat brown ugly thing still made me feel
creepy). And on the field, I saw the double images again
and felt the chill creep up my spine. If it hadn't been for
Rebecca cheering on the sideline, I'd have . . .

But I didn't, and because of that, sometimes I think I
might have caused what happened, partly anyhow.

We won, of course. In fact, it seemed too easy. Maybe
that was why the next game Coach Hayes didn't cuss us
out and didn't show us Mumbo Jumbo.

As soon as I noticed he was changing the pattern, I said
to myself, "It's tonight," only then realizing I'd heard the
same thing last year from a kid who'd been on the team
the year before that. The kid had graduated now, and I
suddenly realized that next year after my own graduation

some other kid would repeat what I'd just said. And I wondered how many others had said it before me.

"No!" Joey shouted, furious.

"One more word, and you're benched!" Coach Hayes shouted back.

Joey shut up. But leaving the locker room, I heard him mutter, "God damn him. I'll show him. We don't need that frigging statue. We'll win anyhow."

But we didn't. And I didn't see the double images. And Joey went nearly out of his mind with rage. He didn't go to the after-game dance, and he didn't say a word in Saturday's game analysis or Sunday's practice. All he did was keep glaring at Coach Hayes.

And me? How did I help cause all the trouble? I got curious is all. I started thinking about patterns.

And patterns.

So what do you do when you're curious? What I did, I went to the school newspaper. Your school probably had one just like ours. The student reporters were the same bunch who put together the yearbook and belonged to the creative writing club. A gossip column, a hit parade column, a humor column. Plenty of announcements. A report from the student council.

And a sports column.

All of this stuff was typed on stencils and run off on a mimeograph machine. Three pages, on both sides, orange sheets stapled together. *The City High Examiner.* Original, huh? It came out every Monday morning. Mostly I think the school administration set aside money for it because of the weekly "Report from the Principal". School spirit and all that.

Anyhow I decided to do some checking, so I went to the newspaper office, which was also the yearbook office, etc.

A cluttered room on the third floor between the typing classroom and the janitor's closet. The place smelled sickish-sweet, like that white liquid goop you put on stencils to hide your typing mistakes. The editor was a kid named Hathaway, and I guess he'd seen too many newspaper movies. He was always talking about the student council beat and the drama club beat and going to press. All of us called him "Scoop," and he took it as a compliment instead of a putdown.

He was sitting at a desk, shoving his glasses back on his nose, glancing back and forth from a handwritten sheet of paper to the stencil he was typing. He had a pen behind his ear and a zit on his chin. He turned as I walked in.

"How's tricks, Scoop?"

"I just got the word on the nominations for homecoming queen."

"Nobody's supposed to know that till next week's assembly."

"No kidding." He grinned. "Maybe you'll be interested. Rebecca Henderson's one of them."

"My, my." I grinned right back. "Somebody's got good taste. So listen, have you got any old editions of the paper?"

"All the ones I edited. Plus a bunch from a couple editors before me."

"How far back do they go?"

He was proud. "Fifteen years."

"Hey, swell. So where do you keep them?"

"In the morgue."

"Huh?"

"That's what newspapers call where they store old issues. Over there." He pointed past some boxes to a rickety bookshelf in one corner.

"You mind?"

He spread his arms. "Hey, be my guest. What do you want to look at them for?"

I'd figured he'd ask. "A couple of us on the football team have been thinking about a reunion game with former players. An exhibition game. You know. The old guys against the new."

"Yeah?" Scoop's eyes brightened. He reached for his pencil.

"Now wait a minute. We're still just talking, Scoop. If you put this in the paper and it doesn't happen, you'll look dumb. You might even screw up our chances of convincing those guys."

"Right." He nodded. "I'll make you a deal. You look at the former issues, but if the plans for the game look definite, let me know so I can break the story."

"Anything you say."

So I went to the corner and started sorting through the papers. They smelled like a mouldy cellar. I almost sneezed.

Fifteen years of them. How many weeks in a school year? Forty? A lot of issues. But looking through them wasn't as hard as you'd think. See, the only issues I wanted were the ones in the football season. And I only wanted the issues since Coach Hayes had come to the school eleven years ago. It took me less than half an hour. And this is what I learned.

The first two seasons when Hayes had coached were awful. Worse than that. Disastrous. The team never won a game. A total zip.

But after that? Winning season after winning season.

With these facts in common. The games we won had lopsided scores in our favor, but the opposing team always managed to get on the board. And every season, we lost one game, the first or the seventh or the third, no consistent pattern there. And the teams that beat us varied. But the score was always zero for us.

Because he didn't bring out Mumbo Jumbo?

I know that's crazy. Next thing you'll figure I believe in horoscopes and fortune telling and all that crap. But I swear it made me wonder; and remember, you weren't on the field to see those creepy double images. In my place, you'd have started to wonder too.

By then, Scoop was leaning over my shoulder, squinting at the paper in front of me.

"Something the matter, Scoop?"

"Just nosey."

"Yeah."

"I see you're reading about the game the team lost three years ago."

"I wasn't playing then."

"I know. But I was the editor of the paper then. I was there that night. I remember thinking how weird that game was."

"Oh?"

"All those perfect games, and then a real dog."

"Well nobody plays good every game. Hey, thanks, Scoop. Anything I can do for you, just—"

"Let me know about the reunion game."

"Believe me, you'll be the first."

And that's what started things. With some bad moves from a new kid on the team whose name was Price. See, he wouldn't keep his grades up. Maybe he was just stupid. He soon started acting that way.

Coach Hayes followed through on his threat. No grades, no play. So Price got kicked off the team.

But Price had a father with a beergut who'd been a jock when he was in high school, and when Price started whin-

ing, the father went whacko over what he said was an
insult to his kid. "I don't care about his grades. You think
I want him to grow up with ulcers, trying to be a brain.
Football's been good for me. It gave me character, and I
know it's good for my boy's."

No major problem. Just your basic asshole father stick-
ing up for his kid. But Coach Hayes wouldn't budge, and
that's when Price broke the rule.

You might remember reading about it back then, and
I'm not talking about the high school paper. The local
Courier. Then the major paper in the state. Then . . .
FATHER OF HIGH SCHOOL FOOTBALL PLAYER AC-
CUSES TEAM OF DEVIL WORSHIP.

Well, you can imagine, there wasn't any stopping it
after that. The city council wanted to know what the hell
was going on. The school board demanded an explanation.
The principal got angry phone calls.

My father put down the *Courier* and frowned at me. "Is
this story about the statue true? Mumbo Jumbo?"

"It's not like Price says. It's just a mascot."

"But you touch it before you go out to play?"

"Hey, it's nothing. It's only sort of for good luck."

My father frowned harder.

The other guys on the team got the same bit from their
parents. Joey told me his father was so upset he wanted
Joey to quit.

"Are you going to?" I asked.

"Are you kidding? Christ, no. The team means too
much to me."

Or winning does, I thought.

By then, the week was over. Friday night had come
around. Another game. One of the first-aid guys came
down to the locker room, excited. "The bleachers are

packed! A record crowd!'' Sure, all the publicity. Everybody wanted to see the team with the voodoo statue.

At first, I thought Coach Hayes would leave it in the cabinet. Because of the controversy. But as soon as he started insulting us, I knew he didn't intend to break the routine. Looking back to that night, I wonder if he guessed that he wouldn't have many more chances to bring it out. He meant to take advantage of every one of them.

So he went to the cabinet. I held my breath as he unlocked it. The publicity made me self-conscious. Certainly all the talk about devil worship made me nervous about the double images I'd seen.

I watched as he opened the door.

His throat made a funny sound, and when he stepped to the side, I understood why.

''Where is it?'' Joey blurted.

Several players gasped.

''Where's Mumbo Jumbo?'' Joey's cleats scraped on the concrete floor as he stalked to the empty cabinet. ''What happened to—?''

Coach Hayes looked stunned. All at once his neck bulged. ''Harcourt.'' His lips curled. He made the principal's name sound like a curse. ''The school board must have told him—''

''But the cabinet was locked,'' someone said.

''The janitor could have opened it for him.'' Coach Hayes stomped across the room toward the door.

And suddenly stopped as if he'd realized something. ''We've got a game to play. I can't chase after him while—'' Turning, he stared at us. ''Get out there and show them. I'll find the statue. You can bet on that.''

So we went out, and maybe because we'd been spooked, the other team killed us. We couldn't do anything right. Fumbles, interceptions, major penalties. It must have been the worst game any team from City High ever played. The fans started hissing, booing. A man shouted, "Devil worship, my ass! These guys don't need a voodoo statue! They need a miracle!" The more we screwed up, the more we lost confidence and screwed up worse. I saw Rebecca wiping tears from her eyes and felt so humiliated I couldn't wait for the game to end so I could hide in the locker room.

Coach Hayes kept scurrying around, talking to the principal and anybody else he suspected, gesturing angrily. They shook their head. By the end of the game, he still hadn't found the statue.

We sat in the locker room, bitter, silent, when somebody knocked on the door.

I was closest.

"Open it," Coach Hayes said.

So I did.

And stared at Mumbo Jumbo on the floor. There wasn't anyone in the hall.

Sure, we heard rumors, but we could never prove that the other team had taken it. We even heard that stealing the statue had been the rival coach's idea, a practical joke on his good old friend Coach Hayes.

Scoop put all this in the school newspaper Monday morning. Don't ask me how he found out. He must have been a better reporter than any of us gave him credit for. He even had a drawing of the statue, so accurate that whoever had stolen it must have shown it to him. Or maybe Scoop was the one who stole it.

Whoever, I feel partly responsible for the story he wrote. I must have made him curious that time I went to see him and asked to look at the former issues of the paper. Maybe he checked and found out I'd handed him a line about a reunion game.

For whatever reason, he seems to have gone through the same issues I did—because he came up with the same pattern I'd noticed. Two losing seasons, then all of a sudden an unbroken string of winners. Because of Mumbo Jumbo? He didn't come right out and link the statue with the team's success, but you could tell he was trying to raise the issue. In every winning season, we'd lost only one game, and our score was always zero. In our winning games, however, we'd always had a lopsided spread in our favor, but the other team had always somehow managed to gain a few points. Coincidence, Scoop asked, or was there a better explanation? For evidence, he quoted from an interview he'd had with Price. He didn't bother mentioning that he had no witness for what had happened in the locker room in the years when Price wasn't on the team. His whole story was like that, making guesses seem like facts. Then he talked about Friday's game and how in the years since Coach Hayes had been showing the statue this was the first time we'd lost two games in one season. Perhaps because somebody stole the statue Friday night? Scoop repeated the rumor that the rival team had been responsible for the theft. We'd probably never know the truth, he said. He'd already described the few tiny holes in the statue, ''the size of a pin, one of them over the statue's heart.'' Now several paragraphs later, he ended the story by mourning the rival coach who'd died from a heart attack on his way home from the game.

I wanted to get my hands on Scoop and strangle the little shit. All everybody in the lunch room talked about was how creepy it would be if the statue had really caused that coach's death, if someone had stuck a pin in Mumbo Jumbo's chest.

I don't know if Coach Hayes wanted to strangle Scoop, but for sure he wanted Scoop expelled. Every kid at school soon heard about the argument Coach Hayes had in the principal's office, his shouts booming down the hall, "Irresponsible, libelous!" Scoop was smart enough to stay home sick all week. He drowned the following summer out at the quarry.

By next Friday's game, though, Scoop was the least of our problems. The churches in town got worked up over Mumbo Jumbo. I read in the local paper how the school had received at least a dozen letters from local ministers, priests, and rabbis. One of the letters was quoted: ". . . superstition . . . unwholesome atmosphere . . . Satanism . . . counterproductive to education." My parents were so upset that they didn't want me to play in the game that night. I told them I couldn't let the other guys down, and as far as education was concerned, what about the B's and A's I'd been bringing home? If anything, the team had been good for me.

But this superstition crap was beginning to get to me, maybe because I still felt bothered by the weird things I'd been seeing on the field, things that seemed to happen before they happened. Could the statue really . . . ? Or was Joey right, and I was only caught up in the speed and excitement of the game?

Enough already, I thought. Mumbo Jumbo. That describes it all right. It's a lot of bullshit. I had no way to know, of course, that this would be the last time Coach Hayes was allowed to bring out the statue. I did know this—I was sick of touching that creepy thing, and if I needed it to make me a good football player, I didn't belong in the game.

So after we dressed in the locker room and Coach Hayes

insulted us and brought out the statue, I didn't touch it as the other guys did when we went out to play.

My right arm still aches when the temperature drops below freezing. The cast stayed on for almost three months. I hadn't been on the field more than thirty seconds, my first play of the game. I got the ball and drew my arm back to throw, but I couldn't find an opening. And I never saw the four guys who hit me, all together at once, really plowing into me, knocking my wind out, taking me down, my arm cocked behind my shoulder, all that weight on it. I fainted. But not before I heard the cracks.

Saturday morning, Joey came to visit me in the hospital. He'd scored three touchdowns, he said. Through a swirl of pain, I tried to seem excited for him.

"Did we win?" I asked.

"Does the Pope live in Italy?" His grin dissolved. "About your arm . . ."

"I know."

He said he was really sorry. I told him thanks.

He fidgeted. "How long are they going to keep you here?"

"Till tomorrow afternoon."

"Well, look, I'll visit you at home."

I nodded, feeling sleepy from the painkiller a nurse had given me. Rebecca came in, and Joey left.

He and I drifted farther apart after that. He had the team, and I had my cast. After the football season, he got a big role in a murder mystery the drama club put on, *Ten Little Indians*. Everybody said he was wonderful in it. I have to admit he was.

And me? I guess I let things slide. I couldn't take notes or do class assignments with my writing arm in a cast. Rebecca helped as much as she could, but she had to do her own work too. I started getting C's again. I also got back in the habit of going down to the Chicken Nest, with Rebecca this time instead of Joey. Those cherry Cokes and fries with ketchup can really put weight on you, especially if you're not exercising.

The city newspaper reported on the meeting between the school board and Coach Hayes. They asked him to explain. He found the statue at a rummage sale, he said. Its owner claimed it was a fertility symbol that the Mayans or the Polynesians or whoever (the name of the tribe kept changing) had used in secret rituals. Coach Hayes said he hadn't believed that—not when its price was fifteen dollars. But he'd been looking for a gimmick, he said, something to work up team spirit, especially after two horrible seasons. A kind of mascot. If the team believed the statue brought them good luck, if the statue gave them confidence, so what? No harm was done. Besides, he said, he sometimes didn't bring the statue out—to teach the players to depend on themselves. The team had lost on those occasions, true, but as a consequence they'd tried harder next time. There was nothing mysterious about it. A dramatic gimmick, that's all. The point was it worked. The team had been winning championships ever since. School spirit had never been better.

"What about the statue's name?" a school board member asked.

"That came later. In the third winning season. One of the players made a joke. I forget what it was. Something about good luck and all that mumbo jumbo. The phrase sort of stuck."

The school board heard him out. They held up the stacks of letters from angry parents and clergy. Their decision was final.

To show that they were willing to compromise, they let

him put the statue in the glass case with the trophies the
team had won in the school's front lobby.

The rest of the season was brutal. We lost every game.
Sitting with Rebecca on the sidelines, trying to show
enthusiasm for the team, I felt terrible for Joey. You could
see how depressed he was, not being a winner.

West High won the championship. Monday, the big
news was that over the weekend somebody had smashed
the glass in the trophy case and stolen Mumbo Jumbo.
Nobody knew who had it, though all of us suspected
Coach Hayes. He resigned that spring. I'm told he teaches
now in upstate New York. I think about him often.

Joey's grades were good enough that Yale accepted him
on a scholarship. With my C's, I won't even tell you what
college accepted me. I didn't go anyhow. Rebecca got
pregnant that summer. In those days, abortions weren't
easy to arrange. I'm not sure I'd have wanted her to have
one anyhow. The child, a daughter, breaks my heart with
love every time I look at her. Rebecca and I got married
that Halloween. Both sets of parents were good about it.
We couldn't have made a go without their help.

We have three children now, two girls and a boy. It's
tough to pay rent and feed and dress and give them everything we want to. Both Rebecca and I have jobs. She's a
secretary at our high school. I work at the chemical plant
in town.

And Joey? You know him as Joseph "Footwork" Sum-
mers. He played receiver for Yale and was picked up by
the NFL. You saw him play twice in the Superbowl. For
sure, you saw him in plenty of beer commercials. The one
where he beats up five motorcycle guys, then walks to the
bar and demands a beer.

"What kind?" the bartender asks. "What those guys were drinking?"

And Joey says, "That stuff's for losers. When I say I want a beer, I mean the best."

And you know what brand he means. The commercial got him into the movies. I saw *Dead Heat* last week and loved it. The action was great. His acting gets better and better.

But a part of me . . .

I'll try to explain. Three years ago, Joey came back to town to see his folks. Imagine how surprised I was when he called me up. I mean he hadn't exactly been keeping in touch. He asked me over to his parents' house for a beer, he really drinks the brand he advertises, and while I was there, he took me up to his old bedroom. A lot of good memories. He gestured toward his battered dresser. I was so busy looking at him (hell, he's a movie star, after all) that I didn't know what he meant at first.

Then I really looked.

And there it was. In his open suitcase. Mumbo Jumbo. As ugly and shitty and creepy as ever. I felt spooked the way I'd used to.

And abruptly realized. "No. You don't mean . . . You're the one who stole it?"

He just grinned.

"But I thought it was Coach Hayes. I thought . . ."

He shook his head. "No, me."

My stomach felt hollow. I don't remember what we talked about after that. To tell the truth, the conversation was kind of awkward. I finished my beer and went home. And Joey returned to Hollywood.

But this is what I think. The other night, my son and I were watching a movie on television. *David Copperfield*. I never watch that kind of stuff, but my son had a book report due, and he hadn't read the book, so he was cheating, sort of, watching the movie. And I was helping him.

At the end, after David Copperfield becomes a success and all his friends have turned out losers, there's a part in this movie where you hear what he's thinking. "It isn't enough to have the luck," he says. "Or the talent. You've got to have the character."

Maybe so. But I keep thinking about Mumbo Jumbo and how, when I didn't touch the statue, I got my arm broken in the game. That was a turning point. If I'd stayed on the team and kept my grades up, could I have gone to Yale like Joey? Could I have been a winner too?

I keep thinking about Coach Hayes and his winning streak. Was that streak caused by the statue? I can't believe it.

But . . .

I remember Joey—the movie star—pointing at the statue he stole from the glass case in the school's front lobby. In his senior year. And everything kept getting better for him after that.

Then I think about myself. I love my kids and my wife.

But I felt so tired tonight when I got home from work . . . The bills . . . My son needs braces on his teeth, and . . .

Maybe Joey understood. Maybe David Copperfield was wrong.

Maybe it doesn't take talent. Or character.

Maybe all it takes is Mumbo Jumbo.

Dead Image

"YOU KNOW WHO he looks like, don't you?"

Watching the scene, I just shrugged.

"Really, the resemblance is amazing," Jill said.

"Mmm."

We were in the studio's screening room, watching yesterday's dailies. The director—and I use the term loosely—had been having troubles with the leading actor, if acting's what you could say that good-looking bozo does. It wasn't enough that Mr. Beefcake wanted eight million bucks and fifteen points to do the picture. It wasn't enough that he changed my scene so the dialogue sounded as if a moron had written it. No, he had to keep dashing to his trailer, snorting more coke (for "creative inspiration", he said), then sniffling after every sentence in the big speech of the picture. If this scene didn't work, the audience wouldn't understand his motivation for leaving his girlfriend after she became a famous singer, and believe me, nothing's more unforgiving than an audience when it gets confused. The word-of-mouth would kill us.

"Come on, you big dumb sonofabitch," I muttered.

"You make me want to blow my nose just listening to you."

The director had wasted three days doing retakes, and the dailies from yesterday were worse than the ones from the two days before. Sliding down in my seat, I groaned. The director's idea of fixing the scene was to have a team of editors work all night patching in reaction shots from the girl and the guys in the country-western band she sang with. Every time Mr. Wonderful sniffled . . . cut, we saw somebody staring at him as if he was Jesus.

"Jesus," I moaned to Jill. "Those cuts distract from the speech. It's supposed to be one continuous shot."

"Of course, this is rough, you understand," the director told everyone from where he sat in the back row of seats. Near the door. To make a quick getaway, if he had any sense. "We haven't worked on the dubbing yet. That sniffling won't be on the release print."

"I hope to God not," I muttered.

"Really. Just like him," Jill said next to me.

"Huh? Who?" I turned to her. "What are you talking about?"

"The guitar player. The kid behind the girl. Haven't you been listening?" She kept her voice low enough that no one else could have heard her.

That's why I blinked when the studio v.p. asked from somewhere in the dark to my left, "Who's the kid behind the girl?"

Jill whispered, "Watch the way he holds that beer can."

"There. The one with the beer can," the v.p. said.

Except for the lummox sniffling on the screen, the room was silent.

The v.p. spoke louder. "I said who's the—?"

"I don't know." Behind us, the director cleared his throat.

"He must have told you his name."

"I never met him."

"How the hell, if you . . . ?"

"All the concert scenes were shot by the second-unit director."

"What about the reaction shots?"

"Same thing. The kid only had a few lines. He did his bit and went home. Hey, I had my hands full making Mr. Nose Candy feel like the genius he thinks he is."

"There's the kid again," Jill said.

I was beginning to see what she meant now. The kid looked a lot like—

"James Deacon," the v.p. said. "Yeah, that's who he reminds me of."

Mr. Muscle Bound had managed to struggle through the speech. I'd recognized only half of it—partly because the lines he'd added made no sense, mostly because he mumbled. At the end, we had a closeup of his girlfriend, the singer, crying. She'd been so heartless clawing her way to the top that she'd lost the one thing that mattered—the man who'd loved her. In theory, the audience was supposed to feel so sorry for her that they were crying along with her. If you ask me, they'd be in tears all right, from rolling around in the aisles with laughter. On the screen, Mr. Beefcake turned and trudged from the rehearsal hall, as if his underwear was too tight. He had his eyes narrowed manfully, ready to pick up his Oscar.

The screen went dark. The director cleared his throat again. He sounded nervous. "Well?"

The room was silent.

The director sounded more nervous. "Uh . . . So what do you think?"

The lights came on, but they weren't the reason I suddenly had a headache.

Everybody turned toward the v.p., waiting for the word of God.

"What I think," the v.p. said. He nodded wisely. "Is we need a re-write."

"This fucking town." I gobbled Dy-Gel as Jill drove us home. The Santa Monica freeway was jammed as usual. We had the top down on the Porsche so we got a really good dose of car exhaust.

"They won't blame the star. After all, he charged eight million bucks, and next time he'll charge more if the studio pisses him off." I winced from heartburn. "They'd never think to blame the director. He's a God-damned artist as he keeps telling everybody. So who does that leave? The underpaid schmuck who wrote what everybody changed."

"Take it easy. You'll raise your blood pressure." Jill turned off the freeway.

"Raise my blood pressure? Raise my—? It's already raised! Any higher, I'll have a stroke."

"I don't know what you're so surprised about. This happens on every picture. We've been out here fifteen years. You ought to be used to how they treat writers."

"Whipping boys. That's the only reason they keep us around. Every director, producer and actor in town is a better writer. Just ask them, they'll tell you. The only problem is they can't read, let alone write, and they just don't seem to have the time to sit down and put all their wonderful thoughts on paper."

"But that's how the system works, hun. There's no way to win, so either you love this business or leave it."

I scowled. "About the only way to make a decent

picture is to direct as well as write it. Hell, I'd star in it too if I wasn't losing my hair from pulling it out.''

"And twenty million bucks," Jill said.

"Yeah, that would help too—so I wouldn't have to grovel in front of those studio heads. But hell, if I had twenty million bucks to finance a picture, what would I need to be a writer for?"

"You know you'd keep writing, even if you had a hundred million."

"You're right. I must be nuts."

"Wes Crane," Jill said.

I sat at the word processor, grumbling as I did the re-write. The studio v.p. had decided that Mr. Biceps wasn't going to leave his girlfriend. Instead his girlfriend was going to realize how much she'd been ignoring him and give up her career for love. "There's an audience out there dying for a movie against women's lib," he said. It was all I could do not to throw up.

"Wes what?" I kept typing on the keyboard.

"Crane. The kid in the dailies."

I turned to where she stood at the open door to my study. I must have blinked stupidly because she got that patient look on her face.

"The one who looks like James Deacon. I got curious. So for the hell of it, I phoned the casting office at the studio."

"All right, so you found out his name. So what's the point?"

"Just a hunch."

"I still don't get it."

"Your script about mercenary soldiers."

I shrugged. "It still needs a polish. Anyway it's strictly

on spec. When the studio decides we've ruined this picture
sufficiently, I have to do that Napoleon mini-series for
ABC."

"You wrote that script on spec because you believed in
the story, right? It's something you really wanted to do."

"The subject's important. Soldiers of fortune employed
by the CIA. Unofficially, America's involved in a lot of
foreign wars."

"Then fuck the mini-series. I think the kid would be
wonderful as the young mercenary who gets so disgusted
that he finally shoots the dictator who hired him."

I stared. "You know, that's not a bad idea."

"When we were driving home, didn't you say that the
only way to film something decent was to direct the thing
yourself?"

"And star in it." I raised my eyebrows. "Yeah, that's
me. But I was just making a joke."

"Well, lover, I know you couldn't direct any worse
than that asshole who ruined your stuff this morning. I've
got the hots for you, but you're not good-looking enough
for even a character part. That kid is, though. And the man
who discovers him . . ."

". . . can write his own ticket. If he puts the package
together properly."

"You've had fifteen years of learning the politics."

"But if I back out on ABC . . ."

"Half the writers in town wanted that assignment. They'll
sign someone else in an hour."

"But they offered a lot of dough."

"You just made four hundred thousand on a story the
studio ruined. Take a flyer, why don't you? This one's for
your self-respect."

"I think I love you."

"When you're sure, come down to the bedroom."

She turned and left. I watched the doorway for a while, then swung my chair to face the picture window and thought about mercenaries. We live on a bluff in Pacific Palisades. You can see the ocean forever. But what I saw in my head was the kid in the dailies. How he held that beer can.

Just like James Deacon.

Deacon. If you're a film buff, you know who I'm talking about. The farm boy from Oklahoma. Back in the middle sixties. At the start a juvenile delinquent, almost went to reform school for stealing cars. But a teacher managed to get him interested in highschool plays. Deacon never graduated. Instead he borrowed a hundred bucks and hitch-hiked to New York where he camped on Lee Strasberg's doorstep till Strasberg agreed to give him a chance in the method acting school. A lot of brilliant actors had come out of that school. Brando, Newman, Clift, Gazzara, McQueen. But some say Deacon was the best of the lot. A bit part on Broadway. A talent scout in the audience. A screen test. The rest as they say is history. The part of the younger brother in *The Prodigal Son*. The juvenile delinquent in *Revolt on Thirty-Second Street*. Then the wildcat oil driller in *Birthright* where he upstaged half a dozen major stars. There was something about him. Intensity, sure. You could sense the pressure building in him, swelling inside his skin, wanting out. And authenticity. God knows, you could tell how much he believed the parts he was playing. He actually was those characters.

But mostly the camera simply loved him. That's the way they explain a star out here. Some goodlooking guys come across as plain on the screen. And plain ones look gorgeous. It's a question of taking a three-dimensional

face and making it one-dimensional for the screen. What's
distinctive in real life gets muted, and vice versa. There's
no way to figure if the camera will like you. It either does
or doesn't. And it sure liked Deacon.

What's fascinating is that he also looked as gorgeous in
real life. A walking movie. Or so they say. I never met
him, of course. He's before my time. But the word in the
industry was that he couldn't do anything wrong. That's
even before his three movies were released. A guaranteed
superstar.

And then?

Cars. If you think of his life as a tragedy, cars were the
flaw. He loved to race them. I'm told his body had practi-
cally disintegrated when he hit the pickup truck at a hundred miles an hour on his way to drive his modified
Corvette at a race track in northern California. Maybe you
heard the legend. That he didn't die but was so disfigured
that he's in a rest home somewhere to spare his fans the
disgust of how he looks. But don't believe it. Oh, he died,
all right. Just like a shooting star, he exploded. And the
irony is that, since his three pictures hadn't been released
by then, he never knew how famous he became.

But what I was thinking, if a star could shine once . . .

"I'm looking for Wes. Is he around?"

I'd phoned the Screen Actor's Guild to get his address.
For the sake of privacy, sometimes all an actor will give
the Guild is the name and the phone number of his agent,
and what I had in mind was so tentative that I didn't want
the hassle of dealing with an agent right then.

But I got lucky. The Guild had an address.

The place was in a canyon out near the desert. A dusty
winding road led up to an unpainted house with a sundeck
supported on stilts and a half-dozen junky cars in front

along with a dune buggy and a motorcycle. Seeing those clunkers, I felt self-conscious in the Porsche.

Two guys and a girl were sitting on the steps. The girl had a butch cut. The guys had hair to their shoulders. They wore sandals, shorts, and that's all. The girl's breasts were as brown as nutmeg.

The three of them stared right through me. Their eyes looked big and strange.

I opened my mouth to repeat the question.

But the girl beat me to it. "Wes?" She sounded groggy. "I think . . . out back."

"Hey, thanks." But I made sure I had the Porsche's keys in my pocket before I plodded through sand past sagebrush around the house.

The back had a sundeck too, and as I turned the corner, I saw him up there, leaning against the rail, squinting toward the foothills.

I tried not to show surprise. In person, Wes looked even more like Deacon. Lean, intense, hypnotic. Around twenty-one, the same age Deacon had been when he made his first movie. Sensitive, brooding, as if he suffered secret tortures. But tough-looking too, projecting the image of someone who'd been emotionally savaged once and wouldn't allow it to happen again. He wasn't tall, and he sure was thin, but he radiated such energy that he made you think he was big and powerful. Even his clothes reminded me of Deacon. Boots, faded jeans, a denim shirt with the sleeves rolled up and a pack of cigarettes tucked in the fold. And a battered stetson with the rims curved up to meet the sides.

Actors love to pose, of course. I'm convinced that they don't even go to the bathroom without giving an imaginary camera their best profile. And the way this kid leaned against the rail, staring moodily toward the foothills, was certainly photogenic.

But I had the feeling that it wasn't a pose. His clothes didn't seem a deliberate imitation of Deacon. He wore them too comfortably. And his brooding silhouette didn't seem calculated either. I've been in the business long enough to know. He dressed and leaned that way naturally. That's the word they use for a winner in this business. He was a natural.

"Wes Crane?" I asked.

He turned and looked down at me. At last, he grinned. "Why not?" He had a vague country-boy accent. Like Deacon.

"I'm David Sloane."

He nodded.

"Then you recognize the name?"

He shrugged. "Sounds awful familiar."

"I'm a screenwriter. I did *Broken Promises*, the picture you just finished working on."

"I remember the name now. On the script."

"I'd like to talk to you."

"About?"

"Another script." I held it up. "There's a part in it that I think might interest you."

"So you're a producer too?"

I shook my head.

"Then why come to me? Even if I like the part, it won't do us any good."

I thought about how to explain. "I'll be honest. It's a big mistake as far as negotiating goes, but I'm tired of bullshit."

"Cheers." He raised a beer can to his lips.

"I saw you in the dailies this morning. I liked what I saw. A lot. What I want you to do is read this script and tell me if you want the part. With your commitment and

me as director, I'd like to approach a studio for financing.
But that's the package. You don't do it if I don't direct.
And I don't do it unless you're the star.''

"So what makes you think they'd accept me?"

"My wife's got a hunch."

He laughed. "Hey, I'm out of work. Anybody offers
me a job I take it. Why should I care who directs? Who
are you to me?"

My heart sank.

He opened another beer can. "Guess what, though? I
don't like bullshit either." His eyes looked mischievous.
"Sure, what have I got to lose? Leave the script."

My number was on the front of it. The next afternoon,
he called.

"This script of yours? I'll tell you the same thing you
said about my acting. I liked it. A lot."

"The script still needs a polish."

"Only where the guy's best friend gets killed. The hero
wouldn't talk so much about what he feels. The fact is, he
wouldn't say anything. No tears. No outburst. This is a
guy who holds himself in. All you need is a closeup on his
eyes. That says it all. He stares down at his buddy. He
picks up his M-16. He turns toward the palace. The
audience'll start to cheer. They'll know he's set to kick
ass."

Most times when an actor offers suggestions, my stomach cramps. They get so involved in their parts that they
forget about the story's logic. They want more lines. They
want to emphasize their role till everybody else in the
picture looks weak. Now here was an actor who wanted
his largest speech cut out. He was thinking story, not ego.
And he was right. That speech had always bothered me.

I'd written it ten different ways and still hadn't figured out what was wrong.

Till now.

"The speech is out," I said. "It won't take fifteen minutes to redo the scene."

"And then?"

"I'll go to the studio."

"You're really not kidding me? You think there's a chance I can get the part?"

"As much chance as I have to direct it. Remember the arrangement. We're a package. Both of us, or none."

"And you don't want me to sign some kind of promise?"

"It's called a binder. And you're right. You don't have to sign a thing."

"Let me get this straight. If they don't want you to direct but they offer me the part, I'm supposed to turn them down. Because I promised you?"

"Sounds crazy, doesn't it?" The truth was, even if I had his promise in writing, the studio's lawyers could have it nullified if Wes claimed he'd been misled. This town wouldn't function if people kept their word.

"Yeah, crazy," Wes said. "You've got a deal."

In the casting office at the studio, I asked the woman behind a counter, "Have you got any film on an actor named Crane? Wes Crane?"

She looked at me strangely. Frowning, she opened a filing cabinet and sorted through some folders. She nodded, relieved. "I knew that name was familiar. Sure, we've got a screen test on him."

"What? Who authorized it?"

She studied a page. "Nope. Doesn't say."

And I never found out, and that's one of the many

things that bother me. "Do you know who's seen the test?"

"Oh, sure, we have to keep a record." She studied another page. "But I'm the only one who looked at it."

"You?"

"He came in here one day to fill out some forms. We got to kidding around. It's hard to describe. There's something about him. So I thought I'd take a look at his test."

"And?"

"What can I say? I recommended him for that bit part in *Broken Promises.*"

"If I want to see that test, do you have to check with anybody?"

She thought about it. "You're still on the payroll for *Broken Promises,* aren't you?

"Right."

"And Crane's in the movie. It seems to me a legitimate request." She checked a schedule. "Use screening room four. In thirty minutes. I'll send down a projectionist with the reel."

So I sat in the dark and watched the test and first felt the shiver that I'd soon know well. When the reel was over, I didn't move for a while.

The projectionist came out. "Are you all right, Mr. Sloane? I mean, you're not sick or anything?"

"No. But thanks. I'm . . ."

"What?"

I took a deep breath and went back to the casting office.

"There's been a mistake. That wasn't Crane's test."

She shook her head. "There's no mistake."

"But that was a scene from *The Prodigal Son.* James Deacon's movie. There's been a switch."

"No, that was Wes Crane. It's the scene he wanted to do. The set department threw together something that looked like the hayloft in the original."

"Wes . . . ?"

"Crane," she said. "Not Deacon."

We stared.

"And you liked it?" I asked.

"Well, I thought he was ballsy to choose that scene—and pull it off. One wrong move, he'd have looked like an idiot. Yeah, I liked it."

"You want to help the kid along?"

"Depends. Will it get me in trouble?"

"Exactly the opposite. You'll earn brownie points."

"How?"

"Just phone the studio v.p. Tell him I was down here asking to watch a screen test. Tell him you didn't let me because I didn't have authorization. But I acted upset, so now you've had second thoughts, and you're calling him to make sure you did the right thing. You don't want to lose your job."

"So what will that accomplish?"

"He'll get curious. He'll ask whose test it was. Just tell him the truth. But use these words. 'The kid who looks like James Deacon.' "

"I still don't see . . ."

"You will." I grinned.

I called my agent and told him to plant an item in *Daily Variety* and *Hollywood Reporter*. "Oscar-winning scribe, David Sloane, currently prepping his first behind-the-lens chore on *Mercenaries,* toplining James Deacon lookalike, Wes Crane."

"What's going on? Is somebody else representing you? I don't know from chicken livers about *Mercenaries*."

"Lou, trust me."

"Who's the studio?"

"All in good time."

"You sonofabitch, if you expect me to work for you when somebody else is getting the commission . . ."

"Believe me, you'll get your ten percent. But if anybody calls, tell them they have to talk to me. You're not allowed to discuss the project."

"Discuss it? How the hell can I discuss it when I don't know a thing about it?"

"There. You see how easy it'll be."

Then I drove to a video store and bought a tape of *The Prodigal Son.*

I hadn't seen the movie in years. That evening, Jill and I watched it fifteen times. Or at least a part of it that often. Every time the hayloft scene was over, I rewound the tape to the start of the scene.

"For God's sake, what are you doing? Don't you want to see the whole movie?"

"It's the same." I stared in astonishment.

"What do you mean the same? Have you been drinking?"

"The hayloft scene. It's the same as in Wes Crane's screen test."

"Well, of course. You said that the set department tried to imitate the original scene."

"I don't mean the hayloft." I tingled again. "See, here in *The Prodigal Son,* Deacon does most of the scene sprawled on the floor of the loft. He has the side of his face pressed against those bits of straw. I can almost smell the dust and the chaff. He's talking more to the floor than he is to his father behind him."

"I see it. So what are you getting at?"

"That's identical in Wes Crane's test. One continuous

shot with the camera at the floor. Crane has his cheek
against the wood. Every movement, every pause, even that
choking noise right here as if the character's about to start
sobbing—they're identical.''

"But what's the mystery about it? Crane must have
studied this section before he decided to use it in his test.''

I rewound the tape.

"No, not again,'' Jill said.

The next afternoon, the studio v.p. phoned. "I'm disappointed in you, David.''

"Don't tell me you didn't like the rewrite on *Broken
Promises.*''

"The rewrite? The. . . ? Oh, yes, the rewrite. Great,
David, great. They're shooting it now. Of course, you
understand I had to make a few extra changes. Don't
worry, though. I won't ask to share the writing credit with
you.'' He chuckled.

I chuckled right back. "Well, that's a relief.''

"What I'm calling about are the trades today. Since
when have you become a director?''

"I was afraid of this. I'm not allowed to talk about it,
Walt.''

"I asked your agent. He says he didn't handle the
deal.''

"Well, yeah, it's something I set up on my own.''

"Who with?''

"Walt, really I can't talk about it. Those items in the
trades surprised the hell out of me. They might screw up
the deal. I haven't finished the negotiations yet.''

"With this kid who looks like James Deacon.''

"Honestly I've said as much as I can, Walt.''

"I'll tell you flat out. I don't think it's right for you to
try to sneak him away from us. I'm the one who discov-

ered him, remember. I had a look at his screen test yesterday. He's got the making of a star.''

I knew when he'd screened that test. Right after the girl in the casting department phoned him to ask if I had the right to see the test. One thing you can count on in this business. They're all so paranoid that they want to know what everybody else is doing. If they think a trend is developing, they'll stampede to follow it.

''Walt, I'm not exactly trying to sneak him away from you. You don't have him under contract, do you?''

''And what's this project called *Mercenaries?*'' Walt demanded. ''What's that all about?''

''It's a script I did on spec. I got the idea when I heard about the ads at the back of *Soldier of Fortune* magazine.''

''*Soldier of* . . . David, I thought we had a good working relationship.''

''Sure. That's what I thought too.''

''Then why didn't you talk to me about this story? Hey, we're friends, after all. Chances are you wouldn't have had to write it on spec. I could have given you some development money.''

And after you'd finished mucking with it, you'd have turned it into a musical, I thought. ''Well, I guess I figured it wasn't for you. Since I wanted to direct and use an unknown in the lead.''

Another thing you can count on in this business. Tell a producer that a project isn't for him, and he'll feel so left out that he'll want to see it. That doesn't mean he'll buy it. But at least he'll have the satisfaction of knowing that he didn't miss out on a chance for a hit.

''Directing, David? You're a writer. What do you know about directing? I'd have to draw the line on that. But using the kid as a lead. I considered that yesterday after I saw his test.''

Like hell you did, I thought. The test only made you curious. The items in the trades today are what gave you the idea.

"You see what I mean?" I asked. "I figured you wouldn't like the package. That's why I didn't take it to you."

"Well, the problem's hypothetical. I just sent the head of our legal department out to see him. We're offering the kid a long-term option."

"In other words, you want to fix it so no one else can use him, but you're not committing yourself to star him in a picture, and you're paying him a fraction of what you think he might be worth."

"Hey, ten thousand bucks isn't pickled herring. Not from his point of view. So maybe we'll go to fifteen."

"Against?"

"A hundred and fifty thousand if we use him in a picture."

"His agent won't go for it."

"He doesn't have one."

That explained why the Screen Actor's Guild had given me Wes's home address and phone number instead of an agent's.

"I get it now," I said. "You're doing all this just to spite me."

"There's nothing personal in this, David. It's business. I tell you what. Show me the script. Maybe we can put a deal together."

"But you won't accept me as director."

"Hey, with budgets as high as they are, the only way I can justify our risk with an unknown actor is by paying him next to nothing. If the picture's a hit, he'll screw us next time anyhow. But I won't risk money I'm saving by using an inexperienced director who'd probably run the budget into the stratosphere. I see this picture coming in at five million tops.''

"But you haven't even read the script. It's got several big action scenes. Explosions. Helicopters. Expensive special effects. Ten million minimum.''

"That's just my point. If we used a major star, the budget would go up to twenty million, not to mention the percs he'd demand. And you're so close to the concept that you wouldn't want to compromise on the special effects. You're not directing.''

"Well, as you said before, it's hypothetical. I've taken the package to somebody else.''

"Not if we put him under option. David, don't fight me on this. Remember, we're friends.''

Paramount phoned an hour later. Trade gossip travels fast. They'd heard I was having troubles with my studio and wondered if we could take a meeting to discuss the project they'd been reading about.

I said I'd get back to them. But now I had what I wanted—I could truthfully say that Paramount had been in touch with me. I could play the studios off against each other.

Walt phoned back that evening. "What did you do with the kid? Hide him in your closet?''

"Couldn't find him, huh?''

"The head of our legal department says the kid lives with a bunch of freaks way the hell out in the middle of nowhere. The freaks don't communicate too well. The kid isn't there, and they don't know where he went.''

"I'm meeting him tomorrow.''

"Where?''

"Can't say, Walt. Paramount's been in touch.''

*   *   *

Wes met me at a taco stand he liked on Sunset. He'd
been racing his motorcycle in a meet, and when he pulled
up in his boots and jeans, his tee-shirt and leather jacket, I
shivered from deja vu. He looked exactly as Deacon had
looked in *Revolt on Thirty-Second Street*.

"Did you win?"

He grinned and raised his thumb. "Yourself?"

"Some interesting developments."

He barely had time to park his bike before two men in
suits came over. I wondered if they were cops, but their
suits were too expensive. Then I realized. The studio. I'd
been followed from my house.

"Mr. Hepner would like you to look at this," the blue
suit told Wes. He set a document on the roadside table.

"What is it?"

"An option for your services. Mr. Hepner feels that the
figure will interest you."

Wes shoved it over to me. "What's it mean?"

I read it quickly. The studio had raised the fee. They
were offering fifty thousand now against a quarter million.

I told him the truth. "In your position, it's a lot of cash.
I think that at this point you need an agent."

"You know a good one?"

"My own. But that might be too chummy."

"So what do you think I should do?"

"The truth? How much did you make last year? Fifty
grand's a serious offer."

"Is there a catch?"

I nodded. "Chances are you'll be put in *Mercenaries*."

"And?"

"I don't direct."

Wes squinted at me. This would be the moment I'd

always cherish. "You're willing to let me do it?" he asked.

"I told you I can't hold you to our bargain. In your place, I'd be tempted. It's a good career move."

"Listen to him," the gray suit said.

"But do you *want* to direct?"

I nodded. Till now, all the moves had been predictable. But Wes himself was not. Most unknown actors would grab at the chance for stardom. They wouldn't care what private agreements they ignored. Everything depended on whether Wes had a character similar to Deacon's.

"And no hard feelings if I go with the studio?" he asked.

I shrugged. "What we talked about was a fantasy. This is real."

He kept squinting at me. All at once he turned to the suits and slid the option toward them. "Tell Mr. Hepner, my friend here has to direct."

"You're making a big mistake," the blue suit said.

"Yeah, well, here today, gone tomorrow. Tell Mr. Hepner that I trust my friend to make me look good."

I exhaled slowly. The suits looked grim.

I'll skip the month of negotiations. There were times when I sensed that Wes and I had both thrown away our careers. The key was that Walt had taken a stand, and pride wouldn't let him budge. But when I offered to direct for union scale (and let the studio have the screenplay for the minimum the Writer's Guild would allow, and Wes agreed to the Actor's Guild minimum), Walt had a deal he couldn't refuse. Greed budged him in our favor. He bragged about how he'd out-maneuvered us.

We didn't care. I was making a picture I believed in, and Wes was on the verge of being a star.

I did my homework. I brought the picture in for seven million. These days, that's a bargain. The rule of thumb says that you multiply the picture's cost by three (to account for studio overhead and bank interest, this and that), and you've got the breakeven point.

So we were aiming for twenty-one million in ticket sales. Worldwide, we did a hundred and twenty million. Now a lot of that went to the distributors, the folks that sell you popcorn. And a lot of that went into some mysterious black hole of theater owners who don't report all the tickets they sold, and foreign chains that suddenly go bankrupt. But after the sale to Showtime and CBS, after the income from tapes and discs and showings on airlines, the studio had a solid thirty million profit in the bank. And that, believe me, qualifies as a hit.

We were golden. The studio wanted another Wes Crane picture yesterday. The reviews were glowing. Both Wes and I were nominated for—but didn't receive—an Oscar. "Next time," I told Wes.

And now that we were hot, we demanded fees that were large enough to compensate for the pennies we'd been paid on the first one.

Then the trouble started.

You remember that Deacon never knew he was a star. He died with three pictures in the can and a legacy that he never knew would make him immortal. But what you probably don't know is that Deacon became more difficult as he went from picture to picture. The theory is that he sensed the power he was going to have, and he couldn't handle it. Because he was making up for his troubled youth. He was showing people that he wasn't the fuckup his foster parents and his teachers (with one exception) said he was. But Deacon was so intense—and so insecure—

that he started reverting. Secretly he felt he didn't deserve his predicted success. So he did become a fuckup as others had predicted.

On his next-to-last picture, he started showing up three hours late for the scenes he was supposed to be in. He played expensive pranks on the set, the worst of which was lacing the crew's lunch with a laxative that shut down production for the rest of the day. His insistence on racing cars forced the studio to pay exorbitant premiums to the insurance company that covered him during shooting. On his last picture, he was drunk more often than not, swilling beer and tequila on the set. Just before he died in the car crash, he looked twenty-two going on sixty. Most of his visuals had been completed, just a few closeups remaining, but since a good deal of *Birthright* was shot on location in the Texas oilfields, his dialogue needed re-recording to eliminate background noises on the soundtrack. A friend of his who'd learned to imitate Deacon's voice was hired to dub several key speeches. The audience loved the finished print, but they didn't realize how much of the film depended on careful editing, emphasizing other characters in scenes where Deacon looked so wasted that his footage couldn't be used.

So naturally I wondered—if Wes Crane looked like Deacon and sounded like Deacon, dressed like Deacon and had Deacon's style, would he start to behave like Deacon? What would happen when I came to Wes with a second project?

I wasn't the only one offering stories to him. The scripts came pouring in to him.

I learned this from the trades. I hadn't seen him since Oscar night in April. Whenever I called his place, either I didn't get an answer or a spaced-out woman's voice told

me that Wes wasn't home. In truth, I'd expected him to
have moved from that dingy house near the desert. The
gang that lived there reminded me of the Manson clan. But
then I remembered that he hadn't come into big money
yet. The second project would be the gold mine. And I
wondered if he was going to stake the claim out only for
himself.

His motorcycle was parked outside our house when Jill
and I came back from a Writer's Guild screening of a new
Clint Eastwood movie. This was at sunset with sailboats
silhouetted against a crimson ocean. Wes was sitting on
the steps that wound up through a rose garden to our
house. He held a beer can. He was wearing jeans and a
tee-shirt again, and the white of that tee-shirt contrasted
beautifully with his tan. But his cheeks looked gaunter
than when I'd last seen him.

Our exchange had become a ritual.

"Did you win?"

He grinned and raised a thumb. "Yourself?"

I grinned right back. "I've been trying to get in touch
with you."

He shrugged. "Well, yeah, I've been racing. I needed
some down-time. All that publicity, and . . . Jill, how are
you?"

"Fine, Wes. You?"

"The second go-around's the hardest."

I thought I understood. Trying for another hit. But now
I wonder.

"Stay for supper?" Jill asked.

"I'd like to, but . . ."

"Please, do. It won't be any trouble."

"Are you sure?"

"The chili's been cooking in the crockpot all day. Torti-
llas and salad."

Wes nodded. "Yeah, my mom used to like making chili. That's before my dad went away and she got to drinking."

Jill's eyebrows narrowed. Wes didn't notice, staring at his beer can.

"Then she didn't do much cooking at all," he said. "When she went to the hospital . . . This was back in Oklahoma. Well, the cancer ate her up. And the city put me in a foster home. I guess that's when I started running wild." Brooding, he drained his beer can and blinked at us as if remembering we were there. "A home-cooked meal would go good."

"It's coming up," Jill said.

But she still looked bothered, and I almost asked her what was wrong. She went inside.

Wes reached in a paper sack beneath a rose bush. "Anyway, buddy." He handed me a beer can. "You want to make another movie?"

"The trades say you're much in demand." I sat beside him, stared at the ocean, and popped the tab on the beer can.

"Yeah, but aren't we supposed to be a team? You direct and write. I act. Both of us, or none." He nudged my knee. "Isn't that the bargain?"

"It is if you say so. Right now, you've got the clout to do anything you want."

"Well, what I want is a friend. Someone I trust to tell me when I'm fucking up. Those other guys, they'll let you do anything if they think they can make a buck, even if you ruin yourself. I've learned my lesson. Believe me, this time I'm doing things right."

"In that case," I said, vaguely puzzled.

"Let's hear it."

"I've been working on something. We start with several

givens. The audience likes you in an action role. But you've got to be rebellious, anti-establishment. And the issue has to be controversial. What about a bodyguard— he's young, he's tough—who's supposed to protect a famous movie actress? Someone who reminds us of Marilyn Monroe. Secretly he's in love with her, but he can't bring himself to tell her. And she dies from an overdose of sleeping pills. The cops say it's suicide. The newspapers go along. But the bodyguard can't believe she killed herself. He discovers evidence that it was murder. He gets pissed at the coverup. From grief, he investigates further. A hit team nearly kills him. Now he's twice as pissed. And what he learns is that the man who ordered the murder—it's an election year, the actress was writing a tell-it-all about her famous lovers—is the President of the United States.''

"I think"—he sipped his beer—"it would play in Oklahoma.''

"And Chicago and New York. It's a backlash about big government. With a sympathetic hero.''

He chuckled. "When do we start?''

And that's how we made the deal on *Grievance*.

I felt excited all evening, but later—after we'd had a pleasant supper and Wes had driven off on his motorcycle— Jill stuck a pin in my swollen optimism.

"What he said about Oklahoma, about his father running away, his mother becoming a drunk and dying from cancer, about his going to a foster home . . .''

"I noticed it bothered you.''

"You bet. You're so busy staring at your keyboard that you don't keep up on the handouts about your star.''

I set down the bowl I'd taken from the dryer. "So?''

"Wes comes from Indiana. He's a foundling, raised in an orphanage. The background he gave you isn't his."

"Then whose . . . ?"

Jill stared at me.

"My God, not Deacon's."

So there it was, like a hideous face popping out of a box to leer at me. Wes's physical resemblance to Deacon was accidental, an act of fate that turned out to be a godsend for him. But the rest—the mannerisms, the clothes, the voice—were truly deliberate. I know what you're thinking—I'm contradicting myself. When I first met him, I thought that his style was too natural to be a conscious imitation. And when I realized that his screen test was identical in every respect to Deacon's hayloft scene in *The Prodigal Son*, I didn't believe that Wes had callously reproduced the scene. The screen test felt too natural to be an imitation. It was a homage.

But now I knew better. Wes was imitating, all right. But chillingly, what Wes had done went beyond conventional imitation. He'd accomplished the ultimate goal of every method actor. He wasn't playing a part. He wasn't pretending to be Deacon. He actually *was* his model. He'd so immersed himself in a role which at the start was no doubt consciously performed that now he *was* the role. Wes Crane existed only in name. His background, his thoughts, his very identity, weren't his own anymore. They belonged to a dead man.

"What the hell is this?" I asked. *"The Three Faces of Eve? Sybil?"*

Jill looked at me nervously. "As long as it isn't *Psycho*."

What was I to do? Tell Wes he needed help? Have a heart-to-heart and try to talk him out of his delusion? All we had was the one conversation to back up our theory, and anyway he wasn't dangerous. The opposite. His manners were impeccable. He always spoke softly, with humor. Besides, actors used all kinds of ways to psych themselves up. By nature, they're eccentric. The best thing to do, I thought, was wait and see. With another picture about to start, there wasn't any sense in making trouble. If his delusion became destructive . . .

But he certainly wasn't difficult on the set. He showed up a half hour early for his scenes. He knew his lines. He spent several evenings and weekends—no charge—rehearsing with the other actors. Even the studio v.p. admitted that the dailies looked wonderful.

About the only sign of trouble was his mania for racing cars and motorcycles. The v.p. had a fit about the insurance premiums.

"Hey, he needs to let off steam," I said. "There's a lot of pressure on him."

And on me, I'll admit. I had a budget of eighteen million this time, and I wasn't going to ruin things by making my star self-conscious.

Halfway through the shooting schedule, Wes came over. "See, no pranks. I'm being good this time."

"Hey, I appreciate it." What the fuck did he mean by "this time"?

You're probably thinking that I could have stopped what happened if I'd cared more about him than I did for the picture. But I did care—as you'll see. And it didn't matter. What happened was as inevitable as a tragedy.

Grievance became an even bigger success than *Mercenaries*. A worldwide hundred and fifty million gross. *Variety* predicted an even bigger gross for the next one.

Sure, the next one—number three. But at the back of my head, a nasty voice was telling me that for Deacon three had been the unlucky number.

I left a conference at the studio, walking toward my new Ferrari in the executive parking lot, when someone shouted my name. Turning, I peered through the Burbank smog at a longhaired bearded man wearing beads, a serape, and sandals, running over to me. I wondered what he wore, if anything, beneath the dangling serape.

I recognized him—Donald Porter, the friend of Deacon who'd played a bit part in *Birthright* and imitated Deacon's voice on some of the soundtrack after Deacon had died. Porter had to be in his forties now, but he dressed as if the sixties had never ended and hippies still existed. He'd starred and directed in a hit youth film twenty years ago—a lot of drugs and rock and sex. For a while, he'd tried to start his own studio in Santa Fe, but the second picture he directed was a flop, and after fading from the business for a while, he'd made a comeback as a character actor. The way he was dressed, I didn't understand how he'd passed the security guard at the gate. And because we knew each other—I'd done a rewrite on a television show he was featured in—I had the terrible feeling that he was going to ask me for a job.

"I heard you were on the lot. I've been waiting for you," he said.

I stared at his bare legs beneath his serape.

"*This*, man?" He gestured comically at himself. "I'm in the new TV movie they're shooting here. *The Electric Kool-Aid Acid Test*."

I nodded. "Tom Wolfe's book. Ken Kesey. Don't tell me you're playing—"

"No. Too old for Kesey. I'm Neal Cassidy. After he split from Kerouac, he joined up with Kesey, driving the bus for the Merry Pranksters. You know, it's all a load of crap, man. Cassidy never dressed like this. He dressed like Deacon. Or Deacon dressed like him.''

"Well, good. Hey, great. I'm glad things are going well for you." I turned toward my Ferrari.

"Just a second, man. That's not what I wanted to talk to you about. Wes Crane. You know?"

"No, I . . ."

"Deacon, man. Come on. Don't tell me you haven't noticed. Shit, man. I dubbed Deacon's voice. I knew him. I was his *friend*. Nobody else knew him better. Crane sounds more like Deacon than I did."

"So?"

"It isn't possible."

"Because he's better?"

"Cruel, man. Really. Beneath you. I have to tell you something. I don't want you thinking I'm on drugs again. I swear I'm clean. A little grass. That's it." His eyes looked as bright as a nova. "I'm into horoscopes. Astrology. The stars. That's a good thing for a movie actor, don't you think? The stars. There's a lot of truth in the stars."

"Whatever turns you on."

"You think so, man? Well, listen to this. I wanted to see for myself, so I found out where he lives, but I didn't go out there. Want to know why?" He didn't let me answer. "I didn't have to. 'Cause I recognized the address. I've been there a hundred times. When Deacon lived there."

I flinched. "You're changing the subject. What's that got to do with horoscopes and astrology?"

"Crane's birth date."

"Well?"

"It's the same as the day Deacon died."

I realized I'd stopped breathing. "So what?"

"More shit, man. Don't pretend it's coincidence. It's in the stars. You know what's coming. Crane's your bread and butter. But the gravy train'll end four months from now."

I didn't ask.

"Crane's birthday's coming up. The anniversary of Deacon's death."

And when I looked into it, there were other parallels. Wes would be twenty-three—Deacon's age when he died. And Wes would be close to the end of his third movie—about the same place in Deacon's third movie when he . . .

We were doing a script I'd written, *Rampant*, about a young man from a tough neighborhood who comes back to teach there. A local street gang harasses him and his wife until the only way he can survive is by reverting to the violent life (he once led his own gang) that he ran away from.

It was Wes's idea to have the character renew his fascination with motorcycles. I have to admit that the notion had commercial value, given Wes's well-known passion for motorcycle racing. But I also felt apprehensive, especially when he insisted on doing his own stunts.

I couldn't talk him out of it. As if his model behavior on the first two pictures had been too great a strain on him, he snapped to the opposite extreme, showing up late, drinking on the set, playing expensive pranks. One joke involving fire crackers started a blaze in the costume trailer.

It all had the makings of a death wish. His absolute identification with Deacon was leading him to the ultimate parallel.

And just like Deacon in his final picture, Wes began to look wasted. Hollow-cheeked, squinty, stooped from lack of food and sleep. His dailies were shameful.

"How the hell are we supposed to ask an audience to pay to see this shit?" the studio v.p. asked.

"I'll have to shoot around him. Cut to reaction shots from the characters he's talking to." My heart lurched.

"That sounds familiar," Jill said beside me.

I knew what she meant. I'd become the director I'd criticized on *Broken Promises*.

"Well, can't you control him?" the v.p. asked.

"It's hard. He's not quite himself these days."

"Dammit, if you can't, maybe another director can. This garbage is costing us twenty million bucks."

The threat made me seethe. I almost told him to take his twenty million bucks and . . .

Abruptly I understood the leverage he'd given me. I straightened. "Relax. Just let me have a week. If he hasn't improved by then, I'll back out gladly."

"Witnesses heard you say it. One week, pal, or else."

In the morning, I waited for Wes in his trailer when as usual he showed up late for his first shot.

At the open trailer door, he had trouble focusing on me. "If it isn't teach." He shook his head. "No, wrong. It's me who's supposed to play the teach in—what's the name of this garbage we're making?"

"Wes, I want to talk to you."

"Hey, funny thing. The same goes for me with you. Just give me a chance to grab a beer, okay?" Fumbling, he shut the trailer door behind him and lurched through shadows toward the miniature fridge.

"Try to keep your head clear. This is important," I said.

"Right. Sure." He popped the tab on a beer can and left the fridge door open while he drank. He wiped his mouth. "But first I want a favor."

"That depends."

"I don't have to ask, you know. I can just go ahead and do it. I'm trying to be polite."

"What is it?"

"Monday's my birthday. I want the day off. There's a motorcycle race up near Sonora. I want to make a long weekend out of it." He drank more beer.

"We had an agreement once."

He scowled. Beer dribbled down his chin.

"I write and direct. You star. Both of us, or none."

"Yeah. So? I've kept the bargain."

"The studio's given me a week. To shape you up. If not, I'm out of the project."

He sneered. "I'll tell them I don't work if you don't."

"Not that simple, Wes. At the moment, they're not that eager to do what you want. You're losing your clout. Remember why you liked us as a team?"

He listened blearily.

"Because you wanted a friend. To keep you from making what you called the same mistakes again. To keep you from fucking up. Well, Wes, that's what you're doing. Fucking up."

He finished his beer and crumbled the can. He curled his lips, angry. "Because I want a day off on my birthday?"

"No, because you're getting your roles confused. You're not James Deacon. But you've convinced yourself that you are, and Monday you'll die in a crash."

He blinked. Then he sneered. "So what are you, a fortune teller now?"

"A half-baked psychiatrist. Unconsciously you want to

complete the legend. The way you've been acting, the parallel's too exact.''

''I told you the first time we met—I don't like bullshit!''

''Then prove it. Monday, you don't go near a motorcycle, a car, hell, even a go-cart. You come to the studio sober. You do your work as well as you know how. I drive you over to my place. We have a private party. You and me and Jill. She promises to make your favorite meal. Homemade birthday cake. The works. You stay the night. In the morning, we put James Deacon behind us and—''

''Yeah? What?''

''You achieve the career Deacon never had.''

His eyes looked uncertain.

''Or you go to the race and destroy yourself and break the promise you made. You and me together. A team. Don't back out of our bargain.''

He shuddered as if he was going to crack.

In a movie, that would have been the climax—how he didn't race on his birthday, how he had the private party and he hardly said a word and went to sleep in our guest room.

And survived.

But this is what happened. On the Tuesday after his birthday, he couldn't remember his lines. He couldn't play to the camera. He couldn't control his voice. Wednesday was worse.

But I'll say this. On his birthday, the anniversary of Deacon's death, when Wes showed up sober and treated our bargain with honor, he did the most brilliant acting of his career. A zenith of tradecraft. I often watch the video of those scenes with profound respect.

And the dailies were so truly brilliant that the studio v.p. let me finish the picture.

But the v.p. never knew how I faked the rest of it. Overnight, Wes had totally lost his technique. I had enough in the can to deliver a print—with a lot of fancy editing and some uncredited but very expensive help from Donald Porter. He dubbed most of Wes's final dialogue.

"I told you. Horoscopes. Astrology," Donald said.

I didn't believe him till I took four scenes to an audio expert I know. He specializes in voice prints.

He spread the graphs in front of me. "Somebody played a joke on you. Or else you're playing one on me."

I felt so unsteady that I had to press my hands on his desk when I asked him, "How?"

"Using Deacon's scene from *The Prodigal Son* as the standard, this other film is close. But this third one doesn't have any resemblance."

"So where's the joke?"

"In the fourth. It matches perfectly. Who's kidding who?"

Donald Porter had been the voice on the second clip. Close to Deacon's, dubbing for Wes in *Rampant*. Wes himself had been the voice on the third clip—the dialogue in *Rampant* that I couldn't use because he didn't sound like Deacon at all.

And the fourth clip? The voice that was identical to Deacon's, authenticated, verifiable. Wes again. His screen test. The imitated scene from *The Prodigal Son*.

So what's the bottom line?

Wes dropped out of sight. For sure, his technique had collapsed so badly that he would never again be a shining star.

I began to hear rumors, though. So for a final time I

drove out to his dingy place near the desert. The Manson
lookalikes were gone. Only one motorcycle stood outside.
I climbed the steps to the sun porch, knocked, received no
answer, and opened the door.

The blinds were closed. The place was in shadow. I
went down a hall and heard strained breathing. Turned to
the right. And entered a room.

The breathing was louder, more strident and forced.

"Wes?"

"Don't turn on the lights."

"I've been worried about you, friend."

"Don't . . ."

But I did. And what I saw made me swallow vomit.

He was slumped in a chair. Seeping into it would be
more accurate. Rotting. Decomposing. His cheeks had
holes that showed his teeth. A pool that stank of leaking
potatoes spread on the floor around him.

"I should have gone racing on my birthday, huh?" His
voice whistled through the gaping flesh in his throat.

"Oh, shit, friend." I started to cry. "Jesus Christ, I
should have let you."

"Do me a favor, huh? Turn off the light now. Let me
finish this in peace."

I had so much to say to him. But I couldn't. My heart
broke.

"And buddy," he said, "I think we'd better forget
about our bargain. We won't be working together anymore."

I stumbled out of there, blinded by the sun, unable to
clear my nostrils of the stench. I threw up beside the car.

And this is how it ended, the final dregs of his career.
His talent was gone, but how his determination lingered.

Movies. Immortality.

See, special effects are expensive. Studios will grasp at any means to cut the cost.

He'd told me, "Forget about our bargain." I later found out what he meant—he worked without me in one final feature. He wasn't listed in the credits, though. *Zombies from Hell*. Remember how awful Bela Lugosi looked in his last exploitation movie before they buried him in his Dracula cape?

Bela looked great compared to Wes. I saw the Zombie movie in a four-plex out in the valley. It did great business. Jill and I almost didn't get a seat.

Jill wept as I did.

This fucking town. Nobody cares how it's done, as long as it packs them in.

The audience cheered when Wes stalked toward the leading lady.

And his jaw fell off.

JOSEPH PAYNE BRENNAN

Wanderson's Waste

ONE OF THE strangest cases I have ever encountered in association with my investigator friend, Lucius Leffing, occurred in the summer of 1977.

Leffing telephoned to tell me that a Mr. Fraser Hullmont of Cedarville, Connecticut had scheduled an appointment with him for the following afternoon. He admitted that he knew very little concerning Mr. Hullmont's problem but he felt there was a possibility the case might have some features of interest. Would I care to attend?

I agreed without hesitation. Early the next afternoon Leffing welcomed me into his familiar little house at seven Autumn Street.

I was grateful to observe that nothing had changed. Leffing's favorite Morris chair, the colorful Godey fashion prints, the flowered Victorian carpet, were like old friends. I noticed only one new addition: a Mt. Washington Peach-blow decanter in delicate pink of which Leffing appeared inordinately proud. My friend's collection of carefully-chosen art glass, though not extensive, was impressive enough to excite the envy of collectors.

Mr. Hullmont had not yet arrived. We sat quietly chatting and sipping cold sarsaparilla until the door chimes sounded.

Hullmont hitched through the living room with the assistance of two canes. Leffing helped ease him into the Morris chair.

He sank down with a sigh, hanging a cane on either chair arm. "Comfortable chair. Can't stand new-fangled furniture. Makes my bones ache!"

Although an obvious victim of arthritis or some other insidious ailment, Hullmont retained a look of vigor and alertness. His searching eyes, prominent hooked nose and compressed lips made me think of an old eagle, grounded and incapacitated, but still dangerous.

After I was introduced, Hullmont sat silently for a few moments while his quick eyes roved the room.

"Nice decanter you've got there, Mr. Leffing. Pretty penny went into that, eh?"

Leffing smiled. "Actually I acquired it at a bargain price. Quite a nice little find, I believe."

Hullmont nodded. "I'm sure it is. I don't collect but I recognize quality when I see it."

He cleared his throat rather portentously and leaned forward. "Before I—launch into my problem—we had better settle the matter of fees. The natives of Cedarville think I'm a millionaire, but that's nonsense. My income goes down every year and my expenses go up. I've had to retire from active business of course. Too much trouble dragging these twisted legs around."

Leffing nodded sympathetically. "My fees are flexible, Mr. Hullmont. Charges depend on the time required for a case, the effort expended, the expenses involved and so on. I can assure you, however, that I keep fees at a most reasonable level."

I knew this to be true. Hullmont did not seem entirely satisfied but at length he shrugged. "I'll chance it then. I'm determined to get at the root of this business."

Leffing tented his long fingers and leaned back in his chair. "What is the problem, Mr. Hullmont?"

"I own a spread of land up in Cedarville, six hundred acres, give or take a few. A big chunk of this land, about half, belonged formerly to a local family named Wanderson. It's a dismal sort of place, swampy, inhospitable, brackish pools in one place, barren ridges in another. Hardly anything seems to thrive except clumps of fern in the swamps and conifers along the higher ground. The last Wanderson was found dead in a pool there about sixty years ago. It appeared he fell in and drowned, but there were—still are—rumors that something else happened. I don't know. Don't much care. But the place has got an evil name and I think the native loafers are behind it all. Foolish gossip and probably more than that."

Leffing's eyebrows lifted. "More than that, Mr. Hullmont?"

"Yes, I am convinced so. While I have no immediate plans for selling out, I have few illusions concerning my future. I may become so crippled that I can no longer cope with the place. I manage now with a housekeeper-cook and a gardener-handyman, but if it gets so that I can't walk at all, I'll need a full-time nurse. Too expensive, too complicated. In that event, I'd sell out and move into a so-called convalescent home."

Leffing frowned. "Of what concern is this to the—natives?"

"Well, you see, several times during the past year, I've had developers in to look at the property. It was the same story every time. They came full of enthusiasm but after prowling over the land and snooping about the town, their enthusiasm cooled remarkably. Their tentative offers were so preposterously low that I more or less dismissed them on the spot. Two of them who had poked quite a distance into Wanderson's Waste hinted that they had had some kind of very disagreeable experiences there.''

"Wanderson's Waste?'' Leffing repeated quizzically.

Hullmont flushed angrily. "That's what the nitwit natives call the old Wanderson land holdings. Been referring to it that way for years.''

Leffing sat silently for a few moments. "You just said, Mr. Hullmont, that two of the developers hinted at a 'very disagreeable experience' while looking over the old Wanderson holdings. Could you elaborate on that?''

Hullmont scowled. "They were both vague about it. Seems they felt they were being followed, spied on, threatened. Made them feel uncomfortable, frightened even.''

He leaned forward. "I'll tell you what I think. Some of the nosier—and more unscrupulous—natives followed the developers into Wanderson's Waste in a deliberate attempt to scare them off! It's a—a conspiracy, that's what it is! And I won't put up with it!''

"I must at this point admit to some confusion,'' Leffing conceded. "Why on earth should the Cedarville people conspire to frighten off possible purchasers of your property?''

Hullmont looked up in surprise. "I thought that was obvious, Mr. Leffing. Don't you see? The natives know what will happen if my land is sold to developers. Roads will be cut through, houses will go up, city folk will pour in. Actually, it would put Cedarville on its feet—just what it needs. But the natives don't view it that way. Bitterly opposed. A lot of nonsense about the consequences: new schools, rising taxes, old ways of life changed. What they're too dim-witted to see is that new jobs would be created, new opportunities. Everybody in the town would ultimately benefit.''

"I believe I have the situation in focus," Leffing commented. "It is by no means an uncommon one. But what is it you wish us to do about it, Mr. Hullmont?"

Hullmont leaned forward with a grim look. "Come up to Cedarville disguised as land developers. Ask questions around the village. Make yourself conspicuous. Act eager. And then prowl around my place, Wanderson's Waste in particular. With any luck at all, you'll catch those half-wit connivers red-handed!"

Leffing appeared to ponder this suggestion. At length he nodded. "Your plan sounds sensible, Mr. Hullmont, but I must warn you—nothing at all may come of it. I cannot predict results, and certainly not success, in any of these matters."

Hullmont took hold of his canes. "I'll risk it. I've heard of your abilty."

He struggled to his feet. "And even if you fail, I'll be no worse off."

He turned at the door. "Except for your fee," he added with a sardonic smile.

Leffing escorted him down the porch steps to his car. It was agreed that we would visit Cedarville the following week. Apparently the village boasted a small inn where rooms could be engaged. It was used by a few "summer people" plus an occasional traveling salesman. Hullmont grudgingly conceded that the food and service were acceptable.

As we drove toward Cedarville the following Tuesday, I glanced at my companion. "I hate to admit it, Leffing, but I think we're embarked on the proverbial wild-goose chase. I believe Hullmont is the victim of a very ordinary type of persecution mania. He probably sits around brooding about his affliction, worrying about his future and inwardly cursing the 'half-wit natives', as he calls them."

Instead of taking offense (as I feared he might) Leffing merely shrugged. "You may be right, Brennan, but meanwhile we are enjoying the Connecticut scenery, and a bit of country air can do us no harm."

Cedarville, if not entirely a typical New England village, was of an order with which I was familiar: a general store with a gas pump, a white-steepled church, a clapboard building with a sign reading "Social Hall", a small inn (The Hickory Arms) and about a dozen other buildings, most of them private frame houses, centered around a grassy common set off by a flagpole and two wooden benches whose green paint was beginning to peel. Farmhouses, barns, and a few other structures could be glimpsed in the distance.

We parked alongside The Hickory Arms and were soon settled in clean but rather cramped quarters: two small rooms and a bath obviously designed for a dwarf.

Cedarville, luckily, was situated in the hilly section of northwest Connecticut. In spite of the summer heat, a refreshing breeze stirred the curtains on the screened windows of our cubicle quarters.

After driving for an hour or more, I usually enjoy a walk. Leffing fell in with my suggestion and we strolled around the common.

"How do land developers act?" I asked.

"Just pretend you are one," Leffing answered. "Peer at buildings and plots with a speculative eye. Stand about reflectively with hand on chin, eyes narrowed."

I looked at him, but he maintained a poker face.

"We are supposed to make ourselves conspicuous, Brennan. Let us sit on one of these benches for a few minutes."

As we sprawled on a bench in the little green, the absurdity of the situation grew on me.

"This whole business is farcical, Leffing! Wanderson's Waste is nothing more than Hullmont's Hallucination!"

"Well said, Brennan, but we had best make sure, at all events."

An occasional car drove past and three or four pedestrians cut through the common but nobody paid us any particular attention.

At Leffing's suggestion, we finally arose and wandered over to the general store.

Here Leffing's conduct amazed me. In no time at all he had cornered the proprietor behind the counter. His manner was effusive and brash. He plied the old man with questions in a rather loud voice, inquiring about houses and farms for sale, road conditions, the tax rate. Several times he mentioned Hullmont by name. He was polite, yet subtly aggressive and disagreeable. Several loungers in the store edged up to listen.

I was considerably relieved when he thanked the old storekeeper and we left. I had hovered uncomfortably in the background, feeling awkward and ill at ease.

As we walked down the store steps, I noted an expression of satisfaction on his face.

"You have uncovered something of import?" I asked.

"Absolutely!" he replied. "I have ascertained that Kell's General Supply Store stocks sarsaparilla!"

Leffing's evasive flippancy often annoyed me but I ignored the remark. "You certainly acted like a land developer. You might make a successful career of the business!"

"I believe not. I rather think the successful land developer approaches his prospects in a far smoother and less conspicuous manner. As a matter of fact, I acted more like a liniment salesman! But we have now made our presence and purported field of interest apparent. In a day or two—if not by nightfall—everyone in the village and its environs will know about us.''

The next afternoon we drove out to Hullmont's home. He lived in a sprawling clapboard farmhouse about three miles from the village center. Although the house itself gleamed with a fresh coat of white paint, there was evidence of growing neglect in the unkempt yard and among the outbuildings. Grass needed mowing; some windows were cracked; lumber, kegs and papers lay scattered about.

Five minutes passed before there was any response to Leffing's application of the brass knocker. Hullmont himself opened the door.

"Sorry to keep you waiting. Housekeeper's out shopping and—wouldn't you know—the gardener's been off sick all week.''

He shook his head. "I sometimes think the both of them are in on the—conspiracy. Place is going down hill. Used to keep everything spic and span, but no more.''

Muttering, he directed us down a carpeted hallway to a cool farmhouse "parlor", shades drawn against the sun and a faint mustiness pervading the atmosphere.

With an effort, he hitched his way to an armchair and carefully lowered himself into it. "Infernal nuisance, hobbling around. When your legs go, you're only half a man!''

He motioned us toward chairs and sat forward. "You have—made yourselves known—amongst the local snoopers and idiots?''

"At this point," Leffing replied, "I would hazard the guess that scarcely a soul in the village is unaware of our presence. I questioned Mr. Kell at the General Store rather closely.''

Hullmont grinned approval. "Just as good as announcing yourselves from the church steeple with a bullhorn!"

His suspicious eyes searched our faces. "Were you followed here?"

Leffing shook his head. "I saw no evidence of it."

"Humpf!" Hullmont seemed disappointed.

He pulled at his canes impatiently. "If you were followed, I don't think you *would* see any evidence of it. Give the devils their due—those yokels can fade into the underbrush along the roads like so many ropes of smoke. Clever at that kind of thing. Are you planning to take a prowl over my land today?"

"I think not today, Mr. Hullmont. It might be a bit premature. Best let the situation ripen a bit. We will remain in the village another day or two before exploring your estate."

Hullmont was obviously displeased. I believe he had mental visions of Leffing's fee mounting daily.

He frowned but inclined his head. "As you see fit, Mr. Leffing. Is there anything you want me to do?"

Leffing stood up. "Nothing, Mr. Hullmont. I came out to keep you apprised of developments. And even though I do not think we were followed, I believe our presence here will be made known in the village in due time!"

Hullmont's shaggy eyebrows met above his bony nose. "I'm sure of that! Those loafers will learn of it before you get back!"

As we drove along toward the village, Leffing, as was often the case, remained uncommunicative.

"It seems odd to me," I ventured, "that both Hullmont's housekeeper and handyman were absent when we arrived. Could it be that they deliberately arranged to be absent?"

Leffing shook his head. "Hullmont said that the gardener had been off sick for a week. I fail to see how he could have anticipated our visit to Cedarville.''

I shrugged and said no more.

Dinner at The Hickory Arms was plain but substantial: boiled potatoes, roast beef, corn on the cob and a dish of sliced tomatoes. Apple pie and coffee rounded out the meal.

After a stroll around the common, we sat on the inn porch for a half hour and then retired to our rooms. The evening was cool and we went to bed early.

Leffing remained taciturn the next morning. After breakfast, he lounged about the inn porch. At length his lethargic manner and mood of apathy got on my nerves.

"I'm going for a hike," I announced abruptly. He merely nodded.

After a long ramble along the country roads, I returned in time for lunch. I was gratified to notice that Leffing appeared more animated.

When lunch was over, we sat on the common. "How did your morning go?" I asked.

Leffing smiled. "I acted like a liniment salesman again in Kell's store and I also elicited a nugget of information from Mrs. Cowdran, the gossipy wife of our good boniface."

"What was the nugget of information?"

"I took the bull by the horns, Brennan, and asked her what she knew about Wanderson's Waste. She repeated what Hullmont had already told us. Sixty-odd years ago the last Wanderson was found dead, apparently drowned in a pool or small pond situated in the so-called 'Waste'. Although she did not use the word 'autopsy', Mrs. Cowdran informed me that an 'examination' had been held on the remains. There was no water in the lungs and the entire cadaver was covered with strange-looking bruises. 'Like big welts they was, all purplish-colored', to quote Mrs. Cowdran. A perfunctory investigation was made, but nothing ever came of it. Since that time, Wanderson's Waste has been shunned by the local people. Hullmont got his property at rockbottom because it included the old Wanderson holdings.''

"An odd enough incident," I admitted, "but I can't see that it has any particular relevance after sixty years."

Leffing stood up, brushing off some flakes of peeling green paint which adhered to his trousers. "You may be right, Brennan. I think, however, it is high time we had a look at this property of ill repute."

"Drive slowly," he instructed, as we headed back toward Hullmont's place. "If local mischief makers want to shadow us, we shall give them every advantage!"

He smiled as we cruised along the winding country road. "I am sure Mrs. Cowdran knows where we are going and a greater gossip never wagged tongue!"

Hullmont's housekeeper, a faded woman in her fifties who wore her grey-streaked hair in an old-fashioned bun, opened the door for us.

Hullmont hitched along behind her, ushered us into the parlor and closed the door.

"We have now made ourselves sufficiently conspicuous, I believe," Leffing told him. "We must not overdo the act. With your approval, we will take a little ramble about your property. You might just indicate which portion consists of Wanderson's Waste, as it is called."

Hullmont slumped into his armchair. "You'll have no trouble recognizing it. Miserable terrain. Bogs and barren hillocks."

After giving us general directions, he leaned forward in his chair. His sharp eyes scrutinized us. "See any of those village half-wits sneaking out here after you?"

"We saw none, but we drove slowly and I am certain that Mrs. Cowdran surmised our destination."

Hullmont nodded his satisfaction. "If that old bellwether knows, then the whole of Cedarville knows! Silly old sheep!"

I was perversely tempted to point out that a bellwether is always a male but prudently refrained.

We left him sitting in the musty parlor, like a dyspeptic old eagle shackled in a dingy cage.

It was warm and windless as we started out across the meadow which lay behind Hullmont's farmhouse. Grasshoppers whirred over the clumps of ox-eye daisies; plump bees explored the clover patches and a barn swallow skimmed over our heads.

At the far end of the meadow, we climbed over a weathered stone wall and entered what appeared to be a former cow pasture, overgrown now with brush, sumac and maple saplings. According to Hullmont, Wanderson's Waste bordered the distant edge of this neglected pasture.

As we pushed our way through the crowded brush and clumps of small trees, insect and bird sounds gradually subsided. The pasture was a sizable one; by the time we reached the near end of it, almost complete silence had descended.

There was no sharp demarcation line between the pasture and Wanderson's Waste. We passed gradually from patches of briers and brush into swamp ground where the pasture bushes straggled out, to be replaced by clumps of fern and reeds.

The first thing I noticed was the oppressive humidity. Tongues of mist curled above the quaggy pools, hung over the clusters of wood and cinnamon ferns.

Silence seemed absolute. The cicadas had grown still; the warblers and finches had disappeared; I could no longer hear the scurry of squirrels nor the buzzing of searching bees.

Very shortly we were carefully probing through a depressing bog-like area which appeared to nourish only fern fronds, reeds and spears of swamp grass.

Along occasional ridges of higher ground, various kinds of conifer trees had sunk in stubborn roots. For the most part, pines, cedars and larch had claimed the raised ribs of dryer soil. Low-growing yew and juniper clung to the slopes of these ridges.

Glimpsed suddenly through the rising mist, these conifer-crowned hillocks had a strange spectral appearance.

It occurred to me that neither Leffing nor myself had uttered a word since entering the desolate expanse known as Wanderson's Waste.

"The place is aptly named," I commented.

My own voice somehow sounded hollow and detached. Leffing nodded. "That is so," he replied absently.

We moved along slowly, skirting the misty pools and reed-circled ponds as well as we could. Ferns grew everywhere in lush profusion. I noticed bladderfern, wood fern, sensitive fern and half a dozen others I was unable to identify. The majority seemed enormous, thickly spread, all out of proportion to their normal size.

As we advanced, I was filled with a disturbing sense of apprehension. I tried to shrug it off, well aware that I am often unduly influenced by the atmospheric effects of landscape. But the apprehension persisted.

"Do you think we are being followed?" I finally asked Leffing, in what I'm sure was a sepulchral voice.

He paused and glanced aside at me. I thought I detected both alarm and puzzlement on his perspiring features.

"I am—not sure," he answered shortly.

He edged ahead and I followed reluctantly. The pools

became more numerous, the mist thickened and the hill-ocks crowned by fir and pine loomed less often through the hazy air.

We had stopped, faced by a pond larger than any we had previously encountered, when I thought I detected movement somewhere ahead. It was at first elusive but finally unmistakable. The air itself appeared to tremble and then coalesce into an amorphous core of motion which moved through the mist toward us at a frightening speed. It seems impossible to describe the thing. It had no definite outline or contours; its lineaments melted together as it moved, liquescent, gaseous. Briefly, I tried to convince myself that it was only a figment of my overactive imagi-nation, but I sensed and felt the thing's malignancy. That could not be imagination.

It rushed in our direction, an appalling funnel of energy. It reminded me of a huge spinning top in motion.

As we stood rooted, it was almost upon us.

"Down, Brennan!" Leffing commanded, flinging him-self prone.

I was an instant too late. A burning sensation sliced down my left side, from shoulder to thigh. I felt as if I had been suddenly branded with a hot iron.

I hurled myself down and hugged the ground next to Leffing.

I had the conviction that although the thing had passed over after attacking me, it still hovered somewhere above. It was, I felt sure, searching for us.

After a minute or two, Leffing spoke. "Are you hurt?"

I grimaced, my face against the damp ground. "Not seriously, I think. Just lashed a bit."

We waited a minute longer and then cautiously got up.

Leffing peered through the heavy mist which hung above

the pond just ahead. "We must leave here at once. There may be—more of them!"

As we turned to retrace our footsteps, I felt, rather than heard, a kind of humming in the air.

Without ceremony, Leffing seized me and we dropped to earth together. The air above us seemed to vibrate with furious energy. We lay almost without breathing. After a few seconds—which felt to us like long minutes—the intensity of the vibration diminished. In another minute or so the air was calm again.

Once more we regained our feet.

Taking my arm, Leffing plunged forward. "Hurry, Brennan. We have ventured into a veritable hornets' nest!"

I thought the metaphor an apt one. My left side felt as if half a hundred hornets had left their stingers in it.

It was impossible to run straight ahead out of that sprawling morass. There were too many ponds and pools, too many encumbering clumps of fern, too many abrupt ridges. Our route was necessarily circuitous, our speed, under the circumstances, maddeningly limited.

Twice more, before we finally reached the environs of the old cow pasture, that fearful funnel of malignant, searching energy swirled through the heavy mist to seek us out. Each time, it appeared to me, we escaped, literally, by inches.

I gained the distinct impression that the force, whatever it was, could not actually *see,* in a literal sense. I gathered that it somehow apprehended *motion* and that if we lay perfectly still, scarcely daring to breathe, the thing found it difficult to detect us.

But I felt at the time that there might well be more than one of the things and that the odds were decidedly against us.

We were soaked, lacerated, covered with mud and slime,

and breathing like long-distance runners by the time we staggered into the first straggling line of saplings which ran along the edge of the pasture.

Once well into the pasture, the sense of imminent danger and pursuit left us. By the time we had clambered over the stone wall into the meadow, we were breathing normally again.

But we must have presented an alarming appearance when we arrived back at Hullmont's farmhouse. The faded housekeeper stared at us as if she might faint. Hullmont himself hitched up behind her with a concerned yet half-triumphant expression.

"Those village bounders attacked you in the swamp?"

"We were attacked, Mr. Hullmont, but I am convinced that the villagers had nothing to do with it. If you can supply us with hot baths and a bit of merthiolate for our cuts, we will give an account of our little adventure."

The housekeeper led us upstairs to an old-fashioned bathroom which contained an enormous galvanized tub. She laid out fresh towels and soap, pointed out the medicine cabinet and left.

As I undressed to bathe, I glanced in the floor-length mirror. An ugly purple welt, or weal, ran from my left shoulder to my thigh. It burned with brief but agonizing intensity when I lowered myself into the hot water.

Later, when we had both toweled down, Leffing examined it closely. "Ugly enough, Brennan. If any sign of infection shows, you had better hurry to a doctor's."

With a sudden shudder, I recalled Mrs. Cowdran's account of the last Wanderson who was found dead in a pool, covered with strange-looking bruises. 'Like big welts they was, all purplish-colored', Mrs. Cowdran had told Leffing.

Hullmont was waiting for us in the musty parlor. He had

had the housekeeper set out glasses and a decanter of whiskey. He fidgeted impatiently as we gratefully helped ourselves to drinks.

After a succinct but graphic description of our encounter in the swamp, Leffing set aside his glass. "I am by now fully convinced, Mr. Hullmont, that Wanderson's Waste is indeed infested—but not by spiteful villagers. I believe that the area harbors an elemental—or elementals—and has done so for many decades—perhaps centuries!"

Hullmont stared at him. "An—*elemental?* You mean a ghost?"

Leffing smiled faintly. "Not exactly, Mr. Hullmont. A ghost is the revenant of a deceased person. An elemental is a primitive life form, ordinarily invisible, which may have existed for millennia."

Hullmont scowled, obviously unconvinced.

Leffing went on patiently. "Nature experimented with many primitive life forms—the various kinds of dinosaurs, the mammoth, the pterodactyl, the sabertooth tiger, and hosts of other creatures too numerous to mention. Many of these ancient life forms, I am convinced, have never been identified. Is it so surprising then, that nature created as well early life forms which exist outside the range of our rudimentary and limited sensory apparatus? Elementals have been reported, feared, and written of for centuries—for thousands of years actually. They would appear to be impervious to the passage of time as we know it."

Hullmont shifted his canes restlessly. "Even accepting your premise—which I'm not sure I do—why has this infernal creature settled in my swamp? What does it want?"

Leffing explained. "As Brennan and I advanced into the swamp section known locally as Wanderson's Waste, I was immediately struck by one singular observation. We might as well have been entering a forest of the Paleozoic, the age of ferns and conifers. Wanderson's Waste resembles a patch of Paleozoic swamp somehow preserved into the present time. There are vast differences, of course, but the resemblance remains: the humidity, the ever-present mist, the great fern fronds, the conifers clinging to the otherwise barren ridges, the gleaming pools, the all-pervading silence. The resemblance was striking, overwhelming in its implications.

"The elemental which we encountered may well have evolved or at least attained its own bizarre maturity in Paleozoic times. It may have survived in this kind of environment for millions of years. Although it obviously maintained its existence long after its familiar milieu vanished, it apparently attached itself to Wanderson's Waste, once it located that eerie expanse. In many respects the Waste is like a Paleozoic swamp in miniature.

"I am now convinced that the last Wanderson was killed in the swamp by this same elemental and I think your two land developers were lucky to escape with their lives when they went in to inspect this unprepossessing property."

Hullmont sat sunk in thought for long minutes. He appeared to be impressed by Leffing's story but by no means ready to accept it without qualification.

He looked up at length. "What course of action would you suggest I take, Mr. Leffing?"

"Drain the entire swamp, Mr. Hullmont. Cut down the conifers. Level the ridges and fill in the empty pools. If possible, secure a permit and finally burn over the entire area. The malignant entity—or entities—which at present infests this accursed bog will almost certainly disappear."

Hullmont looked doubtful. "You suggest a pretty expensive procedure, Mr. Leffing!"

Leffing stood up. "I see no other, Mr. Hullmont. Have

the workmen start at the edges and gradually push toward the center. Warn them they are to be on the alert at all times.''

Hullmont had not risen as we walked toward the door. ''What about your fee, Mr. Leffing?''

Leffing turned. ''If you act on my suggestion, send me whatever amount you consider suitable, after six months have elapsed. If I fail to hear from you at the end of that period of time, I will mail you my own invoice for basic expenses.''

We left him sitting there, a stubborn, narrow-minded old man, disappointed because he could not blame the villagers for his troubles, skeptical in the face of something he could not readily comprehend.

As we drove back to New Haven, I turned to my friend.

''Two things are bothering me, Leffing. You say elementals are invisible—yet I am sure I saw the thing, amorphous though it was, advancing on us. And how could something invisible, with no physical body as we understand it, inflict this nasty weal on me?''

''Elementals are ordinarily invisible, Brennan, but it may be that in times of stress—fury, agitation, directed rage, the very intensity of their emotions make them at least partially visible. They are *forces*, Brennan, forces not fully understood certainly, but forces which might agitate the air, 'make it tremble', as it were, forces which might briefly impress upon the air their own outline and image. And force would explain that welt you received. Force can wound, or kill, without being visible.''

As was not infrequently the case, Leffing's explanation did not entirely satisfy me, but I had no other.

Nearly five months had passed, when my friend telephoned me one afternoon and asked me to visit him that evening.

After my arrival, he sat back in his Morris chair with an air of contentment. "Yesterday I received a note from Mr. Hullmont. He has followed my advice. The swamp has been drained and filled, the ridges leveled, the drying ferns, reeds and bog grasses burned off, the cut trees hauled away. The aura of unpleasantness and menace has entirely disappeared and Hullmont has already received several handsome offers for his property, including, of course, the tract known as Wanderson's Waste."

He got up, languidly, and moved to the sideboard where he poured two glasses of brandy.

"Mr. Hullmont's check," he commented, "should keep us supplied with decent brandy for quite some time to come!"

Pick-Up

HE WAS IN a restless, edgy mood and the intermittent sheets of rain which slashed across the windshield did not help matters. His foot pressed heavily against the gas pedal even though he knew it hadn't rained long enough for the slippery scum of oil and grease to be washed off the road.

Speed suited his mood. As so often in the past, he was bored with his paper-shuffling job, with his patient, routine-rut wife, with his lawn-girt suburban house. All his life, it seemed, he had been casting about for adventure, variety, a break in tedium—with some success.

When he saw the woman standing alongside the highway in the rain, arm extended, he slowed down from force of habit.

Years ago, he had got into the potentially exciting and hazardous habit of picking up female hitchhikers. He was aware of the risks; he had survived a few hairy encounters; but he had never entirely given up the practice.

Some of his most rewarding affairs had been triggered by an outstretched thumb.

He braked carefully, stopping only a few feet beyond

the woman. He was still reaching for the door when she
opened it and hopped in beside him.

He saw at once that he had made a mistake. She was not
merely old; she was haggard, mottled, puffy-lipped. Her
eyes looked out-of-focus. He wondered if she was high on
drugs.

He shrugged. He couldn't very well shove her back out
into the rain. Well, it might prove mildly amusing, he told
himself. He'd dump her at the nearest bus stop on some
pretext. Meanwhile she might help alleviate the boredom.

She turned toward him with a half-toothless grin. "Hello,
handsome! Goin' my way, honey?"

For some reason which he couldn't immediately fathom,
the greeting left him oddly disturbed.

Dismissing this, he started on. "I'm just traveling along
a few miles," he commented casually. "Get you to a bus
shelter anyway. Looks like it might rain all night."

"All night," she repeated. "Maybe forever."

Frowning, he glanced at her. A real kook, he concluded. Well, it was always pot luck when you picked up
one of the road people.

Rain streamed against the car as if it might indeed drum
down interminably. His wipers were efficient enough but
the rushing downpour made him concentrate on the road
ahead. Visibility was limited to a few feet.

Soon however, sensing that she was staring at him, he
looked around again. She was no longer grinning. Her
glazed eyes were fastened on him; her expression puzzled
him. Something about him appeared to intrigue her.

He swung his eyes back toward the road. Have to stay
alert. You never knew about these floozies. She might pull
a gun or yell Rape if she saw people at a bus stop.

Five minutes later he spotted an empty bus shelter and
drew abreast of it.

"I turn off just ahead," he told her. "You'll have a roof here anyway. The bus runs hourly, I guess."

She sat there unmoving, staring at him.

He reached across and opened the door. "I'm sorry, lady. I'm in a hurry."

She slid backwards out of the car, filmy eyes still fixed on him.

She was standing there, staring, when he slammed the door. Looking back, just as he drove off, he saw that she was gone.

"Half-witted old hag," he muttered. "Too dumb to stay out of the rain."

He drove homeward unwillingly, feeling more frustrated than he had before. Just his luck. Damned old harridan!

In spite of the driving rain, he rolled the window partway down. The wet seat alongside him emitted a sickening odor. Stale rainwater mixed with cheap perfume, he decided.

Papers were piled a foot high on his desk the next day. He was too busy to spend any time thinking about the events of the previous evening.

After dinner and a boring two hours with TV, his wife went to bed. Although he remained restless, he felt tired. Best stay home, he concluded. Switching off the box, he mixed a scotch and soda and picked up the evening paper.

As he scanned the news articles with a perfunctory attention, a one-column headline on page three caught his eye: "Woman Drives into Lake, Drowns."

He read down. "Woman identified as Wilma Crent, 45." "Employed as waitress, check-out clerk." "Address uncertain." "Accident or suicide." "Police not sure." "Investigation continuing." "Car may have been stolen."

His hand shook as he dropped the paper and picked up his drink. Wilma Crent! He had had an off-and-on affair with her for years. One of his most exciting in some

ways. It didn't seem possible that she was 45. Suicide? It
wouldn't surprise him. She had been desolated when he
left her for the last time. Probably gone downhill ever
since. Over fifteen years since he'd seen her last.

He poured another scotch and began to reminisce. She'd
been hitchhiking rides, like most of the others, when he
first saw her. It had started to rain. When he stopped,
she'd given him a cute, come-on smile. 'Hello, handsome!' she'd said. 'Goin' my way, honey?'

He almost dropped his drink when he recalled that initial
greeting. Could that slack-faced tramp he'd picked up the
previous evening . . .? Impossible, he assured himself.
Just a coincidence. Just part of the road floozies' jargon.
Any one of them might say that.

And yet . . . That strange way she'd kept staring at him. . .

He read the article again, more carefully. The police
were vague about the time. ''Late evening or some time
during the night.''

Had it been Wilma after all? Had her chance meeting
with him made her decide to end it all? Maybe because he
hadn't recognized her? Maybe because the good times
they'd had together, contrasted to the miserable existence
she had come to endure, was too much for her to go on
thinking about?

In despair, maybe, she'd darted away from the bus stop,
stolen a car and later deliberately driven into the lake.

By the time he dropped into bed, the scotch was nearly
gone.

He couldn't concentrate on work the next day. Was that
bleary-eyed old woman he'd picked up really Wilma Crent?
How could anyone go downhill so fast? She looked more
like 75 than 45. He was aware of a sense of remorse and it
made him angry. It wasn't his fault. The affair had become

awkward and tiresome. If she'd let herself go to pieces on booze and drugs, she had only herself to blame.

He did his best to dismiss the whole business from his mind. What the hell. Probably wasn't her anyway.

As the days passed, he gradually forgot about it. The job, always somewhat sticky, was getting out of hand. His wife, ordinarily complacent, was becoming increasingly restless and critical. Enough problems.

He'd worked late and he was driving back in the rain. He drove slowly; November leaves made the road treacherous. He felt tired, old. The thought of the evening paper and a few quiet drinks at home was beginning to look better every night.

He didn't see anyone and he certainly didn't hear the car door open or close, but suddenly the smell—like a mixture of stale water and cheap perfume—seemed to permeate the interior of the vehicle.

The hair on his neck began to bristle but he forced himself to turn.

She was sitting there as formerly, staring at him with filmy out-of-focus eyes, that frightful mirthless grin contorting her puffy lips.

"Hello, handsome! Goin' my way, honey?"

Canavan Calling

A QUARTER OF a century had passed since that chill and desolate autumn day when I ran from Canavan's bewitched back yard like a soul possessed—ran headlong through the wind-scoured streets, vowing that I would never again go near the accursed place.

I am not sure what impelled me to return. Morbid curiosity, you might suggest. Possibly. But I believe it was something beyond mere inquisitiveness. I experienced a persistent compulsion to return. An intangible but potent force seemed pressuring me to revisit the scene of poor Canavan's frightening derangement—and disappearance.

Although I had remained away from the area for twenty-five years, from time to time I had heard rumors concerning it: a rabid dog, "foaming at the mouth", had been glimpsed running in circles through the overgrown waste of brindle grass which crowded the back yard; a crazed tramp, wild-eyed and dangerous, lived in the yard, hiding by day, prowling by night; an aged crone, lacerated and screaming imprecations, had been seen rushing through the matted grass and thickets. And so on.

Common sense, simple prudence, and my own nightmare experience warned me to stay away. But something
else—at last irresistible—prompted me to return.

Years before, I had assumed that Canavan's neglected
house—eventually taken by the city for nonpayment of
taxes—would be demolished and that the back yard would
be cleared to make way for some kind of housing project. I
was wrong. Prospective buyers and developers came, looked
and went away, murmuring various complaints: the area
was not yet "ripe" for development; the tract appeared
swampy-looking and poorly-drained; highway and shopping access was too limited; etc.

So, as the years passed, the house, ramshackle to begin
with, fell into near ruin; stalks of grass in the back yard
grew tougher and more tangled; the jagged shrubs became
nearly impenetrable. And blackened trunks of the dead
apple trees finally rotted away into the weeds and grass.

Canavan, of course, had never been found. I understand
that he was officially listed as a missing person. Inquiries
had been made and a search had been undertaken. But the
inquiries were routine, the search perfunctory.

Thus matters stood when, in defiance of my own better
judgement, I decided to make one final visit to Canavan's
back yard.

At this point, for the sake of those who have not read
my previous account, *Canavan's Back Yard*, first printed
in 1958, I will briefly recapitulate.

In those long-vanished years I had become friendly with
Canavan, an antiquarian book dealer who operated from a
small isolated house on the outskirts of New Haven. Canavan
at first rented and later purchased the place. Behind the
house lay a neglected and overgrown yard, covered with
tall brown grass, briars and a number of rotted apple trees.
The entire lot, scarcely an acre, appeared to offer nothing

of interest but Canavan gradually became intrigued by
what he regarded as some unusual feature of the landscape—
"something about distance and dimensions and perspec-
tives", he told me. After his curiosity had turned into a
compelling obsession, I visited his shop one day to find
that he had apparently disappeared into the back yard.
Following a frightening exploration through the brittle grass
stalks, I found him—changed into a mindless, bestial shell
of his former self. He pursued me—with lethal intent I was
convinced—but I escaped. Although I informed the police,
Canavan was never found. Later, after long research, I
learned that his back yard was the site of a marsh where an
old woman, Goodie Larkins, condemned as a witch in
1692, had been torn to death by starving wild dogs released by her accusers. Before her death, Larkins had
uttered a curse: *"Let this land I fall upon lye alle the way
to Hell! And they who tarry here be as these beastes that
rende me dead!"*

So it was that, finally, one bleak and overcast day in the
late fall of the year, I started out for Canavan's crumbling
house and the blighted, curse-ridden back yard which lay
behind it. Although the distance was considerable, I
walked—as I had a quarter century before. While I made
my way through the damp, half-deserted streets, I seemed
drawn onward by a force beyond myself. Several times I
stopped, intending to turn and go back, but in each instance, after long minutes of indecision, I continued on,
gripped by an apprehension which no amount of realistic
self-assurance would dispell.

I even fingered the .38 automatic which, on an impulse,
I had pocketed just before starting out—even though I had no
permit.

I encountered very few pedestrians. Those I passed
walked swiftly, muffled against moisture-laden air and

occasional chill gusts of a north wind. Even traffic was
unusually light. In some neighborhoods I seemed to be
walking through a forsaken city from which everyone had
fled.

As I approached the section where Canavan's abandoned
house was located, I was surprised at how few buildings
had been erected over a twenty-five-year period. Houses
were still scarce and more or less isolated from one another. Pavements were broken; roads riddled with pot
holes; fences sagged; fields ran to weeds and scrub. Neglect was evident over the entire area.

I was within a quarter mile of my goal when I was filled
with a sense of such intense desolation that, once more, I
very nearly turned back. Yet I went on. I felt like some
kind of metal robot, mindless and without a will of my
own, pulled on by a malign and powerful magnet.

I rounded a final corner and there, scant yards away,
beyond a ragged row of leafless ash trees, lay Canavan's
deserted house. Part of the roof had fallen in; windows
were broken; shingles hung askew. The entire structure
seemed to be sinking into an intermingled mass of overgrown shrubbery, saplings, vines and briars.

As I drew closer, I saw that the former cleared space
behind the house had disappeared in a tangle of towering
grass. The tops of some of the higher stalks leaned through
the shattered windows.

Forcing a passage through the barrier of shrubs and
thorns, I pushed to the rear.

Before me spread a dismal waste of wavering brindle
grass, much as I remembered it. The broken wooden
fences and the rotted apple trees had disappeared; otherwise little had changed.

If anything, the witch-cursed back yard looked more
sinister than ever. The grass stalks were longer, thicker,

more closely clustered. A heavy growth of briars, as if allied with the crowding grass, had spread everywhere. As before, near-silence prevailed. The only sound was the sibilant whisper of the grass stems, stirred by the cold autumn wind.

For some minutes I stood watching that swaying wall of grass, carried back in time. There was an alien, inimical quality about the scene which I could not trace to any single feature. It was like an aura, an invisible miasmic mist generated by that devil's landscape.

As I shuddered and started to turn away, something about the yard drew my attention. It suddenly seemed larger than it had at first—longer, much longer. It appeared to stretch for miles, miles and miles, endlessly . . .

Perhaps it *would* be exciting, I mused, to explore it again. Exciting? Exhilarating! I could plunge in and run on and on, freely, swallowed up in the grass, unseen, unshackled . . . I might even roll in the grass, run on all fours and . . . Yes—*howl!* Howl with wild abandon as I ran on and on toward . . .

"Toward Hell!" I told myself as the madness abruptly drained away from me.

My heart was pounding as I ran quickly toward the front of the house, away from that demonic beckoning expanse. Thorns gashed my face and the jagged branch of a shrub gouged my leg, but I shoved through the snarled growth without stopping until I was free of it.

I paused in front of the place to catch my breath. At that point, I fully intended to leave, but, again, something held me back. I wanted to get away at once, but an obscure yet insistent voice, perhaps welling up from my own stubborn subconscious mind, kept commanding me to stay—*that my mission had not been fulfilled.*

I took out a handkerchief and dabbed at the blood

trickling down my face. As I regained my breath, I became calmer. Perhaps, I thought, it would do no harm to look into the half-wrecked house. Who knows?—even after all the intervening years, there could still be some remaining clue, something that might conceivably indicate whether Canavan was living or dead.

Pushing aside the overhanging branches of a sprawling yew hedge, I faced the entry door. It hung crookedly, half off its hinges, warped and cracked beyond repair.

In spite of its condition, it resisted my efforts to force it further open. I put my shoulder against it and shoved. It swung open suddenly and I staggered off balance into a darkened room.

I stood motionless, letting my eyes adjust to the shadowy interior. Even though nearly all windows were broken, the heavy growth of outside shrubbery, untended for years, shut out most of the light.

I found it hard to believe that this was the same booklined room in which I had enjoyed quiet conversation and many a cup of hot English tea with Canavan. Vandals had removed the shelves and even a few of the floor boards. Cobwebs clotted with dust drooped in the corners. All that remained of furniture was an upended chair with one leg.

I walked down a narrow hall to the rear room where Canavan had stored books and prepared shipments. The room was dark, pungent with the smell of intermingled dust and mould, empty except for a few battered crates which littered the floor. The tops of high stalks of grass hung through the broken window—the window where Canavan had stood a quarter century before, staring out at the enigmatic field of brindle grass until his puzzled preoccupation became a mania which drove him to madness.

As I re-entered the corridor, I noticed a small door just opposite the rear stock room. On impulse, I opened it. In the faint light which filtered through, I saw wooden steps leading down. They looked rickety and certainly unsafe, but it occurred to me that Canavan had never taken me into the cellar of the house. Was it possible that I might find some evidence down there, something overlooked before? Unlikely, but yes, just possible.

Moving with great care, I gingerly crept down the short flight of creaking stairs, expecting at any moment to be precipitated headfirst into black cellar depths.

Luckily, I carried a miniature finger-sized flashlight in one pocket of my jacket. As I reached the bottom of the stairs and stepped onto an earthen floor, I drew out the light and turned on its tiny beam.

There was little to be seen: damp mouldy dirt underfoot; cement walls, cracked, mildewed, beginning to collapse; scraps of wood and paper strewn about; in one corner a pile of torn blankets mixed with gunny sack fragments and miscellaneous rags. The place was permeated by a musty, rancid smell, almost suffocating in intensity.

Closer inspection revealed a small annex to the main cellar room. In this adjacent cubicle, even the walls were earthen. Peering in, I saw that it was empty.

As I prowled about, my sliver of light also picked out the dilapidated remains of a small deal table against one wall. Several candle stubs and a partially-used book of matches lay on its top. I concluded that Canavan's cellar, fetid and filthy though it was, occasionally served as a guest room for roving knights of the road when no better accommodations were readily available.

It was obvious, I decided, that there was nothing at all which might provide any helpful clues pertaining to Canavan's disappearance and ultimate fate.

Shrugging, I started toward the stairs.

My hand was on the wobbly banister when I felt a

draft—which was not coming from above. Curious, I turned,
probing about with my pencil of light again. There were
no cellar windows and though the walls were fissured and
starting to crumble, I found it hard to believe that a draft
could be blowing through them.

I stood still, hand upraised. A weak but unmistakable
current of cold air brushed against it. Groping, hesitating,
pausing every foot or two, I followed it toward its source.
It was coming from the small earthen-walled annex off one
corner of the main cellar room.

Mystified, I stepped into the dank recess and swung my
light around. The dirt walls looked solid, but I felt a flow
of stale damp air. Tracing it to the wall opposite the
entrance, I soon located its source. The bottom of the wall
was not solid earth; a dirt-encrusted gunny sack had been
carefully fixed over an aperture. I had not noticed it before
because the dirt-smeared sack was scarcely distinguishable
from the wall itself.

Stooping down, I pulled aside the sack to reveal a hole
between two and three feet in diameter. Flashing my light
inside, I saw that it was the entrance or exit of a hollowed-
out tunnel which twisted away into darkness beyond the
limited range of my tiny light. It extended under the rear
of the house toward the back yard.

I straightened up and stepped back. Wild, fantastic con-
jectures raced through my head. No woodchuck, gopher or
fox could have burrowed a tunnel like that. What then?

It was a question I could not—or would not—answer.
Perhaps, I speculated, there was one way to solve the
riddle. I could crawl through myself and find where the
passage led—possibly even encounter the industrious
burrower!

But when I bent down again and stared into the hole,
my courage failed me. I simply did not possess the pluck

to crawl inside. Of course, I assured myself, it would be foolhardy in any case. The wet walls might cave in at any moment. I could be buried alive. And if I did meet the tunnel's occupant in that restricted space, I would be at a terrible disadvantage.

Trying to beat back the thought that I was a coward, I groped for a solution. A tramp, I told myself, had dug the tunnel. Wishing to get into the cellar without being seen, he had laboriously scraped out a hidden underground entrance for his own convenience. I didn't believe it for a second. No tramp I had ever heard of would go to all that work for the shelter of an unheated and utterly inhospitable cellar.

As I stood, frowning with indecision and uncertainty, I heard a distant scraping sound. I waited, listening intently. It came again, a scraping, dragging sound. Squatting, I put my ear to the opening. There could be no mistaking it this time. Something was coming through the tunnel.

I am reluctant to admit that my initial impulse was to turn, race up the cellar stairs and rush out of the house itself. It took every half ounce of fortitude I possessed to stand up, step backward from the hole, switch off my light and wait.

My heart pounded so hard I wondered idiotically whether the sound of its beat extended into the tunnel.

I decided I would not switch my light back on until whatever was moving through the tunnel reached my end of it. Moving with great care, I reached forward and dropped the gunny sack back over the hole.

I was reasonably sure that I would hear the sound of the sack being lifted or pushed aside. At that instant, I determined, I would flick on my light.

As the dragging sound grew more distinct, I moved my flash from my right hand to my left and with my right

drew the .38 automatic which I had hastily pocketed just
before leaving home. The cold grip felt like ice in my hand
but under the circumstances I found it infinitely comforting.

The scraping sound grew louder. It quickly became
apparent to me that the approach of a small animal would
not cause such a sound. Something of substantial bulk was
steadily drawing closer.

I waited, unpleasantly aware of the sound of my own
heavy breathing. If the burrower heard it, I wondered,
would it turn and hurry away?

I cannot remember now what I expected to see, but
when I heard the dirt-stiffened gunny sack knocked aside,
and switched on my light, I stood petrified.

I would like to say, simply, that the face squinting out at
me was indescribable and let it go at that. But I suppose
that would not do, so I will make an attempt at description.

I saw skin like mottled parchment stretched over a
queerly-misshapen skull: low, slanting forehead, under-
slung jaw made more hideous by long, crowded, canine-
like teeth which thrust aside the purple lips.

The thing seemed able to see in the dark; it looked
beyond the cone of my miniature light directly into my
face. I saw—with a rush of horror I hope never to experience again—that a flicker of recognition stirred in the
bestial narrowed eyes which inspected me.

While I stood, unable to either move or speak, the
repulsive thing crawled out of the hole on all fours. As the
sack dropped back over the tunnel entrance, the creature
settled on its haunches and began making weird noises,
half growl, half croak. I felt renewed horror stirring the
roots of my hair as I realized the monster was attempting
to communicate!

Insisting to myself that I must be mistaken, I nevertheless played my light over it carefully, trying desperately to

assure myself that it could not be human. Its hide—or skin—resembled a scabrous sheath of dried-out leather, repulsively knobbed, marred with cuts and half covered with random tufts of coarse grey hair. Its appendages resembled those of a wild animal, with curved lethal-looking nails and calloused hairy pads. And yet I was forced to concede that it *might* have been human at one time. If so, it had undergone some fearful metamorphosis beyond comprehension.

As the rasping guttural sounds of the thing continued, I tried to focus my attention on them, concentrating as best I could with that nightmare shape crouching in front of me.

At length, as I listened, I distinctly heard a single word which seemed to burn into the very marrow of my bones. That word was "Frank"—my name.

I was momentarily too overwhelmed with horrified disbelief to reply. I could only run my tongue over my lips while sound froze in my throat.

"Canavan—can it be?" I finally managed.

The thing nodded its dog-like head. "Can-van. Me."

It would be futile for me to make an attempt to reproduce the sounds which issued from that half-atrophied throat for the next half hour or so as the ghastly remnant of a human being struggled to speak. I could at last understand a good part of it, but it would read like gibberish. Finally, however, some semblance of normal speech returned.

During this period, as my flashlight began to flicker, I hurried into the main cellar, retrieved the candle stubs, lit them and set them on the dirt floor near the tunnel mouth.

By guttering candlelight, in a cellar cubicle which seemed like the inside of a tomb, I heard my poor old friend's incredible story.

Twenty-five years before, while the police searched for

him in that bewitched back yard of whispering brindle grass, he had been hidden in the huge hollow trunk of one of the old dead apple trees. He had emerged that night, only to hide again the next day when the searchers returned. Disoriented, fearful and in fact terrified by the growing change in himself, he had remained secreted in the high grass of the yard, subsisting on grubs, worms, mice, roots and even the grass itself. When the clamor and searching dwindled away, he had found himself so changed physically—and psychically—that he had no desire to enter the house and return to his old ways. The curse of Goodie Larkins, accused as a witch—"And they who tarry here be as these beastes that rende me dead!"—had manifested itself with fearful speed and accuracy. He found himself prowling on all fours, howling, snapping, devouring whatever offal or living morsel of food offered itself.

"You should have sought me out," I told him.

He shook his head. "Would—would have—killed you!"

"I came back once," I said. "I didn't see you."

He closed his awful, off-focus eyes, nodding. "Saw you—Frank. Wanted—wanted to run you down—in the grass. You—left."

He had gone on existing in the yard, always hidden, living like a pariah, skulking in the grass, snuffling, scratching for grubs and insects. He said there were sporadic periods of rationality—he was experiencing one now—when he fully understood his condition and suffered mental anguish beyond his powers to describe.

He had endured the first winter by huddling in the cellar of the house after crawling through the back door when he was sure no one was nearby. Several times he had nearly frozen in the yard when tramps took over the house for the night. With the advent of the next spring, he had started the tunnel; it had taken him over six months to dig.

Frequently he was forced to shore up the sides after loose
earth clogged the passageway. No one had ever pursued
him into the tunnel. The occasional transients had apparently never discovered it. It served both as a secret entrance and an escape hatch.

The weeks, months and finally the years passed—and he
went on existing. He told me he was convinced that the
curse inflicted a limited sort of immortality—that is, he
was unable to kill himself.

His glowing, strangely altered eyes stared up at me.
"That—why—called you. Frank. Here."

"Called me? How?"

"Willed you. Mind gained powers—animals have. Hu-
mans lost. Willed you here."

I did not fully comprehend, but I nodded. "I felt
something—someone—calling. Well, that's over. We'll
get you out of here in short order. Now the first thing . . ."

Holding up one claw-like hand, he looked at me as if I,
not he, were mad. "No—get out. Called-you—to kill me."

"Kill you? I couldn't do that! I—"

A wild shine entered his eyes. He glared at me, impa-
tient, possessed by a frenzy which he could not control.

"You—Kill!" he screamed. "Old. Dead. Suffer! Witch-
cursed! No use. Kill! Kill! Kill!"

The light died in his eyes; a glaze spread over them.
Recognition flickered away. Growling deep in his throat,
he lifted on all fours, lips spread far back from long yellow
fangs, twitching muscles tensed for a jugular-slashing upward lunge.

There was no time to think. He was already in mid-air
when I pulled the trigger of the .38. His teeth were inches
from my face when the impact of the slug spun him back
against the cellar wall. He fell forward, sighed once and
lay motionless. I could still smell his putrid reeking breath.

In a state of near shock, I stood looking at him for long minutes, the automatic held in my outstretched hand. I lowered my arm, put away the .38 and bent down. It was obvious at once that he was dead; the bullet had torn through his heart. There was no vestige of a pulse.

I was both appalled at what I had done and relieved that I had done it. Canavan's existence had been a living death. In contrast to it, oblivion could be only a blessing.

But I knew what would happen if the authorities learned the manner of his death. I would be accused of murder, or, at best, manslaughter. Canavan's ghastly ordeal would be exploited by the tabloids. He would be depicted as a ravening monster, instead of a suffering victim. I myself would be accused, condemned, interviewed, grilled and harassed until I became nearly insane from exasperation and exhaustion.

As I remained staring down at the hideously emaciated remains of my friend, I determined that I would not allow this to happen.

With a flickering candle stub in one hand, I prowled through the cellar, collecting scraps of paper and bits of wood. Some pieces were damp and these I discarded. Enough remained dry to suit my purpose.

Piling the gathered pieces on the heap of old blankets and rags which lay in the corner, I set fire to them with the candle end. When the flames began eating well into the rags, I dragged the desiccated body of Canavan from the tunnel entrance and laid it on this improvised pyre.

By the time I fled toward the stairs, coughing and gasping as greasy coils of smoke swirled through the cellar, flames were already lifting toward the wooden floors above.

I climbed the flimsy stairs, groped my way through the

doomed house and through the barrier of close-pressing shrubbery beyond.

I saw no one and I was reasonably sure that I was not seen. I walked swiftly and did not turn until I was blocks away.

At first I noticed nothing; for a moment I had a horrified conviction that my hastily-contrived pyre had flickered out. Then, as I watched, the ruined house of Canavan exploded into flames. The dry wood created an instant inferno.

As I waited, tongues of fire spread into the tall brindle grass at the rear of the house. Within minutes half the yard was a towering sheet of flames. I could hear the crackle and roar where I stood.

I watched until the entire yard was engulfed. The fire moved with a speed and burned with an intensity which I had not thought possible.

"The fires of Hell!" I murmured.

I turned and walked away, confident that, at last, the vengeful curse of Goodie Larkins was finally nullified—forever, I hoped.

Oasis of Abomination

AFTER HER escape from the Arab slavers at the eldritch black temple of the dead, lost for unknown millennia in the sands of an uncharted desert, Kerza, the exiled Celt girl, guided her horse across the stifling dunes toward a plateau of rocky ground. Far beyond the plateau, almost invisible against the shimmering blue air, she glimpsed a wavering fringe of trees.

She was a strange alien figure in that arid waste of burning sands and searing desert winds. Although she possessed the glossy black hair, fair skin and arresting dusky blue eyes of the typical Celt, she was neither slender nor short in stature. She resembled, in fact, the typical Amazon of legend: nearly six feet in height, smoothly muscular, superbly proportioned. She was strikingly handsome. In the past, the virile, buxom wanderer had occasioned lust, envy and feuds leading to swordplay and death—and eventually her own exile.

Aside from a thin cloak thrown loosely over her shoulders, she carried nothing but some partially-filled hide flasks and a heavy curved cutlass which she had appropriated from one of her deceased pursuers.

Her horse, the former mount of an Arab slaver, plodded ahead slowly, still exhausted from the harrowing desert chase which had culminated in her final escape.

When she reached the stony plateau, she stopped, dismounted, drank sparingly from one of the hide flasks and then emptied the contents of another flask down the parched throat of her heaving horse. It was not much water for a beast half dead with burning heat, thirst and fatigue, but she hoped it might be enough to keep the creature on its feet until she reached the tantalizing fringe of trees just discernible far over the tawny sands.

For some reason which she could not fathom, she felt reluctant to approach that tree-encircled oasis—for such she judged it to be. But there was nothing else in sight. To remain on the open desert, under a life-sapping sun, with a stumbling horse and a diminishing water supply, would insure death within a day or two.

As her reeling mount toiled across the stony plateau toward the shimmering belt of trees, blue and beckoning beyond the wrinkled wastes of sand, Kerza was suddenly stricken with the thought that the trees might be only a mirage, an illusion created by layers of heat lifting from the desert's floor.

She urged her horse forward, however, because there seemed no alternative. Twice more she stopped, wet her own cracked lips and poured trickles of the precious water down the throat of her suffering mount.

At length, as the staggering animal threatened to collapse beneath her, she dismounted and led the weakened horse forward by hand.

The wavering ribbon of trees gradually came into sharper focus. To Kerza, the foliage, with its bluish tints and asymmetrical shapes, looked strangely unwelcoming and incongruous, but she knew there was shade and almost certainly water under those nearby branches.

Her horse, which had seemed about to sink on its haunches, suddenly lifted its ears and lurched forward. Kerza urged it across the few remaining yards of sand and stone.

As they slipped under the trees, she felt as if a huge cooling hand had spread itself above them, blocking out the scalding torrents of sun. The horse stopped and stood motionless, head down, flanks heaving.

Tethering it to a nearby tree, Kerza lifted the near-empty flasks from the pommel and pushed through the under-growth in search of water.

Within minutes she located a small, spring-fed pool. After drinking deeply, she bathed her burning face and arms, filled the flasks and returned to get the horse.

The dehydrated beast drank greedily. Kerza leaned back against a tree. A few minutes later, after the animal had cropped some of the straggling blades of bluish-green grass, she tethered it again.

She hesitated to separate herself from the animal, but some instinct warned her that it might be best to inspect the oasis on foot. At present she had no idea of its extent, nor of what it might contain.

The horse would be conspicuous and it might make considerable noise pushing through the undergrowth, un-less there were well-worn paths.

Slinging two of the flasks over her shoulders, she set out to explore the oasis.

The bluish tint of the leaves and grass instilled in the girl a sense of uneasiness. In addition, the silence under the trees evoked in her an unfathomable feeling of eeri-ness. After the fierce sun-glare of the open desert, the light which filtered down through the bluish overhead canopy seemed a sickly saffron.

As she cautiously edged through the undergrowth, she noticed a few subdued and sporadic insect sounds, but no bird song, no scampering or scuttling of small jungle beasts.

She stopped abruptly. There *was* a sound! She stood motionless, listening. There it was again. A whine, almost a whimper. Kerza had the conviction that it was forced out involuntarily from whatever afflicted creature uttered it.

She advanced with infinite deliberation. It might be a ruse, she realized, to lure her on.

Almost absolute silence descended as she slipped forward. She was beginning to believe that the disturbing sound had originated in her own imagination, when she heard it again, much closer at hand.

Dropping to hands and knees, she crept ahead through the tangle of vegetation, cutlass at the ready.

She gasped and quickly gripped a nearby vine as she suddenly teetered on the edge of a steep pit, cleverly camouflaged by a leaf and twig-covered netting.

A gap torn in the fragile covering showed where some unwary walker had fallen through.

Peering into the pit, Kerza saw that its steep, slick sides extended downward for many feet—at least thirty, she judged.

The half-light filtering from above did not reach the bottom of the hole. She frowned, straining her eyes into the shadowy shaft. The outline of some vague form was barely discernible, but she could not say what it was.

As she hesitated, the soft whimper came again. There was no doubt that it was the despairing cry of whatever wretched creature had dropped into the pit.

Although the whimpering, pregnant with distress, touched the springs of her compassion, Kerza continued kneeling motionless at the edge of the trap, torn with irresolution. Too many times in the past, she had been tricked and deceived.

At length, as the whimpering continued, weakening as it went on, she made a sudden decision.

Prowling the perimeter of the pit, she tested various trailing vines until she found a long, sturdy one which had secured a veritable stranglehold on one of the tree trunks. Ripping its tenacious suckers from the yielding earth floor, she hurled it against the light but cleverly-constructed lid of leaves, twigs and lichen which screened the shaft. The long vine tore easily through the netting and spiralled downward. Looking over the edge of the pit, Kerza estimated that it must have snaked to within a few feet of the bottom.

After slipping her cutlass through another length of fiber which she twined tightly around her waist, she gripped the heavy vine which dangled into the pit and climbed down.

As she approached the bottom of the shaft, she saw two eyes shining in the semi-darkness. They watched her unwaveringly.

Grasping her cutlass in one hand, she released her hold on the vine and dropped the few remaining feet. She sank to her waist in a soft mass of leaves and moss.

The purpose of the pit, she immediately understood, was to capture unwary prey alive.

The two shining eyes were now only feet away. They remained fastened on her.

For several minutes, while her own eyes grew accustomed to the shadowy interior of the shaft, she remained motionless. At length she saw that the eyes were set in a long, bony and furry head which barely protruded from the mass of mingled moss and leaves.

Kerza spoke soothingly. The eyes brightened and something stirred under the leaves. Puzzled but intrigued, she went on speaking, her voice a soft crooning.

Finally she pushed toward the trapped animal and held

out her hand. A hot dry tongue flicked across her fingers. The animal emitted a friendly whine and suddenly Kerza understood the source of the stirring sound underneath the leaves. The beast was wagging its tail!

She caressed the long bony head, crooning softly. The animal licked her hands, its mournful eyes never leaving her face.

Feeling the animal's tongue, hot and dry against her skin, Kerza quickly reached for one of the two water flasks she had previously hitched over her shoulder.

She poured water into one cupped palm; the furry captive lapped it up eagerly. She let it drink until the one flask was empty.

Moving awkwardly in the mass of leaves, Kerza began shoving aside the tangle in an attempt to free the half-buried beast.

Finally she was able to reach down under the leaves and lift it up. She was amazed at its weight and bulk. She recognized it for what it was at once: a huge Irish wolf-hound, the largest she had ever seen. She judged that its shoulder height must be nearly five feet.

The great dog was half-starved, dehydrated and appeared to be in fever, but it did not seem to be seriously injured.

Kerza had grown up in the company of formidable but devoted Irish wolfhounds. On more than one occasion as a child, she had fallen asleep with her chubby arms twined around one of the massive animals.

She was determined to free the gigantic dog from the pit, but the feat presented problems. In spite of her exceptional strength, she decided not to risk climbing back up the vine carrying a dog which must have weighed in the region of a hundred and sixty pounds or more.

Crooning to reassure the beast, she rubbed it behind the

ears, leaped, caught the vine and climbed swiftly. The dog watched with resigned, mournful eyes, certain that it was being abandoned. Its tail wagged hopefully a few times and then grew still as Kerza reached the top of the shaft and swung from view.

Working with cutlass, teeth and hands, she wove together a serviceable sling, or harness, made of tough vines and pieces of strong plant fiber. She was convinced that delay might be fatal. Whoever—or whatever—had dug and screened the pit would surely return. And the dog was not far from the final stages of starvation.

Fastening the sling securely to a heavy vine, which she in turn fastened tightly around the base of a tree, Kerza climbed back down the pit. The wolfhound, eyes shining again with renewed hope, shuffled through the leaves and licked Kerza's hand. With the quick intelligence of its kind, it understood at once what was expected of it and stood patiently while the girl fixed the sling around it.

When it was firmly in place, Kerza hastily climbed back out of the pit and hauled up the dog, hand over hand, utilizing a tree branch for leverage.

Freed of the harness, the enormous dog shook itself and happily wagged its long thin tail. Although it limped and favored its left forepaw, Kerza was relieved to see that it could walk unaided.

After letting it lap up the last drop of water from her second hide flask, she touched it gently and started off through the tangle of trees. She was anxious to get away from the vicinity of the pit.

The huge wolfhound followed close at her heels.

As she strode along, Kerza was struck again by the unaccountable eeriness of the place. She sensed, rather than felt, a slow pulsation, a throbbing like that of a muted but somehow monstrous pulse beat, stirring the air. It was disturbing yet strangely pleasurable. Kerza was growing weak with hunger; she could not remember when she had last eaten. The pulsation, which appeared to emanate from within the great oasis, in some unfathomable manner renewed her energy and strength.

Kerza's sense of direction was keen. She located the spring where she had filled her flasks without trouble. She refilled them and then stood aside while the gaunt wolfhound lapped up more water.

She smiled as she watched him drink. "Pit," she thought. "Pulled from the pit. That would make a good name."

She held out her hand. "Here, Pit!"

The big dog quickly trotted to her side. She scratched behind its small rounded ears.

Slinging the hide flasks over her shoulder, she turned and walked toward the tree where she had left her horse tethered.

The horse was gone.

Kerza quickly examined the terrain surrounding the tree. There was no blood on the ground, no sign of a struggle. The horse has not been attacked; it had been led away.

Instinctively, Kerza slipped out of sight into the undergrowth. She moved warily. Whoever had taken the horse might still be lurking nearby.

Pit followed her, only feet away, padding in near silence in spite of his size.

Kerza pushed through the half-jungle for nearly an hour. The expanse of the oasis surprised her.

She continued to feel ill at ease. She disliked the sickly saffron light which filtered down through the blue-tinted vegetation. Although she was growing somewhat accustomed to the vibrations which agitated the air like the echo of a great, far-distant pulse beat, their persistence and strange power perplexed and disturbed her.

As the shadows started to lengthen, she noticed several large trees whose roots had apparently given way in the spongy soil. After the trees had toppled about halfway some time in the past, their branches had locked and meshed. Now they leaned together, covered with creepers, dead leaves and lichen, forming a natural cover.

Kerza surveyed the spot for long minutes before she led Pit under the tent of trees and sat down. She was exhausted. Every step through that alien jungle had been one of deliberation. She had been aware that at any moment she might plunge through a cunningly-concealed net into a shaft from which she could not escape.

In spite of her fatigue, she was famished. As she sat in the growing shadows, she noticed two tiny eyes shining in a nearby shrub. Holding her cutlass in readiness, she got up slowly and stole toward the bush. The eyes did not move.

With a lightning swing, Kerza brought down the flat side of her blade. Reaching into the shrub, she pulled out the still twitching body of a small rodent, a marmot she judged. Several more of the creatures watched nearby. They were inquisitive, but they proved to be incredibly stupid. Within a few minutes, Kreza had killed three more.

Although she preferred cooked meat, she did not have the implements for fire at hand. In any case, she knew that it would be unwise to start a fire.

After skinning and cleaning the animals, she kept one aside for herself and set down the others.

The big wolfhound was literally starving, yet it waited until she called it by name and pointed to the meat. In spite of its hunger, which must have been fierce, it did not bolt the food. It ate slowly, pausing occasionally to gaze across at Kerza with adoration in its brown eyes.

She gave it water from her cupped hands after it was finished and then lay back with her head resting against a

tree root. She kept her right hand closed on the hilt of the
cutlass.

Pit, the wolfhound, lay down at her feet.

Exhausted, Kerza fell asleep almost immediately. She
awoke slowly. Light was begining to break through the
trees. Pit sat nearby, awake and alert. His tail thumped the
ground as she regarded him. He yawned, stretched and
came over to lick her hand.

She scratched behind his ears, wondering how he had
come to the oasis. Probably, she reasoned, he was the sole
survivor of some caravan which had been overtaken by a
roving band of desert wolves in human form.

For two days she and Pit remained at the natural shelter
of the tree tent. She fed the emaciated dog marmot meat
and was overjoyed when she saw that his rib bones no
longer showed and that his rough coat was beginning to
acquire a gloss. He stopped limping, his left forepaw
apparently healed.

Accompanied by her faithful canine companion, Kerza
made several forays into the surrounding jungle in search
of the horse, but found no trace of it.

The unaccountable pulsations continued to agitate the
air. The eerie vibrations seemed to affect her own pulse, to
pound in her blood. She could feel them, she was convinced, not only in her brain but even in the marrow of her
bones.

On the evening of the second day, she decided that she
and Pit would leave in the morning. She sensed that there
was something both unnatural and menacing about the
sprawling oasis. She could not explain the source of her
uneasiness, apart from the pulsations, but she could not rid
herself of it.

Without a horse, it might be madness to leave the oasis
and strike out across the open desert, but she was deter-

mined to risk it. Primitive instincts were at work within her. She could not fully understand them, but she could not dismiss them. The elders of her sept, she told herself, would have said the oasis was mazed.

As she settled down for the night, with Pit at her feet, she had made a firm decision to leave at dawn. The hide water flasks were already filled.

She awoke suddenly to the furious snarling of Pit. She sprang up, cutlass in hand.

The huge dog was a few yards in front of the tree shelter, struggling savagely with a horde of diminutive creatures which in the half-light resembled leaping brown monkeys.

Kerza rushed forward. A heavy net dropped upon her and she fell to her knees. Dozens of the brown dwarfs swarmed about her, grabbed the ends of the net and raced in a narrowing circle.

Kerza writhed in a frenzy of rage but the cutlass became tangled in the tough woven ropework of the net. Within minutes she was hopelessly ensnared, unable to move.

The dwarf creatures knotted together the open end of the net, hoisted her up and started off through the eerie blue aisles of the jungle.

When she passed Pit, tears sprang to Kerza's eyes. The great dog, enmeshed in one of the nets, lay motionless, blood flowing from a wound in his side.

As she was borne along through the trees, Kerza grimly inspected the creatures who had captured her.

They were no more than four feet in height, mahogany-skinned and hairy with fish-like expressionless eyes, small mouths and noses and oversize ears. They wore belted tunics which were made of marmot skins sewn together. Most of them carried short knives under their belts.

As she regarded them with revulsion, Kerza's hand

ached for the hilt of her cutlass. It had been pulled through
the net and was now ceremoniously carried along by one
of the dwarf netmen.

The speech of her captors, a succession of hooted vowel
sounds, was complete gibberish to Kerza.

The procession wound along for what seemed an inter-
minable time, following a faint trail. Light glinted down
through the blue leaves overhead.

The trees thinned out. Quite suddenly Kerza was carried
into a spacious clearing. At first it seemed empty, but
within minutes it was swarming with the brown dwarf
men. They crowded about, hooting softly, their fish-like
eyes showing a trace of excitement.

Kerza stared about with puzzled amazement. On one
side of the clearing stood a great gleaming silvery disk, the
size of a small building. Before it was heaped a mound of
strangely-assorted articles: swords and shields, battle axes,
bows, lances, cudgels, daggers, helmets, banners, and
dozens of other miscellaneous items of attack, defense and
sudden death.

Kerza watched as her own cutlass was ceremoniously
stacked at the top of the pile. It was obvious that many
captives before her had been carried into the clearing.

As she was being borne through the jungle, Kerza had
felt that the weird pulsations which seemed to stir the air
had increased in intensity. At first, she had surmised she
only imagined it, but now she was sure of it.

The disturbing vibrations, in fact, appeared to emanate
from the opposite side of the clearing. She looked around
with curious eyes.

There was a huge enclosure of some kind on the other
side, but it was entirely screened off by a heavy net hung
from a high frame.

Whatever caused the pulsations, Kerza decided, was kept hidden in that enclosure.

After a further period of hooting, Kerza's captors carried her around the side of the gleaming silver disc. Some yards in the rear, a number of wooden cages were visible. Trussed like a jungle fowl, Kerza was thrust into one, propped upright and left.

She could see little—only one gleaming edge of the disc and empty jungle. She presumed there must be other captives in some of the cages. The disc, she decided, was a temple erected in honor of the dwarf people's god. The pile of weapons was tribute.

As the hours passed, Kerza mused about her captors. They all appeared to be the same age and gender. They seemed oddly sexless. She pondered their origin. They had come up out of the earth, she reasoned. They were the stunted survivors of some forgotten race which had gone underground in some far-distant past. The elders of her own sept had spoken of similar strange things.

As the shadows deepened, Kerza's undersized captors began to assemble nearby with what appeared to be primitive cooking utensils. A few small fires were started in shallow depressions which had been dug in a cleared area. These depressions were surrounded by heaps of stones and screened at the top by a plaitwork of green vines. The dwarf people seemed to have an inordinate fear of fire.

As Kerza watched, four of the hateful creatures came to her cage carrying bits of food impaled on a long stick. They opened the caged door and shoved the stick toward her mouth. The food consisted of bits of meat and seeds held together by some kind of waxy substance and lightly toasted over the miniature fires.

Kerza refused the messy lumps, glaring at her captors. After a hooted discussion, the dwarfs stared in at her with their expressionless ichthyic eyes, withdrew the stick, fastened the cage door and departed.

The tiny fires flickered out. Darkness swept down.

Sounds—rustlings, moans, sighs and restless stirrings—emanated from some of the other cages, but Kerza could not see any of the occupants. If her captors had posted sentries, they too remained invisible.

Kerza had eagerly awaited the night. Now, reasonably certain she was not being observed, she began to strain at the tough fiber vines which encircled her arms and legs. Far from breaking, they did not even stretch. They held together like the links in carefully welded chain mail.

After hours of effort, while the sweat streamed from her body, Kerza gave up. If she hoped to conserve any of her remaining strength, she decided, she would need a brief period of sleep.

She dropped off, exhausted, while the weird pulsations went on throbbing through the night. They throbbed in Kerza's brain and in her restless sleep they seemed to contain a new note, a strengthened note, of urgency and menace.

Pale light was penetrating the trees when she woke up. The throbbing pulsations were stronger than ever and the fish-eyed throng scurried about with a subdued but growing excitement.

A weird rhythmic chanting began at the opposite side of the clearing. The sounds made no sense to Kerza but she felt the small hairs on the nape of her neck bristle.

As the chanting grew in volume and intensity, the dwarf men became more and more animated. Their fish eyes began to bulge and shine with excitement.

A phalanx of the creatures suddenly wheeled toward Kerza's cage, pulled open the door and carried her off, past the great gleaming silver disc to the screened enclosure at the far side of the clearing.

Here the hooting host was assembled in force. Rank on squatting rank, they surrounded one side of the enclosure, swaying in unison, rhythmically chanting.

Carried to within a few yards of the enclosure, Kerza was finally set down. She could sit up, but that was all. Her bonds remained inflexible; behind her squatted hundreds of her captors.

The vibrations emanating from within the enclosure beat at Kerza's brain like remorseless drums. Paradoxically, at one moment she wanted to fling off her bonds, leap up and dance with delight—at another she wanted to scream in utter inexplicable terror.

Suddenly a new note entered the rhythmic chanting. It became subdued but expectant. The cold fish eyes fastened on the screen.

Slowly, it lifted.

Kerza stared with incredulous disbelief.

Before her, swaying feet above the ground, stretched a huge iridescent web which resembled a hundred rainbows pulled out of the sky by some wizard and woven together to form a single shimmering sheet.

Kerza blinked, looked away and back, but the glimmering web remained.

As her eyes traveled over it, she saw that the far end terminated at the edge of an oval cave, cut in rock. Here all color ended; the mouth of the cave might as well have been a shield of obsidian.

In spite of the visual appeal of the jeweled web, Kerza's eyes remained fixed on the entrance-way to the curious oval cave. As she stared, she became convinced that the maddening pulsations came from that cave—and that they were steadily growing in force.

The chanting grew louder again and out of the cave mouth groped a thing of horror, an alien entity more

hideous than anything Kerza had ever dreamed could exist.
It was huge and grey, a mottled bulk sprouting coarse
quill-like black hairs which quivered and shook as the
monstrous thing pulsated. Two fixed lidless green eyes,
alive with malignancy, were set above a gaping double
row of disc-shaped suckers which served the ravening
nightmare as a mouth.

Hairy, stick-like legs propelled it across the iridescent
web like some gigantic spider. Racing to the very edge of
the glimmering net, it stared down with hungry, hate-filled
eyes, while its mouth suckers ceaselessly opened and closed.
Its pulsations seemed tangible. The entire web trembled
and glittered. The vibrations redoubled in intensity.

The ranks of Kerza's captors quickly broke. There were
a few moments of frenzied scurrying and then the ranks
reformed. The fish eyes of the brown men stared upward.

Following their gaze, Kerza saw that a kind of pulley
had been erected high over the web. Now something which
squirmed and twisted was hoisted up and hauled along the
pulley until it was directly over the middle of the web.

The thing began screaming shrilly as it was lowered
toward the web. It was a large monkey, or ape, Kerza
judged, which had been taken in the oasis or perhaps
stolen from a passing caravan.

As it neared the web, the monstrous spider creature
raced beneath it and reached up with its repulsive hairy
legs. The ape managed a final squeal of terror before the
suckers fastened onto it.

As Kerza watched with revulsion, the body of the ape
shrivelled and shrank until nothing remained but a slack
bag of skin, a mere empty husk of hide and hair.

Lifting the remnant, the ravenous monstrosity flung it
over the edge of the web into the ranks of its feeders.

The pulley was put into motion again. Staring up, Kerza

was amazed to see a horse kicking in terror as it was hauled along over the web. She recognized the doomed beast as the Arab mount which she had left tethered in the oasis.

The hairy legs clamped over the struggling horse as it was lowered; suckers circled its neck. The horse appeared to collapse, to cave in. Within minutes there was nothing left but the scarecrow of a horse, a skeleton protruding through skin.

But the monster's hunger was not satisfied. The skeleton of the horse hurtled over the edge of the web. The fixed green eyes glared down again.

Once again something was hoisted up and started along the pulley. This time it was a man, an Arab, bound hand and foot and nearly naked.

As he looked down at the horror waiting beneath him, the Arab seemed to go insane. He screamed, writhed, prayed and cursed. As he was lowered toward the web, he gibbered like an idiot thing.

Even though he resembled one of the Arab slavers who had pursued her across the desert only days before, Kerza felt pity for him.

As he reached the web, the monster pounced. The Arab's shrill screams gurgled away; soon the pitiful shell of a man was pitched over the edge of the glimmering net.

Brown hands gripped her and Kerza was jerked to her feet.

As she was carried toward the pulley, all hope left her. Perhaps, she thought numbly, she could fasten her teeth into one of the monster's reaching legs.

She was shoved against a pole. The fish-eyed men hurriedly began fixing a sling about her.

They were so absorbed that not one in the hundreds of them saw the crazed, red-eyed intruder which raced into the clearing like a furry thunderbolt.

The slashing fangs of the giant wolfhound had ripped out a dozen throats before they realized what was upon them. A few of them drew their short knives but the blades might as well have been made of straw. The terrible teeth of the maddened wolfhound literally tore them apart.

In spite of the horror which still waited, unsated, in its web nearby, the brown men broke and scattered in panic. Running for their lives, they bolted across the clearing toward the surrounding trees.

The huge hound was after them like an avenging fury. Leg and arm bones snapped. Savaged jugulars spurted blood.

As the survivors of the terrified throng disappeared among the trees, scattering in every direction, Pit, the wolfhound, abandoned the pursuit and rushed back to the clearing.

Bounding to Kerza, he licked her face ecstatically, squirming with joy.

He was so excited, it took her a minute or two to catch his attention. Bending toward her hands, which were pinioned tightly together in front of her, Kerza bared her teeth and made as if to chew.

Momentarily puzzled, Pit cocked his head and gazed at her questioningly, tail wagging.

She repeated the pantomime.

This time the great wolfhound understood. Carefully but effectively, his sharp teeth cut through the tough fiber vines. Once Kerza's hands were free, the giant dog quickly chewed through the bonds which fastened her feet together.

Glancing toward the web, Kerza saw the spiderlike monster crouched on the edge of it, green eyes baleful with baffled hate and unsatisfied hunger.

Running across the clearing with Pit at her side, Kerza scrambled up the heap of weapons and trophies which were piled in front of the gleaming silver disc.

She had liked the heft of the cutlass and now she quickly recovered it.

Looking back toward the web, she saw that the monster had not left it. Possibly, she reasoned, it could not propel itself easily once off that multicolored net of death.

As she hesitated, she became aware of a growing murmur, of muttering, muted hooting sounds.

Beginning to recover from their panic, the brown men were mustering again.

If she had any momentary impulse to flee, Kerza instantly dismissed it. A wave of fury so intense that it left her trembling swept through her.

The berserker fit of the Viking is legendary, but the uncontrollable blood rage of the Celt is very nearly beyond belief.

With lifted cutlass, Kerza rushed toward the hooting sounds, a blazing incarnation of vengeance and hate.

The brown men, partially overcoming their initial fright, advanced in a body, knives drawn. They fully expected that more of their number would go down under the murderous fangs of the great wolfhound, but they were confident that they could overcome him. He was vulnerable; they had knifed him and left him for dead not long before. And though they feared him, they feared even more the malignant monster which waited in the web, still unsated and almost certainly consumed with ferocious impatience.

The brown men had braced themselves to meet the killer dog again, but they were totally unprepared for the two furies which simultaneously burst upon them. The giant hound was at their throats as before and by his side rushed the towering Celt girl they had left trussed at the pulley.

As they froze in shock and consternation, the cutlass swung right and left with the speed and accuracy of a mamba's strike. Heads spun through the air. A few who lunged half-heartedly with their short knives had their hands or arms lopped off.

A calm and disinterested observer might have mentally compared the spectacle to that of stalks of standing wheat going down under a scythe.

Blood-splattered, so brimmed with fury that the fish-eyed men became a brown blur before her, Kerza cut and slashed, chopped and skewered.

Pit, literally dripping with his victims' blood, worked nearby with the deadly effectiveness of a saber-tooth tiger or the gigantic dire wolf from which his kind derived their name.

It was too much for the demoralized brown men. The survivors broke and ran again, dropping their knives as they fled, their only thought—escape from the ripping teeth and whistling blade which had decimated their ranks.

Kerza and Pit pursued them under the trees, slashing and hacking as they stumbled blindly away.

When Kerza finally halted and called Pit to her side, scarcely a score of the brown men had escaped. The rest, dead, or mangled and dying, lay strewn about the clearing or sprawled in the shadows under the blue-leaved trees.

Warily, the girl returned toward the web. The hairy voracious creature which the brown men must have worshipped as a god, hovered on the edge of it, hate-filled eyes staring toward the trees where his sycophants had scattered in terror.

When it saw Kerza and Pit approaching, its green eyes glowed balefully, but it made no attempt to climb down from the web.

As Kerza watched the monster crouched along the edge of the rainbow web, she had a sudden inspiration. The brown men had appeared to have a deadly fear of fire. Perhaps . . .

With Pit scampering at her side, Kerza hurried to the rear of the great gleaming disc and located one of the carefully-shielded cooking fires. A few embers still glowed in the protected grill. Seizing a tree branch which lay nearby, she thrust it into the embers.

When the end of the branch was blazing, she hurried back toward the web.

The cold green eyes glared at her; the mouth suckers moved incessantly. Afraid the hideous creature might spring, Kerza held her cutlass in readiness even as she hurled the blazing torch toward the web.

As soon as it struck, Kerza knew her hunch had been correct. The shimmering web began to burn furiously.

The monster whirled toward the fire, hesitated briefly and then raced toward the far end of the web. Seconds later it disappeared in the oval cave cut in rock, its lair, apparently, when it was not on the web.

Flames and pungent pink smoke filled the clearing. Kerza backed away, guiding Pit out of the worst area of swirling smoke.

Towering flames reached toward the rock lair; tinted smoke swirled through the entrance.

Kerza waited, watching the cave mouth. She was about to turn away, concluding the monster had suffocated, when the repulsive mottled bulk of the thing dropped heavily from the cave. Its weight and momentum bore it through the burning web to the ground below. It was scorched and some of its ugly quill-like hairs were burning, but it groped clumsily away from under the web. As Kerza had surmised, once off the web, it moved awkwardly and with obvious effort.

As it approached, Kerza heard a deep-throated growling. Glancing aside, she saw that Pit was about to spring. He crouched, lips writhed back.

Kerza was not sure why she put out her hand and held him back. Was it concern for his life—or some inexplicable touch of pity for the burned hideous thing which shambled away from the web?

Although the great dog obeyed, it went on growling savagely.

The mottled thing passed only a few yards away, laboring along the ground like some huge wounded beetle with only half its legs. Hate appeared to have died out in the green lidless eyes, yet the creature seemed moved by some strong compulsion. It crawled across the smoke-filled clearing toward the gleaming disc-shaped structure.

Kerza watched, puzzled, as it circled the mound of weapons and trophies. Hitching ahead, it reached the disc and scrabbled its way up a short flight of steps.

The hairy, spider-like appendages of the thing fumbled at the side of the disc for several minutes and finally a door swung open. The monster slid inside and the door closed behind it.

It had gone into its shrine, its place of worship, Kerza decided, to die.

Smoke drifted off among the trees. The whole blazing sheet of the web had fallen to earth; within minutes only a few blackened strands remained, still flickering with fire.

Kerza was about to turn away when a sudden humming sound returned her attention to the disc.

The entire structure appeared to be spinning. Kerza watched in amazement as the disc lifted off the ground and rose straight into the air. It moved slowly at first, until it had ascended just beyond the tops of the surrounding trees; then it shot swiftly upward.

It had nearly disappeared from sight and Kerza was straining her eyes to catch a last glimpse of it, when it suddenly plummeted back toward the earth. For just a few seconds its descent slowed and it appeared to be leveling off. Abruptly, it dropped again.

There was a tremendous earth-rocking crash somewhere along the edge of the oasis. A mighty explosion which shook the blue leaves from the trees was followed by a flash of light which outlined every twig and pebble. Kerza covered her eyes.

Half-blinded, with ringing ears, she stumbled away from the smouldering remains of the web. She could not comprehend what she had witnessed. An ineffable sense of exhaustion filled her, a weariness beyond description.

The oasis was gripped in eerie silence; the pulsations had ceased.

Making sure that Pit was by her side, Kerza slowly walked out of the clearing into the tangled stand of trees. Here she crept into the brush and lay down. The great wolfhound curled against her.

Before falling asleep, she stroked the massive beast and felt the closed gash in his side where the brown men had knifed him. They had left him for dead, but the wound was already healing. She marvelled at the huge dog's recuperative powers.

She awoke to a silence more profound than any she had ever experienced. She felt as if she had slept for days. She was not sure whether it was morning or afternoon.

She got up shakily, aching in every limb, and stared around her. She stood in a stifling forest of dead and leafless trees. Sand from the surrounding desert blew down the empty aisles. Sprawled about lay the half-covered skeletons of what looked like brown withered monkeys.

Pit stood nearby. He wagged his tail, but whined. He looked old and stiff and gaunt.

Moving with effort, Kerza circled back toward the clearing. The mound of weapons and trophies was slippery with blowing sand, but she managed to climb to the top and retrieve her two water flasks. She shook them. One contained only a few drops; the other was nearly full.

Suspending them from her shoulders, she hastened away, cutlass in hand. Pit moved at her side.

The place was accursed, she felt. It would be better to die on the open desert than in this unearthly oasis of abomination.

As she slipped through the last fringe of leafless trees onto the empty dunes, she pondered on what had happened.

The elders of her sept would have told her the place was bewitched. The weird pulsations of the monster, she concluded, had somehow imbued the oasis and its inhabitants with life and energy. When those pulsations ended, the oasis and all within it were doomed.

Kerza's forehead wrinkled in perplexity. Was it possible, she asked herself, that the monster had somehow created the oasis?

She shook her head. Such thoughts confused her. She was too tired to go on thinking. Perhaps there was no explanation at all for such things as she had experienced.

She was several miles away from the oasis when a sudden impulse impelled her to turn and look back.

Behind her, as far as the eye could see, stretched a still and empty desert, a flat expanse of endless sand, bereft of even a blade of grass.

There was no sign of any oasis.

Starlock Street

THE MOMENT he turned down Starlock Street he sensed that something was wrong; he felt unaccountably excited—and apprehensive.

It was a warm summer afternoon. He was strolling in a distant section of the city where he had seldom walked before. There appeared to be nothing remarkable about the area. The streets, quiet, almost somnolent, seemed chiefly residential although a number of small shops were interspersed among the well-maintained houses. He judged it to be one of the better middle-class neighborhoods, making an unremitting and so far successful effort to preserve its peace and identity. A few miles distant lay a district of dilapidated houses and litter-strewn lots where it was dangerous to walk even during daylight hours.

After starting down Starlock Street, he stopped to wipe perspiration from his face. Glancing about, he saw nothing unusual: the same quiet houses with carefully-tended lawns, a few small shops. About a dozen large elm trees cast welcome islands of shade.

Starlock Street covered only one average block. When

he reached the far end, he saw that he had the choice of either making a left turn into a connecting street or of going back the way he had come.

He hesitated only briefly. As he veered left into the connecting street, he experienced a sense of immediate relief. Apprehension vanished. He breathed more freely and walked more easily, as if he had suddenly removed an over-loaded back pack.

He shrugged off the incident until he reached home and relaxed with a stein of cold beer.

What had made him both excited and agitated when he turned into Starlock Street? The more he thought about it, the more puzzled he became.

He got up and rummaged among the disorderly accumulation which he called "files" only by courtesy, until he found a street map of New Haven.

He was unable to locate a Starlock Street on the map.

Using a magnifying glass, he scanned the map several times and sat back more mystified than ever. In spite of his vague sense of apprehension, there was something about the street which intrigued him.

He recalled that he had seen no parked cars. And the houses had seemed strangely quiet. He found to his annoyance that he was unable to visualize them in any detail. The entire street became blurred and indistinct in his memory.

He decided that he would return to Starlock Street at the first opportunity.

Several days of rain kept him away, but less than a week later, on a clear afternoon, he headed back. He reached the area of his former walk without incident but, to his astonishment, he was unable to find Starlock Street. At length he stopped a passer-by and asked for directions.

The man shook his head impatiently. "Never heard of it. Ain't around here anyway."

Frowning, he continued his quest, wandering down several streets he had never traversed before. He was about to start homeward when, entirely by chance, he glanced up at a sign: "Starlock Street."

Again he felt rising excitement and some degree of oppression as he turned the corner. He walked slowly, determined to scrutinize everything with care.

He appeared to have entered a small isolated part of the city which had remained substantially unchanged for nearly a century. The houses seemed to have survived without alteration since Victorian days. Several of the larger front grass plots boasted decorative iron dogs. Looking into still back yards, he saw syringa bushes, grapevine trellises, lilac hedges and wisteria, along with neat gardens bearing lemon lilies, musk roses and verbena.

He passed one small shop whose diamond-paned window display featured spools of vari-colored thread, needles, thimbles, wooden toy soldiers and penny candy—peppermints, twists of sugared caraway seed, gumdrops.

Most of the sidewalks were brick, he noticed, and as he looked along the street, the only vehicle in sight was a horse-drawn sulky in the shade of an elm.

He was totally entranced. All his life he had longed for the past, for Victorian times especially. In a sense, he had lived in the past instead of the present. He had little or no interest in current events and contemporary problems. He had acquaintances but no friends. The people he met bored and repelled him. He hungered for a long-vanished milieu, for a leisurely and genteel way of life which he felt the present denied him.

In spite of a faint pulse of apprehension somewhere

deep within him, Starlock Street was like a long-cherished dream suddenly come alive.

He moved along the brick sidewalks slowly, savoring details with relish. The very air, filled with the fresh perfume of flowering back yard gardens, stirred him strangely. He paused frequently, peering about, afraid that he might miss something of interest.

A few persons sat on porch swings, or moved about in the leafy yards, but no one paid any attention to him. He approached the end of the street with reluctance and turned the corner only when he realized that his walk was far behind schedule and that his evening rituals would be disrupted unless he hurried. Although his study was a spectacle of disorder, he was nevertheless a creature of habit and routine.

Instead of subsiding, his excitement grew as the evening wore on. He ate only fragments of a cold supper, found himself unable to concentrate on the book he was reading and, finally, lay awake for hours after going to bed. The memory of Starlock Street crowded out all other concerns. He could scarcely wait for the next day and a return trip to the near-magical place he had chanced upon.

Unless wet weather or occasional business affairs interfered, he began making daily visits to the street. The quaint charm of the place never palled on him. Nothing ever seemed to change. A leafy somnolence, blissful and unbroken, held the street as in some kind of spell. He seldom passed anyone strolling along the brick sidewalks. Occasionally he glimpsed someone tending flowers in one of the back yard gardens or sitting quietly on one of the wisteria-screened front verandas. Cars appeared to avoid the street. He wondered if some little-known city ordinance, enacted to preserve the Victorian ambience of the place, was being strictly enforced.

The street became a persistent obsession. What little interest he had in contemporary events entirely vanished. He cut off his few acquaintances, reduced his business activity to the bare minimum which maintained a roof over his head, and neglected everything else.

He did undertake some historical research on the city and he was vaguely troubled to find no reference to Starlock Street, but he shrugged off the omission, assuring himself that, at best, municipal histories were sketchy and incomplete.

As the summer wore on, his only interest in life remained Starlock Street. He spent hours walking up and down the brick sidewalks, studying the houses, peering into the back yards, always, it seemed, partially hidden behind arbors, trellises and hedges. Time after time he stopped and gazed into the diamond-paned window of the small shop whose window display never changed. The spools of colored thread always looked new; the wooden soldiers were never touched with dust; the peppermints and the twists of sugared caraway always looked fresh and appetizing.

At times he was grateful that no one on the street paid any attention to him; on other occasions he was disappointed. There were afternoons when he would have welcomed a greeting or a brief chat. He decided it would be pleasant to rest for a few minutes on one of the porch swings or perhaps to be invited for a stroll through one of the back gardens.

One afternoon when the scent of the flowering plots imbued the summer air with a gentle sweetness beyond any perfume he had ever known, his wistful desire for some kind of recognition was finally achieved.

A young woman, bending over a front-lawn lilac bush

only feet away, straightened up suddenly and looked him full in the face.

He stood transfixed, heart pounding. He felt, he knew, that he had been searching for her all his life. The perfect oval face, the quiet eyes, the mouth firm yet ready with a tentative smile, the perfectly coiffured honey-colored hair. She stood calmly, expectantly, waiting for him to speak if he wanted to do so.

Trembling like a schoolboy, he bowed and managed a whispered "Good afternoon."

Smiling, she replied, and he found himself able to make a reasonably audible remark—something about the scent of lilacs.

They chatted for a few minutes. Afterward, he could not recall the conversation.

He walked home in a state of wild excitement and agitation. What was her name? Had she introduced herself? He could not remember. Had he told her his name? He didn't know. How long had they talked? He had no idea. When he entered his own door, he suddenly realized that he had walked all the way back without seeing anything.

He sat for hours, recalling every detail of that magical figure materialized, as it were, by the lilac bush. Suppose she were only visiting and never returned? How would he ever find her again? Why had he never seen her before? Would she talk to him again? Had he been too bold? too assertive? *What had he said anyway?* He could not recall a word.

Toward midnight, stomach pangs reminded him that he had forgotten dinner. He munched a sandwich absently, tasting not a morsel. He went to bed finally and lay wide awake until morning.

He got up hurriedly, finished his morning routine like a

robot, and then paced the floor restlessly, watching the clock.

Shortly after noon, he started out for Starlock Street, forcing himself not to hurry. If he arrived too early, he told himself, she would be at lunch. She would not see him. He could not very well hover outside, nor walk up and down the street dozens of times. Someone might summon the police and point out a "suspicious character." How horrible! He would be commanded to stay off the street, to remain away permanently! He might never see her again!

He paused frequently to look into shop windows but he saw nothing. He took a number of deliberate detours until he remembered the day when he had spent hours trying to find Starlock Street. If that happened again, he might arrive too late to see her. If it were late afternoon, it was unlikely that she would be sauntering about outside. She would probably be inside, preparing a meal, sewing or reading. Of course he might not see her in any event, but he sensed that his best opportunity for doing so would be during the hours of early or mid-afternoon.

He reached Starlock Street about one-thirty, tense with both anticipation and apprehension. As he approached the house where he had seen her, disappointment overwhelmed him. She was not outside.

He walked as slowly as he dared and boldly (for him) turned to survey the house. No one was in sight.

He had passed the house, with bent head and faltering steps, when she called his name.

She was standing near the lilac bush, smiling. She waved.

He hurried back, almost stumbling over his own feet.

This time, he made sure they exchanged names. Hers was Alison, Alison Annerton. As they talked, the worst of his tension ebbed away. She invited him to sit on the porch swing and brought out glasses of cold lemonade. They talked about lilacs, summer gardens, the effect of weather on the fragrance of flowers. He learned that she lived with a brother, Philip, who worked in a carriage factory on State Street.

Before he finally left, she had agreed to meet him again the next afternoon. She would be outside, she told him, about two o'clock.

He returned home in a near-ecstatic state. The evening dragged and the night, during which he slept only for brief intervals, seemed endless.

She was there by the lilac bush when he arrived. They sat together on the porch swing and talked. She had accepted him as a friend. He learned she had no plans for leaving, for going anywhere. He was free to visit her when he wished.

A rare happiness came to him. He sat relaxed, conversing eagerly. The street was quiet, a serene refuge surrounded by areas of clamor, traffic and confusion. Occasionally a horse-drawn wagon creaked past. Once a gleaming phaeton whirled smartly down the street, polished wheel spokes reflecting the afternoon sun in spinning arcs of light. He was entranced. The people on Starlock Street, he concluded, were bent on preserving every possible semblance of the past, of Victorian times vanished long ago.

He left reluctantly as late afternoon sun began building shadows in the back yards. Alison stood on the porch, waving, as he walked away.

As he turned home, he reflected that at times she wore an enigmatic expression which puzzled and even disturbed him. He imagined her to be the possessor of secret sorrows which she would never mention, sorrows which showed in her quiet eyes even when she was smiling.

He slept badly, awakening near midnight as the fragments of a sentence she had spoken earlier kept repeating themselves in his mind. 'My brother Philip,' she had said, 'works in a carriage factory on State Street.'

He sat up abruptly. A carriage factory? There were no carriage factories in the city. The last one had closed its doors seventy years ago!

He got up and prepared a pot of tea. Perhaps he had not heard her correctly. He would question her that very afternoon. Was it possible that a mischievous sense of misplaced humor lurked behind those calm eyes?

The next afternoon she treated the question casually. "Well, you see," she explained, "a few of us here on Starlock Street like to carry on the old traditions. It's not, I suppose, a factory. A small shop really, catering to a limited clientele—people who prefer old-fashioned living, you might say."

Her explanation left him unsatisfied, but he did not press her for more detail. Was it possible, he asked himself later, that there might be some things he did not want to know?

He decided he would accept Starlock Street and Alison without further queries or reservations. He had found life's first happiness and he did not intend to jeopardize it if he could help it.

He was in love and nothing else mattered.

At length, as the summer wore on, he walked to Starlock Street every afternoon, regardless of the weather. One afternoon as he and Alison sat on the porch swing, he mentioned that he was growing increasingly dissatisfied with his living quarters and hoped to move. He hinted that he would like to find suitable accommodations closer to Starlock Street.

Alison's quiet eyes met his own. "We have two rooms upstairs which we seldom use. The furniture is not sumptuous, but sturdy and functional. The rooms are yours, if you wish."

He accepted instantly, overwhelmed. It was like a secret dream come true. He could scarcely believe his good luck. When he finally inquired about terms, she shrugged impatiently.

"We'll discuss it some other time. It's too nice a day to talk about business things."

Later, she led him upstairs to inspect the rooms. He merely glanced inside the chambers, a bedroom with attached living room plus a small bath. Ten minutes later he could not have described them. He carried away an impression of order and scrubbed cleanliness but he could remember little else.

After selling the best of his own furniture for a nominal sum, he gave away the rest and arrived at Starlock Street with only clothing, personal items and two huge trunks into which he had swept, helter skelter, the more important contents of his study.

Once ensconced in his new rooms on Starlock Street, he felt that he was as close to heaven as it was possible for anyone to get. His dearest was in the same house. He would see her every day. His former fears of being unable to locate the street, or of finding her gone once he arrived, would no longer gnaw at him.

Sometimes he awoke suddenly, after dreaming that he was back in his former quarters. At such times some aspects of the new situation frightened him. He would get up, inspect the room and peer out the front window. The sight of Starlock Street lying still and deserted in the moonlight would reassure him and he would return to bed with his fears diminished, if not entirely dispelled.

Days passed before he met Alison's brother, Philip, a friendly but reticent young man who seemed peculiarly reluctant to discuss his job at the carriage shop. It was becoming a specialty project, he explained. There was less and less demand for the product.

He would shake his head sadly. "It will all end one of these days. Very soon, I expect."

The days passed quietly. He arose early, strolled in the back garden and then walked on Starlock Street, up one side and down the other. He had no desire to venture further. He scarcely glanced beyond. Beyond lay a seething world of noise, confusion and vulgarity. He had never felt himself an integral part of it and he had no wish to return to it.

When he arrived back at the house, he and Alison would share breakfast, talking quietly of trivial things. She always looked immaculate and composed; she smiled frequently; she was alert and quick-witted. But the growing sorrow in her eyes began to haunt him.

After breakfast, he went upstairs to write letters and read, while Alison busied herself at household tasks. After a light lunch, sometimes consumed on the porch, they sat together in the swing or wandered through the garden.

It was usually enough to be with her. He asked for nothing else. But he sometimes told himself he was living in a dream which must end. The thought demoralized him. At such times, he would seek her out and take her in his arms, holding her for long minutes until his panic subsided.

Yet he remained troubled. Something he could not readily identify, something intangible and elusive, continued to disturb him. After long thought, he finally decided it was simply the *lack of discernible change* which puzzled and worried him.

In his own mind, he began listing things. The garden looked the same day after day. Although she invariably looked fresh and scrubbed, Alison always seemed to be wearing the same clothes, a white shirtwaist with ruffled collar and cuffs and some kind of stiff crinoline-like skirt. Her brother Philip always wore the same work clothes, a grey cap, a short corduroy coat and corded work trousers. Although he could seldom recall the meals an hour after dining, he knew they were always the same. And all the days seemed to run together, weekends included.

His first near-delirious happiness became shadowed by a haunting and ineffable sadness.

He kept his apprehension to himself. Alison already seemed burdened with some unspoken tragedy. He had no wish to burden her further.

Nevertheless, he remained relatively content. The world as he had known it continued to recede. He lost track of time. His former concerns now seemed trivial and grotesque. He retained no wish to walk beyond Starlock Street.

One fine summer morning he got up unusually early, feeling peculiarly lightheaded. The house was quiet. Alison was not yet up. Dressing quietly, he stole downstairs and let himself out.

The sun had not yet reached into Starlock Street. A summer morning held the street in a hush of sleep and silence. The air was cool, gently scented with the aroma of dew-drenched back gardens.

He walked slowly down the brick sidewalks, still feeling oddly detached. The gnawing apprehension which never left him, abruptly, unaccountably, flared into sudden panic.

He had to get out, he told himself. Out! Before it was too late!

Too late? Too late for what? he asked himself. But he didn't know.

He began to run, knowing only that when he came to the end of Starlock Street, he was going to keep on running, to continue on until, until . . .

As he reached the far end of the street, however, vertigo overcame him. The brick sidewalk seemed to swing from beneath his feet. The streets beyond appeared to melt into a kind of glittering mist which gradually winked away. He felt himself gliding down a narrowing funnel of darkness, faster and faster . . .

He was sitting on the porch next to Alison when he roused himself.

He rubbed his eyes. "I must have had a—a nightmare—I guess," he managed weakly.

She shook her head. "It was no nightmare. You died."

He stared at her, horrified. "But—I don't feel—much different!"

"Death is merely a dimension. You moved from one to another. Actually, one you have been close to all this time."

"I don't—understand!"

Her calm eyes met his. Her face was a mask of sorrow, of final acceptance.

"You created your own dimension of death. All your life you longed to escape into another time, into a vanished world, a milieu of the past. Your desire, prolonged and intense, recreated the time you longed to enter, to return to. Starlock Street does not exist in your former world. You brought it into existence—on another plane of perception. Now it represents actuality for you. It cannot be destroyed or dismissed."

Bewildered, he remained silent.

"You rejected your own life," she went on. "You scorned its values, the experiences it offered, the rich and varied chances for living which it virtually thrust into your hands—had you only reached for them. You turned away. You preferred the past—the past, vanished but still existing in a dimension of time beyond your earthly laws."

He managed to speak again. "But I have—no regrets. Everything I want is here. You are here! The Victorian past which I treasure! The peace and tranquillity of a time I have always revered!"

Slowly, she shook her head again. "Nothing will ever change here. You will finally come to detest the tranquillity, the quiet routine, the gardens, the very bricks in the sidewalk. And you will grow to hate me. Why do you think you tried to rush away, past the end of Starlock Street, back to your former life? It was subconscious knowledge within yourself trying to warn you to escape. But it was too late. The shock of your sudden realization, plus the unaccustomed exertion, brought your death."

Aghast, he faced her. "But how can I come to—to detest—to *hate* even, in heaven?"

Her eyes met his with final, infinite sadness. "My dear," she said, "whatever made you think this was heaven?"

The Haunting
at Juniper Hill

IN LATE AUGUST of 1981 my last surviving uncle, Loren Holborn, died in Juniper Hill, leaving his entire estate to a neighbor, a total stranger to me. When I learned the contents of the will, I was shocked. The entire Holborn holdings, once quite substantial, had now passed into the hands of persons completely unknown to me.

When I wrote, inquiring for details, I received no response. A visit proved useless. I received no information of consequence or significance. I felt that I was regarded with either amusement or contempt.

My attitude toward Juniper Hill began to change. While I still loved the land, I came to appraise the villagers with misgivings.

By one of those coincidences which are not permitted in fiction, but which often occur in actual life, my attitude of distrust was reinforced only a short time later by an adventure which I shared with my private investigator friend, Lucius Leffing.

I had stopped at 7 Autumn Street one September afternoon, with no particular purpose in mind. Although a few yellow leaves were already drifting down, it was a warm, windless day. Leffing served cold sarsaparilla and we sat relaxed in his restful Victorian living room, conversing at intervals.

When the door chimes sounded, Leffing, sighing, arose reluctantly. "Even money, Brennan—a salesman or someone soliciting funds."

I shook my head. "You'd have to give me odds on that."

I heard him conversing at the door. He returned with a stranger, whom he introduced as a Mr. Julius Morling, formerly of Hartford but now residing in Juniper Hill.

Morling was middle-aged, in fine condition, lean and alert, bronzed by outdoor activity. He had an air of impatience and he told his story with obvious exasperation.

A helpful inheritance, plus his own acumen as an insurance executive, had enabled him to retire early. Tired of urban crime, pollution and city life in general, he had sold his house in Hartford and purchased a neglected, but picturesque, old saltbox house on the outskirts of Juniper Hill. Although he did not directly say so, his decision may have been brought about, in part, by the fact that his wife, long an invalid, had died in the Hartford house only a year or so before.

The Juniper Hill saltbox, he told us, was in an advanced state of disrepair. It had been totally neglected for decades. Although he himself undertook and completed much of the renovation work, specialized contractual labor involving electricity, plumbing, carpentry, insulation and so on, plus the purchase of lumber, fixtures, paint, window-glass, etc., as well as furnace installation, furnishings, and endless miscellanea, had cost him nearly forty thousand dollars.

He leaned his head against the flowered antimacassar on the back of Leffing's antique chair and scowled.

"And now I think someone—or something—is trying to drive me out of the place!"

Leffing tented the tips of his long fingers and settled back in his Morris chair. "Let us have all the details, in sequence, Mr. Morling."

Our visitor sat forward. "For a week or so, after I finally moved in, I slept soundly. I had worked hard on the house and I was pretty tired. But about ten days after I'd been there, I began waking up several times during the night. I couldn't account for it at first. At length I realized that I was listening for something—whatever it was that kept invading my sleep. I heard it, finally, when I was fully awake. It was quite a strident racket in a way, yet strangely muffled and subdued. I imagine that sounds like a contradictory statement, but I don't know how else to say it. At intervals there seemed to be a series of mingled screams, moans and muttered imprecations. At times these disconcerting noises seemed to be right outside the house. Again, I could have sworn they came from some little distance."

Morling frowned and shook his head. "I am a sensible man, not given to foolish imaginings. After my sleep had been broken for the better part of a week, I determined to find the source of the disturbance. I searched the house, cellar to attic, and found nothing. I searched outside, with the same result. There are no outbuildings. There are a few old elm trees near the house and a stand of halfgrown maples crowded in with brush and weeds about fifty yards away. I could find nothing at all out of the ordinary."

He leaned back, looking grim. "I finally decided the damned natives were up to something. From the beginning, I got the feeling that they resented my buying the house. And I had acquired the continuing conviction that they resented my presence among them. I wasn't sure

why. Possibly one or more of them had planned to purchase the place. Or perhaps they just disliked strangers on
principle—with that ingrown attitude of suspicion and sly
spite which one sometimes encounters in small towns and
backward communities.''

He shrugged impatiently. ''I tried being friendly, perhaps over-friendly, whenever I met one of the villagers,
but it did no good. They were polite but it was all surface.''

He shook his head again, scowling. ''I started to sit up
nights, watching through darkened windows, but I never
saw anyone approach the house. I didn't see anyone even
at a distance. Yet, at intervals, the nightly sounds went
on—moans, cries, subdued yet somehow distinct. I can
tell you—sometimes the hair on my head stirred!''

He sighed. ''I have always thought that I am one of the
most matter-of-fact men in the world, but at last I had to
admit that there might be something, well—something
unexplainable in material terms—at work. I knew it would
be useless to question the natives. I didn't even try. I was
certain that if any of them could have suggested an explanation, they would not have shared it with me.''

Morling spread his hands in a gesture of defeat. ''One
evening I drove in to Hartford for a few drinks at my old
club. Over scotch, I told my troubles to a friend of mine. I
didn't expect him to offer help. The nagging business was
uppermost in my mind, that's all. I suppose I just wanted
to let it out. Anyway, he listened carefully, asked some
sensible questions, and when I was finished, suggested
that I get in touch with you.''

He grimaced. ''I must admit it took me some time to
follow his advice. But the infernal racket went on and I'm
still losing sleep. Even though I've sunk a lot of money in
that house, I'm not at all sure it would be easy to sell in
today's market.''

He sat back. "Well, that's the gist of it. And here I am."

For some minutes Leffing sat without speaking, his eyes half-closed, obviously pondering the problems which Morling had presented.

He looked up, finally. "I cannot, of course, suggest any solution at this time. I believe a visit to the premises is definitely in order."

Morling nodded. "Any time you'd like to come."

"Good. I am wondering, in fact, if you could manage to put us up overnight. Possibly, if we ourselves heard this nocturnal 'racket', as you call it, we might have some success in discovering its source."

"No trouble at all, Mr. Leffing. The place has four bedrooms."

Leffing turned to me. "You will be available day after tomorrow, Brennan?"

"Name the hour. I need a few days away from routine and the car was tuned up just last week."

"Capital, Brennan!"

My friend stood up. "It is settled then, Mr. Morling. We will arrive after lunch on Thursday."

Our visitor arose and extended his hand. "I am grateful. I'll be awaiting you."

He turned at the door. "You'll have no trouble finding the place. Take the west road out of Juniper Hill center. About four miles. Only house on the left, set back off from the road."

After he departed, Leffing returned to his chair. "Well, Brennan, any theories?"

"I think it's a plain case of harassment. The unfriendly natives are scheming to drive him out. They've undoubtedly figured out some way to transmit that racket to his

area at night. Once we learn what kind of device they're
using . . ." I shrugged. "Well, that will end the business,
I presume."

Leffing looked thoughtful. "Your theory may be the
correct one, Brennan. If so, I might as well admit I will be
disappointed. It would be all so—mundane."

I laughed. "I know your penchant for the bizarre, Leffing!
But I doubt that this case will supply it."

I stood up to leave.

Remaining seated, Leffing waved a languid farewell.
"Thursday morning then?"

"About nine-thirty. A leisurely drive. We'll stop for
lunch along the way."

He nodded approval and I left.

By Thursday morning the weather had turned cold and
wet. After skidding once on slippery leaves, I drove more
slowly through the gray, gleaming streets to Leffing's
house.

The rain increased as we drove north. Leffing had little
to say. I made no attempt to coax him into conversation.
We stopped in Simsbury for a sandwich lunch. As we
drove through Granby, the rain slanted down in relentless
sheets.

It was still pouring when we passed through Juniper Hill
center and headed west.

Because of the poor visibility, we had some little trouble
locating Morling's house. I finally spotted a chimney top
lifting above a screen of trees and turned up the drive.

Morling opened the door before we reached it. "Beastly
weather! I wasn't sure you'd come!"

He took our coats in the entrance hall and led us into a
pine-panelled living room. A welcome blaze leaped brightly
in a capacious field-stone fireplace.

Morling waved us to adjacent armchairs. "Furniture's a bit seedy, I'm afraid. Mean to replace it—if I stay here."

Leffing settled back in his chair and stretched his long legs toward the fire. "This chair is eminently comfortable, Mr. Morling. Were it mine, I would never replace it."

Morling smiled his appreciation. "A bit of brandy, gentlemen?"

After our hearty response, he crossed to a sideboard.

As we settled down with our drinks, Leffing scrutinized our host. "You look a trifle tired, Mr. Morling. Any new developments?"

Morling stared moodily into his brandy glass. "Well—not really new. Same damnable racket again last night. Broke up my sleep all right."

"Would you say this has become an almost nightly occurrence then?"

Morling hesitated. "I'd say—not quite. Not usually two nights running. But no particular pattern to it, that I can see. I guess it averages three to four nights a week."

He shifted in his chair uneasily and glanced around the room. "Sometimes I think the—whatever it is—abstains a night or so to, well, sort of gather strength!"

He looked questioningly at Leffing. "Does that make any sense at all?"

Leffing inclined his head. "It may indeed make eminent sense, Mr. Morling. There may be causative factors, however, of which, at this point, we are entirely unaware."

Morling nodded. "Of course. Certainly so." He swirled his drink. "You have, ah, formulated plans, Mr. Leffing?"

Leffing stared into the fire. "My only plan, at least at this moment, is to sit up until dawn in the hope that we hear the weird sounds which are disturbing you—even though you just mentioned that they are seldom repeated two nights running."

After we finished our drinks, Morling showed us to our rooms, adjacent bedrooms along an upstairs hall, each with a small bath.

We freshened up and our host took us on a leisurely tour of the entire house. In spite of neglect, it was obviously a sturdily-built old saltbox. Morling's renovations had modernized it without destroying any of its original charm. As I tramped up and down stairs, however, through hallways, pantries, bedrooms, cavernous kitchens (two), unused parlor, storage areas and huge finished-off attic, I was grateful that I was not responsible for the heating arrangements.

The cellar was a gloomy place, rather poorly lighted, I thought, but clean. We peered into storage bins, preserve closets, butteries and so on. Morling had cemented over the original dirt floors.

Leffing kept an alert eye but asked few questions.

Although Morling apologized for his "amateur culinary efforts", lamb chops, sliced broiled potatoes and fresh corn, followed by mince pie and coffee, made a more than satisfactory meal.

After dinner, the three of us sat before the fireplace for a time, sipping liqueurs. Morling, obviously tired, excused himself early.

Leffing and I settled down for the long night's vigil. It was totally unrewarding. Aside from the racket of wind and rain, the only other sound audible was the occasional chirp of a cricket hidden somewhere in the stonework of the fireplace.

Shortly before dawn we gave up and retired to our rooms.

I woke up about nine o'clock and dressed, yawning every two minutes. Leffing, I found, was already up and about. Morling, holding breakfast, served it shortly after I descended.

The rain had stopped toward dawn; sun was starting to glint through the breaking cloud cover.

As we sat in the big kitchen, aromatic with the smells of fresh coffee and frying bacon, I found it hard to believe that Leffing and I were there to investigate something unpleasant, if not sinister.

Morling sipped his coffee with relish, looking relatively rested. Although he was grateful for a night's sleep, he was disappointed that Leffing and I had heard nothing.

"We will try again tonight," Leffing assured him. "Meanwhile we will do a bit of exploring in the area."

After breakfast, Morling showed us around outside. There was not much to see. As yet, he had done little landscaping; the grounds were shaggy and neglected. A half dozen large elm trees surrounded the house. Forty or fifty yards away, a rough rectangle of half-grown maples lifted above a dense mass of briars, grass and weeds.

"I mean to winnow out that mess one day," Morling told us. "Haven't had the time—nor inclination either, I guess."

Leffing insisted on tramping through the tangle. Morling and I followed reluctantly.

We emerged scratched, dishevelled and wet with the residue of the previous day's driving rain.

After we changed clothes, Leffing and I decided to take a hike into "the Center"—the natives' term for the small group of buildings which constituted the shopping and business district of Juniper Hill. There was one general store with a gas pump, a white frame Congregational church, a town meeting-hall, a post office and half a dozen private houses. Incongruously perhaps, the cemetery lay a short distance from the church but alongside the general store.

Morling had warned us that we could not expect to
extract any information from the natives. He was correct.
There were five people in the general store; two nodded,
and one managed a grudging "good morning." The proprietor lurking behind the chipped wooden counter resembled an overdone caricature of the typical old-time Yankee
storekeeper: taciturn, apparently indifferent, but actually
keenly observant of everything that went on. He peered
shrewdly over small half-glasses and had a habit of hook-
ing his thumbs under his striped suspenders.

We bought two bottles of soda and sat down at a small
table across the aisle from the counter. I think that both
Leffing and I felt the utter futility of making any inquiries.
Everyone in the store seemed to ignore us but we knew
they were impatiently waiting for us to leave. I was sure
that they would then air their amused speculations concerning us.

After returning our empty bottles to the counter, we left.
Even as we walked down the creaky outside steps, I
thought I heard the cackle of laughter.

We walked back in relative silence. Leffing had grown
rather morose. I had the conviction that he felt at least
momentarily baffled.

By the time we got back, I was tired. I had walked
nearly eight miles after only a few hours' sleep. I went up
to my room and lay down, leaving Leffing to his own
devices. Morling told us that he had been busy with business correspondence.

I slept for two hours and returned downstairs feeling
somewhat refreshed.

As I descended, I heard a car drive off. A moment or
two later, Morling and Leffing walked in accompanied by
a boy of about nine. Morling introduced him as Steve
Brent, his nephew from Simsbury. Stevie's mother had left

her son with Morling while she drove over to Winsted on
some errand. Morling told us that Stevie would rather
ramble around than ride. Mrs. Brent would stop for her
son on the way back from Winsted later in the day.

Stevie soon went back outside. We sat around the living
room rather listlessly.

Leffing finally got up and paced the floor. "I sincerely
hope tonight proves more rewarding. If I heard—"

He broke off as young Stevie came into the room. He
looked pale and frightened.

Morling stood up. "What's wrong, Stevie?"

Stevie stared at the floor, embarrassment beginning to
overcome his fright.

"Well—what?" Morling coached. "What happened?"

Stevie squirmed. "Oh, nothin', I guess. I just thought I
saw—somethin'."

"Saw what? Where? Where were you?"

"In the brush, under the maple trees. I thought I saw—a
face. Scared me, I guess."

"Enough to scare anybody, I'd venture," Leffing interposed. "Can you describe the face, Stevie?"

Stevie scowled in mock or genuine concentration. "Face
of—of an old lady! Sort of—mean. Sort of—mad at somebody. Face of an old witch!"

Morling frowned. "She came after you?"

Stevie shrugged. "Just—sort of—watched me. Real mean.
Then she kind of faded away—back in the bushes."

"We'll look into it, Stevie," Morling assured him.

"Nothing to worry about. Why don't you go out to the
kitchen and help yourself to some cake and ice cream?
Lots of it in the box!"

"What do you make of it?" he asked Leffing after Stevie
had left for the kitchen.

"It may be a pointer in the right dirrection," Leffing

replied. "Or it may be nothing at all—merely the way a few bushes came together, plus a child's overactive imagination."

He crossed the room toward the foyer. "I will take another little stroll under those maple trees, in any case. Care to come along, Brennan?"

Dutifully, I slipped on my coat and followed my friend outside.

Once again I trailed alongside as he forced his way through the burdocks and brush under the stand of maple trees. He doubled back several times and finally made a complete circuit of the outer edge of the tangle. I could see no evidence that an old woman, nor anyone else save ourselves, had been under those trees recently.

Somewhat grumpily, I accompanied Leffing back toward the house. I had sustained a number of fresh briar scratches.

"That should set the matter at rest," I commented. "I'm afraid little Stevie has an overworked imagination."

Pausing, Leffing looked back toward the trees. "I am not so sure, Brennan. Along all four sides of that overgrown area I discerned a very faint but unmistakable indentation. It may well be the dwindling trace of an old foundation line."

I shrugged. "What could that possibly prove?"

Leffing frowned impatiently. "I am not trying to prove anything! I am trying to clear up a mystery which, so far, manifests itself primarily as an auditory phenomenon. It is just possible that something concerning the brush patch may contain a hidden key to the whole enigma!"

I made no reply. We went to our rooms to remedy our bedraggled appearances. I took the opportunity to paint my scratches with merthiolate.

Stevie, gorged with cake and ice cream, had gone back

outside. Morling told us he appeared to have completely gotten over his fright.

During lunch, Leffing described the dim indentations which might indicate a fading foundation line.

Morling was mystified. He had never heard that another building had once occupied the site. He admitted that it was possible.

Our host sat up with us until nearly midnight and then excused himself. He couldn't decide, it seemed, whether to be relieved or disappointed that we had so far heard nothing of the disturbing sounds which had been destroying his sleep.

The noise began about an hour after Morling retired. At first we heard muffled screams which appeared to originate at some far-distant point. They quickly became louder. As they did so, we heard a shrill voice shouting above them—a maniacal voice filled with fury. The sounds increased in volume until they seemed to be only a stone's throw from the house.

Hurriedly slipping on coats, Leffing and I ran to the front door and dashed outside. It was a cold, clear moonlit night and though I could have taken an oath that the hair-raising cacophony arose in the air only yards away, I saw nothing.

Leffing stood motionless, staring in one direction and then another. Gradually the screams turned to moans, but the shrill voice went on as before, cursing only half-coherently, mouthing savage imprecations we could not fully comprehend.

I stood stricken with horror. Leffing, I am sure, was similarly affected, though probably to a lesser degree.

As we stood riveted, the racket slowly receded. It appeared to move away from the house toward the creeper and briar-tangled copse of maples.

Motioning me to follow, Leffing strode off toward the trees. For a minute or two, as we walked, complete silence descended. Just as we moved into the first fringe of shadows alongside the maple grove, however, the screams and the shrill, furious cursing began again, louder than before.

We both stopped. I could feel my heart pounding. In spite of the chill night air, a sweat of fear broke out on my face.

The screams and wild execrations reached a hysterical crescendo. Suddenly Leffing bolted forward into the brush-grown copse. I followed him in under the trees.

Even as we fought our way forward, the heart-rending cries dwindled into moans again. The ear-piercing imprecations broke off. The moans became faint and then stopped. Abrupt silence gripped the grove.

Puzzled and uncertain, we both paused. As we hesitated, we heard a thing far worse than the screams and curses: the gloating, satisfied sound of steady laughter, a mad chuckling which made the hair on my head stiffen.

As it went on and on, I found it far more unbearable than anything which had preceded it.

Leffing shook his head, as if to rid himself of the foul sound, and moved forward. I followed.

We had pushed about a third of the way through the copse before the monstrous, mirthless cachinnation ended.

The silence which ensued, in itself, seemed unearthly. Shivering, I shoved through the briary tangle behind Leffing as he continued on to the far edge of the grove. We found nothing, no evidence at all that anyone was secreted in the maple woods, nor any indication that anyone had entered the copse recently.

Shaken and silent, we returned to the house, poured stiff brandies and sat before the fire.

Leffing stared moodily into the flames. I had arisen twice to pile on fresh wood before he finally spoke.

"Well, Brennan, I think we have at least narrowed our area of investigation. I am now fully convinced that the disturbance is somehow anchored in the maple grove. I am equally sure that it is unearthly in origin."

I got up and stood before the fire. "Can we be positive it is not some kind of infernal recording device hidden in the trees by the locals—perhaps activated electronically from a distance?"

Leffing set down his drink. "I have already considered and rejected that possibility. No recording device could induce in me the psychic *malaise* which I experienced in that haunted tangle of trees."

I nodded agreement. "I too was acutely aware of some kind of unearthly menace, an evil of enormous intensity."

Leffing finished his drink and stood up. "Well expressed, Brennan. But we can do no more tonight. A mere repetition of our experience would be of little help. A few hours sleep might aid us more."

I did not sleep well. Once I thought I heard agonized screams and frenzied curses arising outside, but apparently I was only undergoing a nightmare. In the morning neither Leffing nor Morling reported a second occurrence.

After breakfast, Leffing abruptly asked me if I could drive him into Hartford. He offered no explanation and I did not ask for one until we were well on our way.

"I might as well admit," Leffing replied, "that we may be making this trip entirely in vain. But it is possible that old newspaper reports or county records of land ownership and real estate transactions may yield a clue. It will be a tiresome day, Brennan. I suggest that you visit friends in Hartford, or West Hartford, or otherwise entertain yourself."

"Can't I help with the research?"

"Thank you but I think not. It will be a plodding, pokey business. I am like an old hound dog at this sort of thing. I may veer off suddenly on a side trail if I catch a certain scent. I like to think I was born with a certain investigative intuition. In any event, it can scarcely be imparted to someone else."

I felt decidedly offended by this response but long experience had taught me not to protest. I remained silent.

About ten o'clock I dropped Leffing off near the main office of the town's leading newspaper. We agreed to meet at the same place about five o'clock that afternoon.

The day dragged. I took a long walk around the central city area, sat for an hour over lunch, drove out to West Hartford to visit a friend who turned out not to be at home, browsed in a local bookstore, a hobby shop and a small museum, imbibed two gin-and-tonics at one of the less noisy bars and drove back to Hartford. There was still time to spare. I window-shopped restlessly until four-thirty and then drove down to meet my friend.

He showed up promptly at five and we started back toward Juniper Hill.

Leffing appeared fatigued, and for some time, in the hopes that he might volunteer information, I confined myself to inconsequential remarks. At length I cautiously inquired if he had met with any success.

"I believe," he replied, "that I may have established the broad outlines of an explanation, though not necessarily a solution, of the case. After a hot shower and a swallow of brandy—which should rinse away some of the newspaper's morgue dust—I will supply details to you and Morling."

In spite of my intense curiosity, I knew better than to press Leffing for more information. He would impart it only later when he was somewhat rested and refreshed and in the proper mood.

When we arrived back at Morling's house, we saw nine-year-old Stevie Brent, our client's nephew, playing outside. Our host explained that Stevie's mother had dropped him off for a day or two, along with some new overnight camping gear which he was extremely anxious to try out.

During dinner Leffing seemed absent-minded and abstracted. I decided he was trying to make some kind of decision. In spite of his previous promise, he had not given either Morling or myself any results of his research. After a shower and a bit of brandy, he had merely said that he preferred to delay an outline of his search until dinner was finished.

Over dessert, he turned to Morling. "You mentioned that Stevie here is anxious to use his new camping gear."

Stevie looked up hopefully. Morling nodded. "Awfully anxious, I'd say! Eh, Stevie?"

Stevie's eyes widened. "Tonight, Uncle Jule?"

Morling hesitated. "I—well, I don't know about tonight. It's some distance out to the woods. It'll be dark pretty soon."

Crestfallen, Stevie returned to his dessert, obviously without much appetite.

Leffing studied the boy a moment. "Stevie, would you settle for a campsite in the maple grove? Remember, something frightened you in there before."

Stevie smiled up at Leffing with renewed hope. "Sure! That old grove's still the woods!"

He toyed with his fork for a moment. "Besides, I'm not frightened anymore. I guessed I just sort of 'magined something."

Gulping down the last of his dessert, he asked to be

excused from the table. "Can I get my stuff together now?"

Hesitating, Morling finally nodded approval. As the lad scuttled from the room, our host turned questioning eyes on Leffing.

"I cannot be sure," Leffing told him, "but Stevie's presence in the maple grove may bring support to the theory my researches have indicated."

Morling frowned. "But is there danger? The boy is in my charge."

Leffing considered his reply. "I believe—I am convinced in fact—there will be no physical danger. The possibility of another—fright—does exist. But Brennan and I will remain close at hand."

For some minutes I thought Morling would refuse his consent. I think what decided him was the reappearance of Stevie, bright-eyed and bursting with excitement, lugging his new overnight camping equipment.

Our client arose with reluctance. "Well—all right. We'd better get Stevie settled in there before it gets dark."

All three of us conducted Stevie out to the grove and got him settled in a small clearing near the middle of the copse shortly before dusk descended.

Stevie snuggled down happily in his sleeping-bag under a small canvas tent, pretending, I suspect, that he was a lone pioneer in a great forest infested by ferocious Indians.

Leffing and I trekked back to the house with Morling. I had sustained some fresh briar scratches but neither Leffing nor Morling appeared to have been lacerated. I concluded that I must be peculiarly susceptible to such things.

We stepped inside briefly for an after-dinner drink.

"Brennan will post himself on one side of the grove, I on the other," Leffing explained. "At the first indication of any commotion or—invasion—we will both rush in. We can be at Stevie's side within minutes."

Morling nodded. "I had best sit up, just in case. Won't one or both of you want to be relieved by me later in the night?"

Leffing shook his head. "I shall remain on post till morning. How about you, Brennan?"

"I'll stay right there with you no matter what!" I replied.

That settled the matter. Just before full darkness, we bid goodnight to Morling, walked once more to the maple copse and took our stands on either side. A few crickets were chirping and occasionally we heard the scampering of some small animal, but otherwise the night was quiet.

The more I glanced at my watch, the more I became convinced that minutes had somehow stretched to six hundred seconds instead of sixty and that hours must be proportionally longer. The rising moon increased visibility, but frequent drifting clouds brought periods of deeper darkness.

The tedium and frustrations of the day intensified my fatigue; I felt that I might easily doze off on my feet. In order to stay alert, I kept walking back and forth alongside the outer fringe of the copse.

No sound came from within. I concluded that Stevie had long since fallen asleep.

I was beginning to believe that our vigil was a wasted one when a sudden shrill cursing broke out followed by a spine-chilling cackle of crazy laughter. A moment later Stevie began to scream hysterically.

Disregarding briars, brush and the possibility of a wrenched ankle or twisted knee, I plunged head on into the overgrown maple grove.

As I fought my way toward the center of the copse, I

heard Leffing crashing through the tangle from the opposite direction. I reached Stevie's little bivouac site first.

The terrified lad crouched half in and half out of his small tent, staring fixedly at a tall figure which hovered only feet away.

The thing, its back toward me, was apparently gazing down at Stevie. It was hatless; strands of long white hair hung past its shoulders. Its clothing appeared to consist of an assortment of tattered rags somehow clinging together.

Obviously sensing my presence, it turned its head in my direction.

During my various adventures with Leffing, and in my own life, I have seen some foul and frightful entities, but none, I think, could surpass in horror the monstrous thing which stood there in the filtered moonlight staring down at me. To say that it was the essence of evil would be an understatement; as I looked into its glaring fiery eyes, I glimpsed the depths of hell itself. If it was something which had once been human, it was now nothing more than a tangible concentration of fury, lust and inexpressible cruelty, a fiend escaped from the pit. Its red eyes held me like two malign magnets. Its face—if such it could be called—was a mottled, wattle-like mass of bloated flesh in which individual features were almost too blurred to discern.

In retrospect, I might as well reluctantly admit that, for one of the very few times in my life, I thought that I might faint as the hate-filled flaming eyes burned into my own.

Mercifully, the thing twisted about as Leffing burst into the clearing from the other side.

For an instant even Leffing hesitated as the nightmare manifestation turned to face him. But only for an instant.

The sight of young Stevie, white-faced and quivering, crouched in the tent opening, seemed to galvanize my friend into purposeful action.

He strode directly toward the hovering horror. His voice, low but distinct, held an imperious edge of command and authority which I had seldom heard before. One hand pointed away toward the outer darkness.

"Return to hell, Lucretia Ploor! Return and begone forever! You died a hundred years ago! Only your lusts outlive you! Back to your grave, foul creature!"

Leffing's handling of the situation heartened me; I edged forward. A discernible snarl distorted the apparition's corruption-covered countenance. A thing of indescribable darkness, it swayed there in the half darkness of the night, riven with rage, a famished predator cheated of its prey. Over Leffing's shoulder, its red eyes fastened again on Stevie.

If Leffing had taken one step backward, if he had even wavered, I am convinced the day would have been lost. But he stood motionless and his eyes never left those of the thing which confronted him.

Suddenly a terrible cry burst from it, a scream of mingled fury, bafflement and, I think, fear—a despairing, long-drawn wail which transfixed me.

As the fearful cry ended, the creature moved slowly backwards until it reached the far edge of the clearing. Here it paused and hesitated, wavering in the dim moonlight like some kind of infernal puppet pulled forward and back by invisible strings. Abruptly the terrible shriek rang out again, louder than before, and the thing rushed off through the trees as if propelled by some force beyond itself. For a few seconds a kind of sobbing howl reached our ears, as if from a far distance, and then there was silence.

For a long minute Leffing and I stood motionless, stricken and speechless. Stevie's whimpering broke the hideous spell. Leffing bent quickly, scooped up the lad in his arms

and started off through the brush toward the house. I
followed quickly. From time to time my friend murmured
words of reassurance to the youngster. Apart from that,
neither of us spoke.

Morling, who obviously had not gone to bed at all, met
us in the door.

"Is he hurt?" he inquired apprehensively.

Leffing shook his head. "Not hurt, but frightened half
to death. I suggest a sedative and a cot in front of the
fireplace."

If I had ever had a son, I would have preferred one like
young Stevie. As before, he seemed embarrassed by his
own quite justifiable terror and he now made every effort
to conceal it. Within a few minutes, only an occasional
shiver betrayed the ordeal which he had experienced.

After a mild sleeping potion, he settled down on a couch
in front of the fireplace. Morling had kept a few logs
smouldering; he now stirred them into a blaze.

Leffing and I, along with Morling, moved to the other
side of the room. Our host provided us with stiff brandies
and left the decanter within arm's reach.

Stevie appeared drowsy, but he was not yet asleep. I
concluded that Leffing did not object if the boy listened to
his account.

"It is late," Leffing began. "I will try to be succinct."

Morling and I settled back in our armchairs and my
friend set down his brandy glass.

"I spent the day sifting through brittle newspaper files
and old real estate transaction records. It seemed hopeless
at first. I kept going backwards into time without finding a
clue. I was convinced that the explanation to the disturbance affecting this area lay somewhere in that maple
grove."

He turned to me. "You will recall, Brennan, that I

mentioned finding the dim remains of an old foundation line alongside the edges of the copse?"

I nodded. "I recall it very well."

"That was the clue that sent me searching through musty Hartford County records. I will not bore you with the tedious details—the false leads and dead ends. I was about to give up when I finally found what I sought."

He paused and refilled his glass.

"And what was that?" Morling asked impatiently.

"It was an article in a hundred-year-old Hartford newspaper about an aged woman, Lucretia Ploor, who had lived in this very house. She had recently died and rumors concerning her were rife at the time."

He smiled rather absently, as if to himself. "I must say," he went on, "that if the libel laws were applied then as they are today, some distant relative of the wretched old creature could have put the paper out of business! Lucretia Ploor was a spinster, hard-working, but ignorant, miserly, secretive, unsociable and—worse than any of these—sadistically cruel. At the time it was not uncommon for farm folk around Juniper Hill to board orphan children in return for monthly payments from the state. I gather there were plenty of orphans to go round, and I fear, once they were 'farmed out', as it were, the authorities did not keep an alert eye on them.

"According to the newspaper article, over the years Lucretia Ploor had taken on a long succession of these poor children—all boys. If local reports are accurate, she worked them from sunup to midnight and fed them only scraps another farm family might have thrown into the hogs' trough. Ploor's board boys appeared at the local schoolhouse only after the authorities made complaints. Invariably they were poorly dressed and obviously half-starved. The backsides of many of them were crisscrossed with scars and unhealed weals. The villagers muttered and shook their heads—but nobody did anything.

"From time to time, one or more of the boys disappeared. Invariably, Lucretia Ploor reported they had run away. Nobody bothered to investigate. The missing boys were replaced by new ones. In six months' time, or a year, the new ones 'ran away'. Incredibly, this went on for decades."

Leffing picked up his glass and surveyed it in the firelight. "It was a different world then. Even today natives of Juniper Hill are secretive, withdrawn, conniving among themselves but sly and uncommunicative to outsiders. In those days an investigator from the orphan home in Hartford would have run into the proverbial brick wall."

"Appalling," I interjected. "But I'm afraid I lost the thread. Where does the old foundation line come in?"

Leffing turned with a frown. "I'm coming to that! Where the maple copse now stands, there used to be a huge old barn, according to old real estate and survey records. The barn went with this house. Rumor had it that Ploor often took one of the boys to the barn to administer punishment for some trivial or imagined transgression. Here the monstrous creature would beat the cringing lad until the blood ran. At intervals, usually around midnight or later, screams could be heard all the way to the center of Juniper Hill."

"That was detailed in the newspaper?" I inquired.

"It was. It was even suggested that some of the boys had died under the merciless floggings and had been buried under the barn floor by the crazed old creature!"

Morling shook his head. "Horrible!"

"Horrible indeed," Leffing agreed. "And all the more horrible because nothing was ever done about it."

He toyed with his empty glass. "Apparently an appetite

for blood grew on the sadistic crone. Heaven alone knows
what crimes were committed in that barn. It is my belief,
in any case, that at least ten or a dozen boys were beaten
to death over the decades, and buried under the barn.
Some, of course, may have in fact run away—if they ever
had the opportunity.''

For some minutes, shocked by the story, Morling and I
sat speechless.

Leffing resumed. ''When the creature finally died, in
her nineties it is said, there was vague talk of digging
under the barn floor, but nothing came of it. The unspeak-
able wretch herself was buried somewhere behind the barn.
At one time a pile of field stones marked the place.
Eventually the barn, half in ruins, was struck by lightning
and burned to the ground. Brush and maple saplings spread
over the site. Distant relatives negotiated the sale of the
house. Over the decades it has changed hands many times.''

He turned to Morling. ''I regret to say it almost invariably brought ill luck to its owner. It was sometimes referred
to as 'the Witch House'.''

Morling scowled. ''Damned natives! Not a one of them
said a word to me about all this.''

Leffing nodded. ''That was to be expected of these folk,
I fear. It merely reflects their narrow crafty nature and
their hostility to outsiders.''

Morling glanced across at the recumbent form of young
Stevie. ''I think I understand now why you wanted my
nephew to camp out in the maple grove. You were hoping
to entice this—revenant? Lure back the filthy thing, as it
were? Sort of like leaving a young goat staked out for the
tiger? Right, Mr. Leffing?''

''The simile is perhaps apt, though exaggerated! The
creature was dangerous only in the psychic sphere, not the

physical. Perhaps I went too far—but I wanted confirmation of my theories.''

"But why does the creature return?" I asked. "After all, a hundred years—and what is it trying to accomplish now?"

"The spirit of this foul thing is earthbound, Brennan. I doubt that it consciously wills to return. *It is still there!* Its evil deeds have anchored it. Time does not exist for the dead. A hundred years is scarcely a shadowy heartbeat. The thing hovers over the scene of its earthly atrocities, still hungry for blood, still imbued with all its old fury and lust!"

"How can I get rid of it then?" Morling asked with a puzzled frown.

"I am not sure," Leffing replied, "but it may be gone after tonight. For the first time, to my knowledge, the horrible manifestation has been *challenged*. And it has been told to return to the grave. It may not have even understood, you see, that it was dead!"

Morling stirred uneasily. "What about the screams? I mean of the victims, the boys? Are the innocent earthbound as well?"

Leffing shook his head. "I think not. The thing brought with it its own psychic milieu. The screams we heard emanated from a vanished and invisible yet still existing plane of time."

He leaned back wearily. "I have one suggestion. If you do not object to the expense involved, have the entire copse dug out. If any remains are discovered, have them reinterred in the churchyard, with appropriate ceremonies. Also, if possible, locate the pile of field stones in the rear of the barn site where Lucretia Ploor is rumored to have been buried. If you find the place, exhume the creature's remains and reinter them also—preferably in a far isolated corner of the local cemetery.''

In spite of his experience and his curiosity, Stevie had long since fallen asleep. We turned lights down, but not out, and quietly left the room.

The next day was bright and sunny. Stevie got up early and devoured a huge breakfast. By noon, such is the resiliency of youth, he had found an old kite in the attic and was out running on the slopes.

Leffing and I departed after lunch. I cannot say that I was sorry to leave Juniper Hill and its denizens, both earthly and otherwise.

A few days later Leffing received Morling's check—a very substantial one—but his client did not write at length until months later. It was the following June before he wrote to say that he had acted on Leffing's suggestions. Digging at the barn site, he explained, had been deferred because of the frozen ground. With spring, excavation had commenced. The huddled skeletons of eleven male children were found under the old barn site, buried only a few feet down. They were reinterred in a row in the local cemetery, with the minister presiding.

The mummified remains of Lucretia Ploor, finally located behind the barn site in a shallow grave under a few scattered field stones, were buried in a corner of the graveyard, without ceremony. Although Morling provided a central granite marker for the boys, some of whose names, surprisingly, were ascertained, the grave of Lucretia Ploor was left entirely unmarked.

Morling added that no further disturbances had occurred after Leffing's visit and that he intended to retain the property and go on living in the house.

One evening Leffing and I sat reminiscing about the case, while we sipped my friend's choice cognac. Piled up nearby were half a dozen Connecticut newspapers, all with glaring headlines about the discovery of the poor little victims' skeletons.

"This is one time," I remarked, "when Juniper Hill received a dose of deserved publicity. I wonder how the locals are taking it?"

Leffing looked up. "Oh, I forgot to mention—I just received another note from Morling. He writes that many of the natives, acting as guides to the site of the barn and the boys' graves, are kept quite busy collecting gratuities from the influx of morbidly curious visitors!"

KARL EDWARD
WAGNER

Shrapnel

IT LOOKED LIKE the wreckage of a hundred stained glass windows, strewn across a desolate tangle of wasteland in a schizophrenic kaleidoscope.

The hood of the '78 Marquis buckled in protest as Harmon shifted his not inconsiderable weight. He smeared sweat from his face with a sweatier arm and squinted against the piercing sunlight. Even from his vantage point atop the rusting Mercury, it was impossible to achieve any sense of direction amidst these thousands of wrecked cars.

At some point this had been farmland, although such was difficult to envision now. Whatever crops had once grown here had long ago leached the red clay of scant nutrients. Fallow acres had lapsed into wild pasture where enough soil remained; elsewhere erosion scourged the slopes with red gashes, and a scrub-growth of pine, sumac, honeysuckle and briar grudgingly reclaimed the dead land. Grey knobs of limestone and outcroppings could almost be mistaken for the shapeless hulls of someone's tragedy.

Harmon wished for a beer—a tall, dripping can of cold, cold beer. Six of them. He promised himself a stop at the first convenience store on the highway, once he finished his business here. But first he needed a fender.

"Left front fender. 1970 or '71 Montego."

"I think it will interchange with a '70-'71 Torino," Harmon had offered—too tired to explain that the fender was actually needed for a 1970 Cyclone Spoiler, but that this was Mercury's muscle car version of the Montego, which shared sheet metal with Ford's Torino, and anyway the woman who ran Pearson's Auto Yard probably knew all that sort of stuff already.

She had just a dusting of freckles, and wheat-colored hair that would have looked striking in almost anything other than the regulation dyke haircut she had chosen. The name embroidered across the pocket of her freshly washed but forever grease-stained workshirt read *Shiloh*. Shiloh had just finished off a pair of redneck truckers in quest of certain axle parts incomprehensible to Harmon, and she was more than capable of dealing with him.

"Most of the older Fords are off along the gully along the woods there," Shiloh had pointed. "If they haven't been hauled to the crusher. There's a row of fenders and quarter panels just beyond that. You wait a minute and Dillon or somebody'll be here to look for you."

The thundering air conditioner in the window of the cramped office might have been able to hold the room temperature at 80 if the door weren't constantly being opened. Harmon felt dizzy, and he further felt that fresh air, however searing, was a better bet than waiting on an office stool for Dillon or somebody.

"You watch out for the dogs," Shiloh had warned him. "If one of them comes after you, you just jump on top of something where they can't get at you until Dillon or somebody comes along."

Hardly comforting, but Harmon knew his way around

junkyards. This was an aquaintance that had begun when Harmon had decided to keep the 1965 Mustang of his college days in running order. It had become part hobby, part rebellion against the lookalike econoboxes or the Volvos and BMW's that his fellow young suburban professionals drove each day from their energy-efficient homes in Brookwood or Brookcrest or Crestwood or whatever. Harmon happened to be an up-and-coming lawyer in his own right, thank you, and just now his pet project was restoring a vintage muscle car whose string of former owners had not been overly concerned with trees, ditches, and other obstacles, moving or stationary.

It was a better way to spend Saturday morning than on the tennis court or golf course. Besides, and he wiped his face again, it was good exercise. Harmon, over the past four years and at his wife's insistence, had enrolled in three different exercise programs and had managed to attend a total of two classes altogether. He kept telling himself to get in shape, once his schedule permitted.

Just now he wished he could find Dillon or somebody. The day was too hot, the sun too unrelenting, for a comfortable stroll through this labyrinth of crumbled steel and shattered glass. He rocked back and forth on the hood of the Marquis, squinting against the glare.

"Yoo hoo! Mister Dillon! There's trouble brewin' on Front Street!"

Christ, enough of that! He was getting lightheaded. That late-night pizza had been a mistake.

Harmon thought he saw movement farther down along the ravine. He started to call out in earnest, but decided that the general clatter and crash of the junkyard would smother his words. There was the intermittent mutter of the machine shop, and somewhere in the distance a tractor or towtruck, innocent of muffler, was dragging stripped hulks to their doom in the jaws of the yard's crusher. Grunting, Harmon climbed down from the wreck and plodded toward where he thought he'd glimpsed someone.

The heat seemed worse as he trudged along the rutted pathway. The rows of twisted sheet metal effectively stifled whatever breeze there might have been, at the same time acting as grotesque radiators of the sun's absorbed heat. Harmon wished he had worn a hat. He had always heard that a hat was a good thing to wear when out in the sun. He touched the spot on the top of his head where his sandy hair was inclining to thin. Unpleasant images of frying eggs came to him.

It *smelled* hot. The acres of rusted metal smelled like an unclean oven. There was the bitter smell of roasting vinyl, underscored by the musty stench of mildewed upholstery basted in stagnant rainwater. The palpable smell of hot metal vied with the noxious fumes of gasoline and oil and grease—the dried blood of uncounted steel corpses. Underlying it all was a sickly sweet odor that Harmon didn't like to think about, because it reminded him of his small-town childhood and walking home on summer days through the alley behind the butcher shop. He supposed they hosed these wrecks down or something, before putting them on the yard, but nonetheless . . .

Harmon's gaze caught upon the sagging spiderweb of a windshield above a crumpled steering wheel. He shivered. Strange, to shiver when it was so hot. He seemed to feel his intestines wriggle like a nest of cold eels.

Harmon supposed he had better sit down for a moment. He did.

"Morris?"
Harmon blinked. He must have dropped off.
"Hey, Morris—you OK?"

Where was he?

"Morris?" The voice was concerned and a hand was gently shaking him.

Harmon blinked again. He was sitting on a ruined front seat in the shade of an eviscerated Falcon van. He jerked upright with a guilty start, like a junior exec caught snoring during a senior staff meeting. Someone was standing over him, someone who knew his name.

"Morris?"

The voice became a face, and the face a person. Arnie Cranshaw. A client. Former client. Harmon decided to stop blinking and stand up. On second try, he made it to his feet.

Cranshaw stared reproachfully. "Jesus! I thought maybe you were dead."

"A little too much sun," he explained. "Thought I'd better sit down in the shade for a minute or two. I'm OK. Just dozed off is all."

"You sure?" Cranshaw wasn't so certain. "Maybe you ought to sit back down."

Harmon shook his head, feeling like a fool. "I'll be fine once I get out of this heat. Christ, I'd kill for a cold beer right now!"

Not a well chosen remark, he suddenly reflected. Cranshaw had been his client not quite a year ago in a nasty sort of thing: head-on collision that had left a teen-aged girl dead and her date hopelessly crippled. Cranshaw, the other driver involved, had been quite drunk at the time and escaped injury; he also escaped punishment, thanks to Harmon's legal talents. The other car *had* crossed the yellow line no matter that its driver swore that he had lost control in trying to avoid Cranshaw, who had been swerving all over the road—and a technicality resulted in the DWI charges being thrown out as well. It was a victory

that raised Harmon's stock in the estimation of his col-
leagues, but it was not a victory of which Harmon was
overly proud.

"Anyway, Morris, what are you doing here?" Cranshaw
asked. He was ten years younger than Harmon, had a
jogger's legs, and worked out at his health club twice a
week. Nonetheless, the prospect of lugging a semicon-
scious lawyer out of this metal wasteland was not to
Cranshaw's liking.

"Looking for a fender for my car."

"Fender-bender?" Cranshaw was ready to show sym-
pathy.

"Someone else's, and in days gone by. I'm trying to
restore an old muscle car I bought back in the spring. Only
way to find parts is to dig through junkyards. How about
you?"

"Need a fender for the BMW."

Harmon declined to press for details, which spared
Cranshaw any need to lie about his recent hit-and-run
encounter. He knew a country body shop that would make
repairs without asking questions, if he located some of the
parts. A chop shop wasn't likely to respond to requests for
information about cars with bloodstained fenders and such
grisly trivia. They'd done business before.

Cranshaw felt quite remorseful over such incidents, but
he certainly wasn't one to permit his life to be ruined over
some momentary lapse.

"Do you know where we are?" asked Harmon. He
wasn't feeling at all well, and just now he was thinking
only of getting back into his little Japanese pick-up and
turning the air conditioner up to stun.

"Well. Pearson's Auto Yard, of course." Cranshaw
eyed him suspiciously.

"No. I mean, do you know how to get out of here?"

"Why, back the way we came." Cranshaw decided the man was maybe drunk. "Just backtrack is all."

Cranshaw followed Harmon's bewildered gaze, then said less confidently: "I see what you mean. Sort of like one of those maze things, isn't it. They ought to give you a set of directions or something—like, 'Turn left at the '57 Chevy and keep straight on till you pass the burned-out VW bug.' "

"I was looking for one of the workers," Harmon explained.

"So am I," Cranshaw said. "Guy named Milton or something. He'll know where to find our fenders, if they got any. Sort of like a Chinese librarian, these guys got to be."

He walked on ahead, tanned legs pumping assertively beneath jogging shorts. Harmon felt encouraged and fell in behind him. "I thought I saw somebody working on down the ravine a ways," he suggested to Cranshaw's back.

They seemed to be getting closer to the crusher, to judge by the sound. At intervals someone's discarded dream machine gave up its last vestiges of identity in great screams of rending, crumpling steel. Harmon winced each time he heard those deathcries. The last remaining left front fender for a '70 Cyclone might be passing into recycled oblivion even as he marched to its rescue.

"I don't think this is where I want to be going," Cranshaw said, pausing to look around. "These are pretty much stripped and ready for the crusher. And they're mostly Ford makes."

"Yes. Well, that's what I'm trying to find." Harmon brightened. "Do you see a '70 or '71 Montego or Torino in any of these?"

"Christ, Morris! I wouldn't know one of those from a Model T. I need to find where they keep their late-model

imports. You going to be all right if I go on and leave you
here to poke around?''

"Sure," Harmon told him. The heat was worse, if
anything, but he was damned if he'd ask Cranshaw to
nursemaid him.

Cranshaw was shading his eyes with his hand. "Hey,
you were right. There *is* somebody working down there.
I'm going to ask directions.''

"Wait up," Harmon protested. *He'd* seen the workman
first.

Cranshaw was walking briskly toward an intersection in
the rows of twisted hulks. "Hey, you!" Harmon heard
him call above the din of the crusher. "Hey, Milton!"

Cranshaw turned the corner and disappeared from view
for a moment. Harmon made his legs plod faster, and he
almost collided with Cranshaw when he came around the
corner of stacked cars.

Cranshaw was standing in the middle of the rutted pathway, staring at the mangled remains of a Pinto station
wagon. His face looked unhealthy beneath its tan.

"Shit, Morris! That's the car that I . . .''

"Don't be ridiculous, Arnie. All burned out wrecks
look alike.''

"No. It's the same one. See that porthole window in
back. They didn't make very many of that model. Shit!''

Harmon had studied photos of the wreck in preparing
his defense. "Well, so what if it is the car. It had to end
up in a junkyard somewhere. Anyway, I don't think this is
the same car.''

"Shit!" Cranshaw repeated, starting to back away.

"Hey, wait!" Harmon insisted.

A workman had materialized from the rusting labyrinth.
His greasy commonplaceness was initially reassuring—faded
work clothes, filthy with unguessable stains, and a billed

cap too dirty for its insignia patch to be deciphered. He was tall and thin, and his face and hands were so smeared and stained that Harmon wasn't at first certain as to his race. The workman carried a battered tool box in one hand, while in the other he dragged a shapeless bag of filthy canvas. The eyes that stared back at Harmon were curiously intent above an expressionless face.

"Are you Dillon?" Harmon hoped they weren't trespassing. He could hear a dog barking furiously not far away.

The workman looked past Harmon and fixed his eyes on Cranshaw. His examination of the other man seemed frankly rude.

"Are you Milton?" Cranshaw demanded. The workman's name across his breast pocket was obscured by grease and dirt. "Where do you keep your late-model imports?"

The workman set down his tool box and dug a limp notebook from a greasy shirt pocket. Licking his fingers, he paged through it in silence. After a moment, he found the desired entry. His eyes flicked from the page to Cranshaw and back again.

"Yep," he concluded, speaking for the first time, and he made a checkmark with a well-chewed pencil stub. Returning notebook and pencil to shirt pocket, the workman knelt down and began to unlatch his tool box.

Harmon wanted to say something, but his mouth was too dry to speak, and he knew he was very much afraid, and he wished with all his heart that his legs were not rooted to the ground.

Ahead of him, Cranshaw appeared to be similarly incapable of movement, although from the expression on his face he clearly seemed to wish he were anyplace else but here.

The tool chest was open now, and the workman expertly

made his selection from within. The tool chest appeared to contain mainly an assortment of knives and scalpels, all very dirty and showing evidence of considerable use. If the large knife that the workman had selected was a fair sample, their blades were all very sharp and serviceable.

The canvas bag had fallen open, enough so that Harmon could get a glimpse of its contents. A glimpse was enough. The arm seemed to be a woman's, but there was no way of telling if the heart with its dangling assortment of vessels had come from the same body.

Curiously, once Harmon recognized that many of the stains were blood, it seemed quite evident that much of the dirt was not grease, but soot.

The sound of an approaching motor was only a moment's cause for hope. A decrepit Cadillac hearse wallowed down the rutted trail toward them, as the workman tested the edge of his knife. The hearse, converted into a work truck, was rusted out and so battered that only its vintage tailfins gave it identity. Red dust would have completely masked the chipped black paint, if there hadn't been an overlay of soot as well. The loud exhaust belched blue smoke that smelled less of oil than of sulfur.

Another grimy workman was at the wheel. Except for the greasy straw cowboy hat, he might have been a double for the other workman. The doors were off the hearse, so it was easy to see what was piled inside.

The hearse rolled to a stop, and the driver stuck out his head.

"Another pick-up?"

"Yeah. Better get out and give me a hand here. They want both right and left leg assemblies, and then we need to strip the face. You got a three-inch flaying knife in there? I left mine somewhere."

Then they lifted Cranshaw, grunting a little at the effort, and laid him out across the hood.

"Anything we need off the other?" the driver wondered.

"I don't know. I'll check my list."

It was very, very hot, and Harmon heard nothing more.

Someone was tugging at his head, and Harmon started to scream. He choked on a mouthful of cold R.C. and sputtered foam on the chest of the man who was holding the can to his lips. Harmon's eyes popped open, and he started to scream again when he saw the greasy workclothes. But this black face was naturally so, the workman's eyes showed kindly concern, and the name on his pocket plainly read *Dillon*.

"Just sip on this and take it easy, mister," Dillon said reassuringly. "You had a touch of the sun, but you're going to be just fine now."

Harmon stared about him. He was back in the office, and Shiloh was speaking with considerable agitation into the phone. Several other people stood about, offering conflicting suggestions for treating heat stroke or sun stroke or both.

"Found you passed out on the road out there in the yard," Dillon told him. "Carried you back inside here where we got the air conditioner running."

Harmon became aware of the stuttering howl of an approaching siren. "I won't need an ambulance," he protested. "I just had a dizzy spell is all."

"That ambulance ain't coming for you," Dillon explained. "We had a bad accident at the crusher. Some customer got himself caught."

Shiloh slammed down the phone. "There'll be hell to pay!" she snapped.

"There always is," Harmon agreed.

Old Loves

HE HAD LOVED her for twenty years, and today he would meet her for the first time. Her name was Elisabeth Kent, but to him she would always be Stacey Steele.

Alex Webley had been an undergraduate in the mid-1960s when *The Agency* premiered on Saturday night television. This had been at the height of the fad for spy shows—James Bond and imitations beyond counting, then counter-moves toward either extreme of realism or parody. Upon such a full sea *The Agency* almost certainly would have sunk unnoticed, had it not been for the series' two stars—or more particularly, had it not been for Elisabeth Kent.

In the role of Stacey Steele she played the delightfully eccentric—"kooky" was the expression of the times—partner of secret agent Harrison Dane, portrayed by actor Garrett Channing—an aging matinee idol, to use the expression of an earlier time. The two were employed by an enigmatic organization referred to simply as The Agency, which dispatched Dane and Miss Steele off upon danger-ous assignments throughout the world. Again, nothing in the formula to distinguish *The Agency* from the rest of the pack—except for the charisma of its costars and for a certain stylish audacity to its scripts that became more outrageous as the series progressed.

Initially it was to have been a straight secret agent series: strong male lead assisted by curvaceous ingenue whose scatterbrained exploits would provide at least one good capture and rescue per episode. The role of Harrison Dane went to Garrett Channing—a fortuitous piece of contrary-to-type casting of an actor best remembered as the suave villain or debonair hero of various forgettable 1950s programmers. Channing had once been labeled ''the poor man's James Mason,'' and perhaps the casting director had recalled that James Mason had been an early choice to portray James Bond. The son of a Bloomsbury greengrocer, Channing's Hollywood-nurtured sophistication and charm seemed ideal for the role of American super-spy, Harrison Dane.

Then, through a casting miracle that could only have been through chance and not genius, the role of Stacey Steele went to Elisabeth Kent. Miss Kent was a tall, leggy dancer whose acting experience consisted of several on-and-off-Broadway plays and a brief role in the most recent James Bond film. *Playboy,* as was its custom, ran a pictorial feature on the lovelies of the latest Bond film and devoted two full pages to the blonde Miss Kent—revealing rather more of her than was permitted in the movies of the day. It brought her to the attention of the casting director, and Elisabeth Kent became Stacey Steele.

Became Stacey Steele almost literally.

Later they would say that the role destroyed Elisabeth Kent. Her career dwindled miserably afterward. Some critics suggested that Miss Kent had been blackballed by the industry after her unexpected departure from the series resulted in *The Agency's* plummeting in the ratings and merciful cancellation after a partial season with a forgettable DD-cup Malibu blonde stuffed into the role of female lead. The consensus, however, pointed out that after her role in *The Agency* it was Stacey Steele who was in demand, and not Elisabeth Kent. Once the fad for secret agent films passed, there were no more roles for Stacy Steele. Nor for Elisabeth Kent. A situation comedy series flopped after three episodes. Two films with her in straight dramatic roles were noteworthy bombs, and a third was never released. Even if Elisabeth Kent succeeded in convincing some producer or director that she was not Stacey Steele, her public remained adamant.

Her only film appearance within the past decade had been as the villainess in a Hong Kong chop-fooey opus, *Tiger Fists Against the Dragon*. Perhaps it lost some little in translation.

Inevitably, *The Agency* attracted a dedicated fan following, and Stacy Steele became a cult figure. The same was true to a lesser extent for Garrett Channing, although that actor's death not long after the series' cancellation spared him both the benefits and the hazards of such a status. The note he left upon his desk: "Goodbye, World—I can no longer accept your tedium," was considered an enviable exit line.

The Agency premiered in the mid-1960s, just catching the crest of the Carnaby Street mod-look craze. Harrison Dane, suave super-spy and mature man of the world though he was, was decidedly hip to today's swinging beat, and the promos boldly characterized him as a "mod James Bond." No business suits and narrow ties for Harrison Dane: "We want to take the stuffiness out of secret agenting," to quote one producer. As the sophisticated counterpart to the irrepressible Miss Steele, Dane saved the day once a week attired in various outfits consisting of

bell-bottom trousers, paisley shirts, Nehru jackets, and lots
of beads and badges. If one critic described Harrison Dane
as "a middle-aged Beatle," the public applauded this "anti-
establishment superspy."

No such criticism touched the image of Stacey Steele.
Stacey Steele was the American viewing public's ideal of
the Swinging London Bird—her long-legged physique perfectly suited to vinyl minidresses and thigh-high boots.
Each episode became a showcase for her daring fashions—
briefest of miniskirts, hip-hugging leather bell-bottoms,
see-through (as much as the censors would permit) blouses,
cut-out dresses, patent boots, psychedelic jewelry, groovy
hats, all that was marvy, fab and gear. There was talk of
opening a franchise of Stacey Steele Boutiques, and Miss
Steele became a featured model in various popular magazines seeking to portray the latest fashions for the Liber-
ated Lady of the Sixties. By this time Elisabeth Kent's
carefully modulated BBC accent would never betray her
Long Island birthright to the unstudied ear.

Stacey Steele was instant pin-up material, and stills of
the miniskirted secret agent covered many a dorm wall
beside blow-ups of Bogie and black-light posters. Later
detractors argued that *The Agency* would never have lasted
its first season without Stacey Steele's legs, and that the
series was little more than an American version of one of
the imported British spy shows. Fans rebutted such charges
with the assertion that it had all started with James Bond
anyway, and *The Agency* proved that the Americans could
do it best. Pin-up photos of Stacey Steele continue to sell
well twenty years after.

While *The Agency* may have been plainly derivative of a
popular British series, American viewers made it their
favorite show against formidable primetime competition
from the other two networks. For three glorious seasons

The Agency ruled Saturday nights. Then, Elisabeth Kent's sudden departure from the series: catastrophe, mediocrity, cancellation. But not oblivion. The series passed into syndication and thus into the twilight zone of odd-hour reruns on local channels and independent networks. Old fans remembered, new fans were born. *The Agency* developed a cult following, and Stacey Steele became its goddess.

In that sense, among its priesthood was Alex Webley. He had begun his worship two decades ago in the tv lounge of a college dorm, amidst the incense of spilled beer and tobacco smoke and an inspired choir of whistles and guffaws. The first night he watched *The Agency* Webley had been blowing some tangerine with an old high school buddy who had brought a little down from Antioch. Webley didn't think he'd gotten off, but when the miniskirted Miss Steele used dazzling karate chops to dispatch two baddles, he knew he was having a religious experience. After that, he watched *The Agency* every Saturday night without fail. It would have put a crimp in his dating if Webley had been one who dated. His greatest moment in college was the night when he stood off two drunken jocks, either of whom could have folded Webley in half, who wanted to switch channels from *The Agency* to watch a basketball game. They might have stuffed Webley into the wastebasket had not other *Agency* fans added their voices to his protest. Thus did Alex Webley learn the power of fans united.

It was a power he experienced again with news of Elisabeth Kent's departure from the series, and later when *The Agency* was cancelled. Webley was one of the thousands of fans who wrote to the network demanding that Stacey Steele be brought back to the show (never mind how). With the show's cancellation, Webley helped circulate a petition that *The Agency* be continued, with or without Stacey Steele. The producers were impressed by such show of support, but the network pointed out that 10,000 signatures from the lunatic fringe do not cause a flicker on the Nielsen ratings. Without Stacey Steele, *The Agency* was out of business, and that was that. Besides, the fad for overdone spy shows was over and done.

Alex Webley kept a file of clippings and stills, promotional items, comic books and paperbacks, anything at all pertaining to *The Agency* and to the great love of his life, Elisabeth Kent. From the beginning there were fanzines—crudely printed amateur publications devoted to *The Agency*—and one or two unofficial fan clubs. Webley joined and subscribed to them all. Undergraduate enthusiasms developed into a lifelong hobby. Corresponding with other diehard fans and collecting *Agency* memorabilia became his preoccupying outside interest in the course of taking a doctorate in neurobiology. He was spared from Viet Nam by high blood pressure, and from any longterm romantic involvement by a highly introverted nature. Following his doctorate, Webley landed a research position at one of the pharmaceutical laboratories, where he performed his duties efficiently and maintained an attitude of polite aloofness toward his coworkers. Someone there dubbed him "the Invisible Man," but there was no malice to the *mot juste*.

At his condo, the door to the spare bedroom bore a brass-on-walnut plaque that read *HQ*. Webley had made it himself. Inside were filing cabinets, bookshelves, and his desk. The walls were papered with posters and stills, most of them photos of Stacey Steele. A glass-fronted cabinet held videocassettes of all *The Agency* episodes, painstakingly acquired through trades with other fans. The day he completed the set, Webley drank most of a bottle of

Glenfiddich—Dane and Miss Steele's favorite potation—and afterward became quite ill.

By now Webley's enthusiasm had expanded to all of the spy shows and films of the period, but old loves die hard, and *The Agency* remained his chief interest. Webley was editor/publisher of *Special Assignment,* a quarterly amateur magazine devoted to the spy craze of the 60's. *Special Assignment* was more than a cut above the mimeographed fanzines that Webley had first begun to collect; his magazine was computer-typeset and boasted slick paper and color covers. By its tenth issue, *Special Assignment* had a circulation of several thousand, with distribution through specialty bookshops here and abroad. It was a hobby project that took up all of Webley's free time and much of his living space, and Webley was content.

Almost content. *Special Assignment* carried photographs and articles on every aspect of the old spy shows, along with interviews of many of the actors and actresses. Webley, of course, devoted a good many pages each issue to *The Agency* and to Stacey Steele—but to his chagrin he was unable to obtain an interview with Elisabeth Kent. Since her one disastrous comeback attempt, Miss Kent preferred the life of a recluse. There was some dignity to be salvaged in anonymity. Miss Kent did not grant interviews, she did not make public appearances, she did not answer fan mail. After ten years the world forgot Elisabeth Kent, but her fans still remembered Stacey Steele.

Webley had several years prior managed to secure Elisabeth Kent's address—no mean accomplishment in itself—but his rather gushing fan letters had not elicited any sort of reply. Not easily daunted, Webley faithfully sent Miss Kent each new issue of *Special Assignment* (personally inscribed to her), and with each issue he included a long letter of praise for her deathless characterization of Stacey

Steele, along with a plea to be granted an interview. Webley never gave up hope, despite Miss Kent's unbroken silence.

When he at last did receive a letter from Miss Kent graciously granting him the long-sought interview, Webley knew that life is just and that the faithful shall be rewarded.

He caught one of those red-eye-special flights out to Los Angeles, but was too excited to catch any sleep on the way. Instead he reread a wellworn paperback novelization of one of his favorite *Agency* episodes, *The Chained Lightning Caper,* and mentally reviewed the questions he would ask Miss Kent—still not quite able to believe that he would be talking with her in another few hours.

Webley checked into a Thrifti-Family Motel near the airport, unpacked, tried without success to sleep, got up, showered and shaved. The economy flight he had taken hadn't served a meal, but then it had been all Webley could manage just to finish his complimentary soft beverage. The three-hour time change left his system rather disordered in any event, so that he wasn't certain whether he actually should feel tired or hungry were it not for his anxiousness over the coming interview. He pulled out his notes and looked over them again, managing to catch a fitful nap just before dawn. At daylight he made himself eat a dismal breakfast in the motel restaurant, then returned to his room to shave again and to put on the clothes he had brought along for the interview.

It was the best of Webley's several Harrison Dane costumes, carefully salvaged from various Thrift Shops and yard sales. Webley maintained a wardrobe of vintage mod clothing, and he had twice won prizes at convention masquerades. The pointed-toe Italian boots were original to the period—a lovingly maintained treasure discovered ten years before at Goodwill Industries. The suede bell-bottoms were custom-made by an aging hippy at an aging leathercrafts shop that still had a few psychedelic posters tacked to its walls. Webley tried them on at least once a month and adjusted his diet according to snugness of fit. The jacket, a sort of lavender thing that lacked collar or lapels, was found at a vintage clothing store and altered to his measurements. The paisley shirt, mostly purples and greens, had been discovered at a yard sale, and the beads and medallions had come from here and there.

Webley was particularly proud of his Dane Cane, which he himself had constructed after the secret agent's famous weapon. It appeared to be a normal walking stick, but it contained Dane's arsenal of secret weapons and paraphernalia—including a radio transmitter, recording device, tear gas, and laser. Harrison Dane was never without his marvelous cane, and good thing, too. Alex Webley had caused rather a stir at the airport check-in, before airline officials finally permitted him to transport his Dane Cane via baggage.

Webley still clung to the modified Beatles haircut that Harrison Dane affected. He combed it now carefully, and he studied his reflection in the room's ripply mirror. The very image of Harrison Dane. Stacey Steele—Miss Kent—would no doubt be impressed by the pains he had taken. It would have been great to drive out in a Shelby Cobra like Dane's, but instead he called for a cab.

Not a Beverly Hills address, Webley sadly noted, as the taxi drove him to one of those innumerable canyon neighborhoods tottering on steep hillsides and the brink of shabbiness. Her house was small and featureless, a little box propped up on the hillside beside a jagged row of others like it—distinguishable one from another chiefly by the degree of seediness and the cars parked in front. Some cheap development from the 1950s, Webley judged, and

another ten years likely would see the ones still standing
bought up and the land used for some cheap condo development. He felt increasingly sad about it all; he had been
prepared to announce his arrival to some uniformed guard
at the subdivision's entrance gate.

Well, if it were within his power to do so, Webley
intended to bring to bear the might and majesty of *Special
Assignment* to pressure these stupid producers into casting
Elisabeth Kent in new and important roles. That made this
interview more important than ever to Webley—and to
Miss Kent.

He paid off the cab—tipping generously, as Harrison
Dane would have done. This was perhaps fortuitous, as the
driver shouted after him that he had forgotten his attache
case. Webley wondered how Dane would have handled
such an embarrassing lapse—of course, Dane would never
have committed such a blunder. Webley's case—also mod-
elled after Dane's secret agent attache case, although
Webley's lacked the built-in machine gun—contained a
bottle of Glenfiddish, his notes, cassette recorder, and
camera. It was essential that he obtain some photographs
of Miss Kent at home: since her appearance in the unfortu-
nate *Tiger Fists* film, current photos of Elisabeth Kent
were not made available. Webley had heard vicious rumors that the actress had lost her looks, but he put these
down to typical show biz backstabbing, and he prayed it
wasn't so.

He rang the doorbell, using the tip of his cane, just as
Dane always did, and waited—posing jauntily against his
cane, just as Dane always did. The seconds dragged on
eternally, and there was no response. He rang again, and
waited. Webley looked for a car in the driveway; saw
none, but the carport was closed. He rang a third time.

This time the door opened.

And Alex Webley knew his worship had not been in vain.

"Hullo, Dane," she said. "I've been expecting you."

"How very good to see you, Miss Steele," said Webley. "I hope I haven't kept you waiting."

And she *was* Stacey Steele. Just like in *The Agency*. And Webley felt a thrill at knowing she had dressed the part just for the interview—just for him.

The Hollywood gossip had been all lies, because she hardly looked a day older—although part of that was no doubt due to her appearance today as Stacey Steele. It was perfect. It was all there, as it should be: the thigh-length boots of black patent leather, the red leather minidress with *LOVE* emblazoned across the breastline (the center of the *O* was cut out, revealing a daring glimpse of braless cleavage), the blonde bangs-and-ironed-straight Mary Travers hair, the beads and bells. Time had rolled back, and she *was* Stacey Steele.

"Come on in, luv," Miss Steele invited, in her so-familiar throaty purr.

Aerobics really can do wonders, Webley thought as he followed her into her livingroom. Twenty years may have gone by, but if *The Agency* were to be revived today, Miss Kent could step right into her old role as the mod madcap Miss Steele. Exercise and diet, probably—he must find some discreet way of asking her how she kept her youthful figure.

The livingroom was a close replica of Stacey Steele's swinging London flat, enough so that Webley guessed she had removed much of the set from the Hollywood soundstage where the series was actually shot. He sat down, not without difficulty, on the inflatable day-glo orange chair—Dane's favorite—and opened his attache case.

"I brought along a little libation," he said, presenting her with the Glenfiddich.

Miss Steele gladly accepted the dark-green triangular bottle. "Ah, luv! You always remember, don't you!"

She quickly poured a generous level of the pale amber whisky into a pair of stemmed glasses and offered one to Webley. Webley wanted to protest that it was too early in the day for him to tackle straight Scotch, but he decided he'd rather die than break the spell of this moment.

Instead, he said: "Cheers." And drank.

The whisky went down his throat smoothly and soared straight to his head. Webley blinked and set down his glass in order to paw through the contents of his case. Miss Steele had recharged his glass before he could protest, but already Webley was thinking how perfect this all was. This would be one to tell to those scoffers who had advised him against wearing his Harrison Dane costume to the interview.

"Here's a copy of our latest issue . . ." Webley hesitated only slightly " . . . Miss Steele."

She took the magazine from him. The cover was a still of Stacey Steele karate-chopping a heavy in a pink foil spacesuit. "Why, that's me! How groovy!"

"Yes. From *The Mod Martian Caper*, of course. And naturally you'll be featured on our next cover, along with the interview and all." The *our* was an editorial plural, inasmuch as Webley was the entire staff of *Special Assignment*.

"Fab!" said Miss Steele, paging through the magazine in search of more photos of herself.

Webley risked another sip of Glenfiddich while he glanced around the room. However the house might appear from the outside, inside Miss Kent had lovingly maintained the ambiance of *The Agency*. The black lights and pop-art posters, the psychedelic color schemes, the beaded curtains, the oriental rugs. Indian music was playing, and strewn beside the vintage KLH stereo Webley recognized early albums from the Beatles and the Stones, from the Who and the Yardbirds, from Ultimate Spinach and Thirteenth Floor Elevator. He drew in a deep breath; yes, that was incense burning on the mantelpiece—cinnamon, Miss Steele's favorite.

"That's the platinum bird you used in *The Malted Falcon Caper,* isn't it?"

Miss Steele touched the silver falcon statuette Webley had spotted. "The very bird. Not really made of platinum, sorry to report."

"And that must be the chastity belt they locked you into in *The Medieval Mistress Caper.*" Again Webley pointed.

"One and the same. And not very comfy on a cold day, I assure you."

Webley decided he was about to sound gushy, so he finished his second whisky. It didn't help collect his thoughts, but it did restore a little calmness. He decided not to argue when Miss Steele refreshed their drinks. His fingers itched for his camera, but his hands were trembling too much.

"You seem to have kept quite a few props from *The Agency,*" he suggested. "Isn't that the steel mask they put over your head in *The Silent Cyborg Caper?* Not very comfortable either, I should imagine."

"At times I did find my part a trifle confining," Miss Steele admitted. "All those captures by the villains."

"With Harrison Dane always there in the nick of time," Webley said, raising his glass to her. If Miss Steele was in no hurry to get through the interview, then neither was he.

"It wasn't all that much fun waiting to be rescued every time," Miss Steele confided. "Tied out in the hot sun across a railroad track, or stretched out on a rack in a moldy old dungeon.''

"The Uncivil Engineer Caper," Webley remembered, "and *The Dungeon To Let Caper.*"

"Or being strapped to a log in a sawmill.''

"The Silver Scream Caper."

"I was brushing sawdust out of my hair for a week.''

"And in *The Missing Mermaid Caper* they handcuffed you to an anchor and tossed you overboard.''

"Yes, and I still have my rubber fishtail from that one.''

"Here?''

"Certainly. I've held on to a museum's worth of costumes and props. Would you like to see the lot of it?''

"Would I ever!'' Webley prayed he had brought enough film.

"Then I'll just give us a refill.''

"I really think I've had enough just now,'' Webley begged.

"Why, Dane! I never knew you to say no.''

"But one more to top things off,'' agreed Webley, unable to tarnish the image of Harrison Dane.

Miss Steele poured. "Most of it's kept downstairs.''

"After all, Miss Steele, this is a special occasion.'' Webley drank.

He had a little difficulty with the stairs—he vaguely felt he was floating downward, and the Dane Cane kept tripping him—but he made it to the lower level without disgracing himself. Once there, all he could manage was a breathless: "Out of sight!''

Presumably the downstairs had been designed as a sort of large family room, complete with fireplace, cozy chairs, and at one time probably a ping pong table or such. Miss Kent had refurnished the room with enough props and sets to reshoot the entire series. Webley could only stand and stare. It was as if an entire file of *Agency* stills had been scattered about and transformed into three-dimensional reality.

There was the stake the natives had tied her to in *The No Atoll At All Caper*, and there was the man-eating plant that had menaced her in *The Venusian Vegetarian Caper*. In one corner stood—surely a replica—Stacey Steele's marvelous VW Beetle, sporting its wild psychedelic paint scheme and harboring a Porsche engine and drivetrain. There was the E.V.O.L. interrogation chair from *The Earth's End Caper*, and behind it one of the murderous robots from *The Angry Android Caper*. Harrison Dane's circular bed, complete with television, stereo, bar, machine guns, and countless other built-in devices, was crowded beside the very same torture rack from *The Dungeon To Let Caper*. Cataloging just the major pieces would be an hour's work, even for Webley, and a full inventory of all the memorabilia would take at least a couple days.

"Impressed, luv?"

Webley closed his mouth. "It's like the entire *Agency* series come to life in one house," he finally said.

"Do browse about all you like, luv."

Webley stumbled across the room, trying not to touch any of the sacred relics, scarcely able to concentrate upon any one object for longer than its moment of recognition. It was all too overpowering an assault upon his sensory mechanisms.

"A toast to us, luv."

Webley didn't remember whether Miss Steele had brought along their glasses or poured fresh drinks from Harrison Dane's art nouveau bar, shoved against one wall next to the mind transfer machine from *The Wild, Wild Bunch*

Caper. He gulped his drink without thinking and moments later regretted it.

"I think I'd like to sit down for a minute," Webley apologized.

"Drugged drinks!" Miss Steele said brightly. "Just like in *The Earth's End Caper*. Quick, Dane! Sit down here!"

Webley collapsed into the interrogation chair as directed —it was closest, and he was about to make a scene if he didn't recover his balance. Automatic cuffs instantly secured his arms, legs, and body to the chair.

"Only in *The Earth's End Caper*," said Miss Steele, "I was the one they drugged and fastened into this chair. There to be horribly tortured, unless Harrison Dane came to the rescue."

Webley turned his head as much as the neck restraints would permit. Miss Steele was laying out an assortment of scalpels and less obvious instruments, recognized by Webley as props from the episode.

"Groovy," he managed to say.

Miss Steele was assembling some sort of dental drill. "I was always the victim." She smiled at him with that delightful madcap smile. "I was always the one being captured, humiliated, helplessly awaiting your last minute mock heroics."

"Well, not all the time," Webley protested, going along with the joke. He hoped he wasn't going to be ill.

"Are these clamps very tight?"

"Yes. Very. The prop seems in perfect working order. I think I really ought to stretch out for a while. Most embarrassing, but I'm afraid that drinking this early . . ."

"It wasn't enough that you seduced me and insisted on the abortion for the sake of our careers. It was your egotistical jealousy that finally destroyed me. You couldn't stand the fact that Stacey Steele was the *real* star of *The*

Agency, and not Harrison Dane. So you pulled strings until you got me written out of the series. Then you did your best to ruin my career afterward.''

"I don't feel very good," Webley muttered. "I think I might be getting sick."

"Hoping for a last-second rescue?" Stacey Steele selected a scalpel from the tray, and bent over him. Webley had a breathtaking glimpse through the cut-out of *LOVE,* and then the blade touched his eye.

The police were already there by the time Elisabeth Kent got home. Neighbors' dogs were barking at something in the brush below her house; some kids went to see what they were after, and then the police were called.

"Did you know the man, Miss Kent?"

Miss Kent nodded her double chins. She was concentrating on stocking her liquor cabinet with the case of generic gin she'd gone out to buy with the advance check Webley had mailed her. She'd planned on fortifying herself for the interview that might mean her comeback, but her aging Nova had refused to start in the parking lot, and the road call had eaten up the remainder of the check that she'd hoped would go toward overdue rent for the one-story frame dump. She sat down heavily on the best chair of her sparsely furnished livingroom.

"He was some fan from back east," she told the investigating officer. "Wanted to interview me for some fan magazine. I've got his letter here somewhere. I used to be in films a few years back—maybe you remember.

"We'll need to get in touch with next of kin," the detective said. "Already found the cabbie who let him out here while you were off getting towed." He was wondering if he had ever seen her in anything. "At a guess, he waited around on your deck, probably leaned against the railing—got a little dizzy, and went over. Might have had a heart attack or something.''

Elisabeth Kent was looking at the empty Glenfiddich bottle and the two glasses.

''Damn you, Stacey Steele,'' she whispered. ''God-damn you.''

Blue Lady,
Come Back

THIS ONE STARTS with a blazing bright day and a trim split-level house looking woodsy against the pines.

Wind shrieked a howling Tocsin as John Chance slewed his Duesenberg Torpedo down the streaming mountain road. A sudden burst of lightning picked out the sinister silhouette of legend-haunted Corrington Manor, hunched starkly against the storm-swept Adirondacks. John Chance's square jaw was grim-set as he scowled at the Georgian mansion just ahead. Why had lovely Gayle Corrington's hysterical phone call been broken off in the midst of her plea for help? Could even John Chance thwart the horror of the Corrington Curse from striking terror on the eve of Gayle and young Hartley's wedding?''

"Humph," was the sour comment of Curtiss Stryker, who four decades previous had thrilled thousands of pulp readers with his yarns of John Chance, psychic detective. He stretched his bony legs from the cramped interior of his friend's brand-new Jensen Interceptor and stood scowling through the blacktop's heat.

"Well, seems like that's the way a haunted house *ought*

to be approached,'' Mandarin went on, joining him on the
sticky asphalt driveway.

Stryker twitched a grin. Sixty years had left his tall,
spare frame gristled and knobby, like an old pine on a
rocky slope. His face was tanned and seamed, set off the
bristling white mustache and close-cut hair that had once
been blond. Mandarin always thought he looked like an
old sea captain—and recalled that Stryker had sailed on a
Norwegian whaler in his youth.

"Yeah, and here comes the snarling mastiff,'' Stryker
obliged him.

A curious border collie peered out from around the
Corvette in the carport, wondered if it ought to bark. Russ
whistled, and the dog wagged over to be petted.

The yard was just mowed, and someone had put a lot of
care into the rose beds that bordered the flagstone walk.
That and the pine woods gave the place a cool, inviting
atmosphere—more like a mountain cabin than a house
only minutes outside Knoxville's sooty reach. The house
had an expensive feel about it. Someone had hired an
architect—and a good one—to do the design. Mountain
stone and untreated redwood on the outside walls; cedar
shakes on the roof; copper flashings; long areas of glass.
Its split-level design adapted to the gentle hillside, seemed
to curl around the grey outcroppings of limestone.

"Nice place to haunt,'' Mandarin reflected.

"I hope you're going to keep a straight face once we get
inside,'' his friend admonished gruffly. "Mrs. Corrington
was a little reluctant to have us come here at all. Doesn't
want folks laughing, calling her a kook. People from all
over descending on her to investigate her haunted house.
You know what it'd be like.''

"I'll maintain my best professional decorum.''

Styker grunted. He could trust Russ, or he wouldn't

have invited him along. A psychiatrist at least knew how to listen, ask questions without making his informant shut up in embarrassment. And Russ's opinion of Gayle Corrington's emotional stability would be valuable—Stryker had wasted too many interviews with cranks and would-be psychics whose hauntings derived from their own troubled minds. Besides, he knew Mandarin was interested in this sort of thing and would welcome a diversion from his own difficulties.

"Well, let's go inside before we boil over," Stryker decided.

Russ straightened from petting the dog, carelessly wiped his long-fingered hands on his lightweight sportcoat. About half the writer's age, he was shorter by a couple inches, heavier by forty pounds. He wore his bright-black hair fashionably long for the time, and occasionally trimmed his long mustache. Piercing blue eyes beneath a prominent brow dominated his thin face. Movie-minded patients had told him variously that he reminded them of Terence Stamp or Bruce Dern, and Russ asked them how they felt about that.

On the flagstone walk the heady scent of warm roses washed out the taint of the asphalt. Russ thought he heard the murmur of a heat pump around back. It would be cool inside, then—earlier he had envied Stryker for his open-collar sportshirt.

The panelled door had a bell push, but Stryker crisply struck the brass knocker. The door quickly swung open, and Russ guessed their hostess had been politely waiting for their knock.

Cool air and a faint perfume swirled from within. "Please come in," Mrs. Corrington invited.

She was blond and freckled, had stayed away from the sun enough so that her skin still looked fresh at the shadow of 40. Enough of her figure was displayed by the backless hostess ensemble she wore to prove she had taken care of herself in other respects as well. It made both men remember that she was divorced.

"Mrs. Corrington? I'm Curtiss Stryker."

"Please call me Gayle. I've read enough of your books to feel like an old friend."

Stryker beamed and bent low over her hand in the continental mannerisms Russ always wished he was old enough to pull off. "Then make it Curt, Gayle. And this is Dr. Mandarin."

"Russ," said Mandarin, shaking her hand.

"Dr. Mandarin is interested in this sort of thing, too," Stryker explained. "I wanted him to come along so a man of science could add his thoughts to what you have to tell us."

"Oh, are you with the university center here, Dr. Mandarin?"

"Please—Russ. No, not any longer." He kept the bitterness from his voice. "I'm in private practice in the university area."

"Your practice is . . . ?"

"I'm a psychiatrist."

Her green eyes widened, then grew wary—the usual response—but she recovered easily. "Can I fix something for you gentlemen? Or is it too early in the afternoon for drinks? I've got ice tea."

"Sun's past the yardarm," Stryker told her quickly. "Gin and tonic for me."

"Scotch for you, Russ?" she asked.

"Bourbon and ice, if you have it."

"Well, you must be a southern psychiatrist."

"Russ is from way out west," Stryker filled in smoothly. "But he's lived around here a good long while. I met him when he was doing an internship at the Center here, and I had an appendix that had waited fifty years to go bad. Found out he was an old fan—even had a bunch of my old pulp yarns on his shelves alongside my later books. Showed me a fan letter one magazine had published: he'd written it when he was about 12 asking that they print more of my John Chance stories. Kept tabs on each other ever since."

She handed them their drinks, poured a bourbon and ginger ale for herself.

"Well, of course I've only read your serious stuff. The mysteries you've had in paperback, and the two books on the occult."

"Do you like to read up on the occult?" Russ asked, mentally correcting her—*three* books on the occult.

"Well, I never have . . . you know . . . believed in ghosts and like that. But when all this started, I began to wonder—so I checked out a few books. I'd always liked Mr. Stryker's mystery novels, so I was especially interested to read what he had to say on the subject of hauntings. Then, when I found out that he was a local author, and that he was looking for material for a new book— well, I got up my courage and wrote to him. I hope you didn't think I was some sort of nut."

"Not at all!" Stryker assured her. "But suppose we sit down and have you tell us about it. From your letter and our conversation on the phone, I gather this is mostly poltergeist-like phenomena."

Gayle Corrington's flair-legged gown brushed against the varnished hardwood floor as she led them to her livingroom. A stone fireplace with raised hearth of used brick made up one wall. Odd bits of antique ironware were arranged along the hearth; above the mantelpiece hung an engraved doublebarrelled shotgun. Walnut panelling enclosed the remainder of the room—panelling, not plywood, Russ noted. Chairs and a sofa were arranged informally about the Couristan carpet. Russ dropped onto a cream leather couch and looked for a place to set his drink.

Stryker was digging a handful of salted nuts from the wooden bowl on the low table beside his chair. "Suppose you start with the history of the house?" he suggested.

Sipping nervously from her glass, Gayle settled cross-legged next to the hearth. Opposite her a large area of sliding glass panels opened onto the sunbright back yard. A multitude of birds and two fat squirrels worked at the feeders positioned beneath the pines. The dogs sat on the patio expectantly, staring back at them through the glass door.

Gayle drew up her freckled shoulders and began. "Well, the house was put up about ten years back by two career girls."

"Must have had some money," Russ interposed.

"They were sort of in your line of work—they were medical secretaries at the psychiatric unit. And they had, well, a relationship together."

"How do you mean that?" Stryker asked, opening his notepad.

Mrs. Corrington blushed. "They were lesbians."

This was heavy going for a Southern Belle, and she glanced at their composed expressions, then continued. "So they built this place under peculiar conditions—sort of man and wife, if you follow. No legal agreement as to what belonged to whom. That became important afterward.

"Listen, this is, well, personal information. Will it be OK for me to use just first names?"

"I promise you this will be completely confidential," Stryker told her gravely.

"I was worried about your using this in your new book on haunted houses of the South."

"If I can't preserve your confidence, then I promise you I won't use it at all."

"All right then. The two women were Libby and Cass." Mandarin made a mental note.

"They lived together here for about three years. Then Libby died. She was only about 30."

"Do you know what she died of?" Russ asked.

"I found out after I got interested in this. How's the song go—'too much pills and liquor.' "

"Seems awfully young."

"She hadn't been taking care of herself. One night she passed out after tying one on, and she died in the hospital emergency room."

"Did the hauntings start then?"

"Well, there's no way to be sure. The house stood empty for a couple of years afterward. Legal problems. Libby's father hadn't cared for her lifestyle, and when she died he saw to it that Cass couldn't buy Libby's share of the house and property. That made Cass angry, so she wouldn't sell out her share. Finally they agreed on selling the house and land, lock, stock and barrel, and dividing the payment. That's when I bought it."

"No one else has ever lived here, then?"

Gayle hesitated a moment. "No—except for a third girl they had here once—a nurse. They rented a third bedroom to her. But that didn't work out, and she left after a few months. Otherwise, I'm the only other person to live here."

"It seems a little large for one person," Stryker observed.

"Not really. I have a son in college now who stays here over breaks. And now and then a niece comes to visit. So the spare rooms are handy."

"Well, what happened after you moved in?"

She wrinkled her forehead. "Just . . . well, a series of things. Just strange things . . .

"Lights wouldn't stay on or off. I used to think I was just getting absent-minded, but then I began to pay careful attention. Like I'd go off to a movie, then come back and find the carport light off—when the switch was inside. It really scared me. There's other houses closer now, but this is a rural area pretty much. Prissy's company, but I don't know if she could fight off a prowler. I keep a gun."

"Has an electrician ever checked your wiring?"

"No. It was OK'ed originally, of course."

"Can anyone break in without your having realized it?"

"No. You see, I'm worried about break-ins, as I say. I've got double locks on all the doors, and the windows have special locks. Someone would have to break the glass, or pry open the woodwork around the doors—leave marks. That's never happened.

"And other things seem to turn on and off. My electric toothbrush, for instance. I told my son and he laughed— then one night the light beside his bed flashed off."

"Presumably you could trace all this to electrical disturbances," Russ pointed out.

Gayle gestured toward the corner of the livingroom. "All right. See that wind-up Victrola? No electricity. Yet the damn thing turns itself on. Several times at night I've heard it playing—that old song, you know . . ."

She sang a line or two: "Come back, blue lady, come back. Don't be blue anymore . . ."

Stryker quickly moved to the machine. It was an old Victrola walnut veneer console model, with speaker and record storage in the lower cabinet. He lifted the hinged lid. It was heavy. Inside, the huge tonearm was swung back on its pivot.

"Do you keep a record on the turntable normally?"

"Yes. I like to show the thing off. But I'm certain I haven't left *Blue Skirt Waltz* on every time."

"It's on now."

"Yes, I leave it there now."

"Why not get rid of the record as an experiment?"

"What could I think if I found it back again?"

Stryker grinned. He moved the starting lever with his finger. The turntable began to spin.

"You keep this thing wound?" Russ asked.

"Yes," Gayle answered uneasily.

Curtiss swung the hinged tonearm down, rested the thick steel needle on the shellac disc.

I dream of that night with you
Darling, when first we met . . .

"Turn it off again—please!"

II

Stryker hastily complied. "Just wanted to see what was involved in turning it on."

"Sorry," Gayle apologized. "The thing has gotten on my nerves, I guess. How about refills all around?"

"Fine," Stryker agreed, taking a final chew on his lime twist.

When their hostess had disappeared into the kitchen with their glasses, he murmured aside to Mandarin: "What do you think?"

Russ shrugged. "What can I say from a few minutes talking, listening to her? There's no blatant elevation of her porcelain titer, if that's what you mean."

"What's that mean?" the writer asked, annoyed.

"She doesn't come on as an outright crock."

Stryker's mustache twitched. "Think I'll write that down."

He did.

"Useful for rounds," Russ explained in apology. "What about the occult angle? So far I'm betting on screwy electrical wiring and vibrations from passing trucks or something."

Stryker started to reply, but then Gayle Corrington rustled back, three glasses and a wedge of cheese on a tray.

"I've been told most of this can be explained by wiring problems or vibrations," she was saying. "Like when the house settles on its foundation."

Russ accepted his drink with aplomb—wondering if she had overheard.

"But I asked the real estate man about that," she went on, "and he told me the house rests on bedrock. You've seen the limestone outcroppings in the yard. They even had to use dynamite putting down the foundation footings."

"Is there a cellar?"

"No. Not even a crawlspace. But I have storage in the carport and in the sparerooms. There's a gardening shed out back, you'll notice—by the crepe myrtle. Libby liked to garden. All these roses were her doing. I pay a man from the nursery to keep them up for me. Seems like Libby would be sad if I just let them go to pot."

"Do you feel like Libby is still here?" Russ asked casually.

She hadn't missed the implication, and Russ wished again Curtiss hadn't introduced him as a psychiatrist. "Well, yes," she answered cautiously. "I hope that doesn't sound neurotic."

"Has anything happened that you feel can't be explained —well, by the usual explanations?" Curtiss asked, steering the interview toward safer waters.

"Poltergeist phenomena, you mean? Well, I've only touched on that. One night the phone cord started swinging back and forth. All by itself—nothing near it. I was sitting out here reading when I saw that happen. Then my maid was here one afternoon when all the paper cups dropped out of the dispenser and started rolling up and down the kitchen counter. Another night that brass table lamp there started rocking back and forth on its base—just like someone had struck it. Of course, I was the only one here. Christ, I felt like yelling, 'Libby! Cut it out!' "

"Is there much truck traffic on the highway out front?" Stryker asked. "Stone transmits vibrations a long way, and if the house rests on bedrock . . ."

"No truck traffic to speak of—not since the Interstates were completed through Knoxville. Maybe a pickup or that sort of thing drives by. I've thought of that angle, too.

"But, darn it—there's too many other things." Her face seemed defiant. She's thought a lot about this, Russ surmised—and now that she's decided to tell someone else about it, she doesn't want to be taken for a credulous fool.

"Like my television." She pointed to the color portable resting on one end of the long raised hearth. "If you've ever tried to lug one of these things around, you know how portable they really are. I keep it here because I can watch it either from that chair or when I'm out sunning on the patio. Twice though I've come back and found it's somehow slid down the hearth a foot or so. I noticed because the picture was blocked by the edge of that end table when I tried to watch from my lounge chair on the patio. And I know the other furniture wasn't out of place, because I line the set up with that cracked brick there—so I know I can see it from the patio, in case I've moved it around someplace else. Both times it was several inches past that brick."

Russ examined the set, a recent portable model. One edge of its simulated walnut chassis was lined up one row of bricks down from where a crack caused by heat expansion crossed the hearth. He pushed at the set experimentally. It wouldn't slide.

"Tell me truck vibrations were responsible for *this*," Gayle challenged.

"Your cleaning maid . . . ?"

"Had not been in either time. Nor had anyone else in the time between when I noticed it and when I'd last watched it from outside."

"No one else that you knew of."

"No one at all. I could have told if there's been a break-in. Besides, a burglar would have stolen the darn thing."

Russ smoothed his mustache thoughtfully. Stryker was scribbling energetically on his notepad.

Gayle pressed home her advantage. "I asked Cass about it once. She looked at me funny and said they used to keep their tv on the hearth, too—only over a foot or so, because the furniture was arranged differently."

Stryker's grey eyes seemed to glow beneath his shaggy eyebrows. Russ knew the signs—Curtiss was on the scent.

Trying to control his own interest, Russ asked: "Cass is still in Knoxville, then?"

Gayle appeared annoyed with herself. "Yes, that's why I wanted to keep this confidential. She and another girl have set up together in an old farmhouse they've redone—out toward Norris."

"There's no need for me to mention names or details of personal life," Curtiss reassured her. "But I take it you've said something to Cass about these happenings?"

"Well, yes. She had a few things stored out in the garden shed that she finally came over to pick up. Most of

the furnishings were jointly owned—I bought them with
the house—but there was some personal property, items I
didn't want." She said the last with a nervous grimace.

"So I came flat out and said to her: 'Cass, did you ever
think this house was haunted?' and she looked at me and
said quite seriously: 'Libby?' "

"She didn't seem incredulous?"

"No. Just like that, She said: 'Libby?' Didn't sound
surprised—a little shaken maybe. I told her about some of
the things here, and she just shrugged. I didn't need her to
think I was out of my mind, so I left off. But that's when I
started to think about Libby's spirit lingering on here."

"She seemed to take it rather matter-of-factly," Russ
suggested.

"I think she and Libby liked to dabble in the occult.
There were a few books of that sort that Cass picked up—a
Ouija board, tarot deck, black candles, a few other things
like that. And I believe there was something said about
Libby's dying on April the 30th—that's Walpurgis Night,
I learned from my reading."

Witches' Sabbat, Russ reflected. So he was going to
find his gothic trappings after all.

It must have showed on his face. "Nothing sinister
about her death," Gayle told him quickly. "Sordid maybe,
but thoroughly prosaic. She was dead by the time they got
her to the emergency room, and a check of her blood-
stream showed toxic levels of alcohol and barbs. Took a
little prying to get the facts on that. Family likes the
version where she died of a heart attack or something
while the doctors worked over her.

"But let me freshen those ice cubes for you. This
show-and-tell session is murder on the throat."

Stryker hopped out of his chair. "Here, we'll carry our
own glasses."

Smiling, she led them into the kitchen. Russ lagged behind to work at the cheese. He hadn't taken time for lunch, and he'd better put something in his stomach besides bourbon.

"There's another thing," Gayle was saying when he joined them. "The antique clocks."

Russ followed her gesture. The ornate dial of a pendulum wall clock stared back at him from the dining room wall. He remembered the huge walnut grandfather's clock striking solemnly in the corner of the livingroom.

"Came back one night and found both cabinets wide open. And you have to turn a key to open the cabinets."

"Like this?" Stryker demonstrated on the wall clock.

"Yes. I keep the keys in the locks because I need to reset the pendulum weights. But as you see, it takes a sharp twist to turn the lock. Explain that one for me."

Russ sipped his drink. She must have poured him a good double. "Have you ever thought that someone might have a duplicate key to one of the doors?" he asked.

"Yes," Gayle answered, following his train of thought. "That occurred to me some time ago—though God knows what reason there might be to pull stunts like these. But I had every lock in the house changed—that was after I had come back and found lights on or off that had been left off or on one time too many to call it absent-mindedness. It made no difference, and both the tv and the clock incidents took place since then."

"You know, this is really intriguing!" Curtiss exclaimed, beaming over his notepad.

Gayle smiled back, seemed to be fully at ease for the first time. "Well, I'll tell you it has me baffled. Here, let me show you the rest of the house."

A hallway led off from the open space between livingroom and dining area. There was a study off one side, another room beyond, and two bedrooms opposite. A rather large tile bath with sunken tub opened at the far end.

"The study's a mess, I'm afraid," she apologized, closing the door on an agreeably unkempt room that seemed chiefly cluttered with fashion magazines and bits of dress material. "And the spare bedroom I only use for storage." She indicated the adjoining room, but did not offer to open it. "My son sleeps here when he's home."

"You keep it locked?" Russ asked, noting the outdoor-type lock.

"No." Gayle hastily turned the knob for them, opened the door on a room cluttered with far more of the same as her study. There was a chain lock inside, another door on the outside wall. "As you see, this room has a private entrance. This is the room they rented out."

"Their boarder must have felt threatened," Russ remarked. He received a frown that made him regret his levity.

"These are the bedrooms." She turned to the hallway opposite. "This was Cass's." A rather masculine room with knotty pine panelling, a large brass bed, cherry furnishings, and an oriental throw rug on the hardwood floor. "And this was Libby's." Blue walls, white ceiling, white deep-pile carpet, queen-sized bed with a blue quilted spread touching the floor on three sides. In both rooms sliding glass doors opened onto the back yard.

"Where do you sleep?" Russ wanted to know.

"In the other bedroom. I find this one a bit too frilly."

"Have you ever, well, seen anything—any sort of, say, spiritual manifestations?" Stryker asked.

"Myself, no," Gayle told them. "Though there are a few things. My niece was staying with me one night not long after I'd moved in—sleeping in Libby's room. Next morning she said to me: 'Gayle, that room's haunted. All night I kept waking up thinking someone else was there with me.' I laughed, but she was serious."

"Is that when you started thinking in terms of ghosts?"

"Well, there had been a few things before that," she admitted. "But I suppose that was when I really started noticing things."

Russ chalked up a point for his side.

"But another time a friend of mine dropped by to visit. I was out of town, so no one answered her ring. Anyway, she heard voices and figured I was in back watching tv, with the set drowning out the doorbell. So she walked around back. I wasn't here, of course. No one was here. And when she looked inside from the patio, she could see that my set was turned off. She was rather puzzled when she told me about it. I told her a radio was left on—only that wasn't true."

"The dog ever act strangely?" Stryker asked.

"Not really. A few times she seems a little nervous is all. She's a good watchdog though—barks at strangers. That's one reason why I don't suspect prowlers. Prissy lets me know when something's going on that she doesn't like.

"Aside from that, the only other thing I can think of is one night when my son was here alone. I got back late and he was sitting in the livingroom awake. Said he'd seen a sort of blue mist taking shape in the darkness of his bedroom—like a naked woman. Well, the only mist was the smoke you could still smell from the pot party he and his friends had had here earlier. We had a long talk about that little matter."

Stryker studied his notepad. "I'd like to suggest a minor experiment of sorts, if you don't mind. I'd like for Russ and myself to take a turn just sitting alone in Libby's room for a few minutes. See what impressions we have—if any."

"I'll take first watch," Russ decided, at their hostess's expression of consent.

Curtiss shot him a warning glance and returned with Gayle to the living room.

Waiting until they were around the corner, Mandarin stepped into the room now occupied by Gayle Corrington. Cass's room. There was a scent of perfume and such, a soft aura of femininity that he hadn't noticed from the hallway. It softened the masculine feel of the room somewhat, gave it sort of a ski lodge atmosphere. The bedroom had the look of having been recently straightened for company's inspection. As was the case. There were crescent scratches about three feet up on the corner panelling next to the head of the bed, and Russ guessed that the pump shotgun did not usually hang from brackets on the bedroom wall as it did now.

The bathroom was out of Nero's mountain retreat. Big enough to play tennis in, with synthetic-fur rugs scattered on the slate-tiled floor, and with a dressing table and elaborate toilet fixtures that matched the tiles and included a bidette. A cross between a boudoir and the Roman baths. The sunken tub was a round affair and like an indoor pool. Russ wondered if the mirror on the ceiling fogged up when things got hot.

Swallowing the rest of his drink, he stepped into the guest room. Libby's room. This would, of course, be the Blue Room in one of those sprawling mansions where pulp mysteries had a habit of placing their murders. Come to think of it, hadn't he seen an old '30s movie called something like *The Secret of the Blue Room?*

Sitting on the edge of the bed, he crunched an ice cube and studied the room about him. Very feminine—though the brightness of the patio outside kept it from becoming cloying. It had a comfortable feel about it, he decided—

not the disused sensation that generally hangs over a guest room. There was just a hint of perfume still lingering—probably Gayle kept clothes in the closet here.

Russ resisted the temptation to lie down. Glancing outside, he reflected that, when drawn, the blue curtains would fill the room with blue light. Might be a point worth bringing up to Curtiss, in case the old fellow got too excited over ectoplasm and the like. Aside from that, Russ decided that the room was as thoroughly unhaunted as any bedroom he'd ever sat in.

Giving it up at length, he ambled back to the livingroom.

Stryker was just closing his notepad. Either he'd got another drink, or else he'd been too interested to do more than sip his gin and tonic. At Mandarin's entry, he excused himself and strode off for the bedroom.

Gayle's face was a trifle flushed, her manner somewhat nervous. Russ wondered whether it was the liquor, or if he'd broken in on something. She had that familiar edgy look of a patient after an hour of soul-bearing on the analyst's couch. As he thought about it, Russ agreed that this interview must be a similar strain for her.

"You've eaten your ice cubes," she observed. "Shall I get you another?"

Russ swallowed a mouthful of salted nuts. "Thank you—but I've got to drive."

She made a wry face. "You look big enough to hold another few. A light one, then?"

"Hell, why not. A light one, please." Probably she would feel more at ease if she supposed his psychiatric powers were disarmed by bourbon.

He paced about the livingroom while she saw to his glass. Coming to the fireplace, he studied the beautifully engraved shotgun that hung there. It was a Parker. Russ started to touch it.

"That's loaded."

He jerked back his hand like a scolded kid. "Sorry. Just wanted to get the feel of an engraved Parker double-barrel. That's some gun you have to decorate your fireplace with."

"Thank you. I know." She handed him his drink.

"Don't you worry about keeping a loaded shotgun in your livingroom?" The drink was at least equal to its predecessors.

"I'd worry more with an empty one. I'm alone here at night, and there aren't many neighbors. Besides, there aren't any kids around who might get in trouble with it."

"I'd think a woman would prefer something easier to handle than a shotgun."

"Come out on the skeet range with me sometime, and I'll show you something."

Mandarin must have looked properly chastened. With a quick grin Gayle drew down the weapon, opened the breech, and extracted two red shells. "Here." She handed the shotgun to him.

"Double Ought," Russ observed, closing the breech.

"It's not for shooting starlings."

He sighted along the barrel a few times, gave it back. Briskly she replaced the shells and returned it to its mounting.

"Might I ask what you do, Mrs. Corrington?"

"Gayle. I assume you mean for a living. I own and manage a mixed bag of fashion stores—two here in Knoxville, plus a resort wear shop in Gatlinburg, and a boutique on the Strip by the University. So you see, Doctor, not all working girls fall into the nurse or secretary system of things."

"Russ. No, of course not. Some of them make excellent psychiatrists."

She softened again. "Sorry for coming on strong for

women's lib. Just that you find yourself a little defensive after being questioned for an hour.''

"Sorry about that." Russ decided not to remind her that this was at her own invitation. "But this has been extremely interesting, and Curtiss is like a bloodhound on a fresh trail."

"But how do you feel about this, Gayle? Do you believe a poltergeist or some sort of spirit has attached itself to the house?''

She gave him a freckled frown and shrugged her shoulders. No, Russ concluded, she wasn't wearing some sort of backless bra beneath her gown—not that she needed one.

"Well, I can't really say. I mean, there's just been so many things happening that I can't explain. No, I don't believe in witches and vampires and ghosts all draped in bedsheets, if that's what you mean. But some of the books I've read explain poltergeists on an ESP basis—telekinesis or something on that order.''

"Do you believe in ESP?''

"Yes, to an extent.''

"Do you consider yourself psychic?''

She did the thing with her shoulders again. "A little maybe. I've had a few experiences that are what the books put down as psychic phenomena. I guess most of us have.

"But now it's my turn. What do you think, Russ? Do you believe in ghosts?''

"Well, not the chain-rattling kind anyway.''

"Then ESP?''

"Yes, I'll have to admit to a weakness toward ESP.''

"Then here's to ESP.''

They clinked glasses and drank.

"I'll second that," announced Stryker, rejoining them.

III

"Jesus!" Stryker swore. "Slow down, Russ!" He braced himself with one hand against the dash, almost slung out of his bucket seat as the Jensen took a curve at 70.

"Use the seat belt," advised Mandarin, slowing down somewhat. After all, he *was* a little high to be pushing the car this hard.

"Don't like them," Curtiss grunted. "The damned harnesses make me claustrophobic."

"They say they're someday going to pass a law making it compulsory to wear them."

"Like to see them try—we're not to 1984 yet! Why don't the prying bastards work to prevent accidents instead of putting all their bright ideas into ways of letting the damn fools who cause them live through it. And speaking of prevention, how about slowing this sports car down to legal velocities. The cops would sure like to nail you on a drunk driving charge."

"Who's drunk?" Russ slowed to 65, the legal limit for non-Interstate highways.

"Son, you had a few before you picked me up this noon—and Gayle Corrington wasn't running up her water bill on those drinks she poured for us."

Russ veered from the ragged shoulder of the old two-lane blacktop. "If she starts the day customarily with drinks like she was pouring for me, I think I know where her poltergeist comes from."

"You weren't impressed?" Stryker sounded amused. "But you'll admit natural explanations get a little forced and tenuous after a while."

A stop sign bobbed over the crest of a hill, and Russ hit the brakes hard. Four disc brakes brought the Jensen up almost in its length. Stryker uncovered his eyes.

"Yeah," Russ went on. "There were a number of things she said that sounded like telling points in favor of a poltergeist. But you have to bear in mind that all this is by her unsupported evidence. Hell, we can't be sure she isn't hallucinating this stuff, or even just making the whole thing up to string you along. Women do get bored at 40ish—to say nothing of what the thought of starting over the hill does to their libidos."

"She didn't look bored—and certainly not headed over the hill. Another few years, my friend, and you'll stop thinking of womanhood withering at 30. Hell, it's just starting to bloom. But do you think she's unreliable? Seemed to be just the opposite. A level-headed woman who was frankly baffled and a little embarrassed with the entire affair."

Russ grunted, unwilling to agree offhand—though these were his own impressions as well. "I'm just saying you need to keep everything in perspective. I've gotten fooled by too many patients with a smooth facade—even when I was expecting things to be different beneath the surface."

"But you'll hazard an opinion that Mrs. Corrington is playing straight with us so far as signs indicate?" Stryker persisted.

"Yeah," Mandarin conceded. "But that's one tough woman lurking beneath all that sweet Southern Belle charm she knows how to turn on. Watch out."

He turned onto the Interstate leading into Knoxville's downtown. In deference to Curtiss's uneasiness with high speed, he held the needle at 80, safely just over the 75 limit of the time.

"What's your opinion of it all, then?" the author prodded.

"Well, I'll maintain scientific neutrality. While I consider poltergeists improbable, I'll accept the improbable when the probable explanations have all been eliminated."

"Nicely phrased, Holmes," Stryker chuckled. "And taking a position that will have you coming out sounding correct no matter what."

"The secret of medical training."

"I knew you'd come in handy for something."

"Well, then, what's your opinion?"

The author decided it was safe to release the dashboard and light his pipe. "Well, I guess I've used the supernatural too often in my fiction to accept it as willingly as I might otherwise. Seems everytime I start gathering the facts on something like this, I find myself studying it as a fiction plot. You know like those yarns I used to crank out for pulps like *Dime Mystery Stories,* where when you get to the end you learn that the Phantom of Ghastly Manor was really Cousin Rodney dressed up in a monster suit so he could murder Uncle Ethelred and claim the inheritance before the will was changed. Something like that. I start putting facts together like I was plotting a murder thriller, you know. Kind of spoils the effect for me. This thing, for instance . . ."

Russ cursed and braked viciously to avoid the traffic stopped ahead at Malfunction Junction. Knoxville's infamous rush hour tangle had the Interstate blocked solid ahead of them. Swerving onto the shoulder, he darted for the upcoming exit and turned toward the University section. Curtiss seemed about to bite his pipe in two.

"Stop off at the Yardarm? I don't want to fight this traffic."

Stryker thought he could use a drink.

* * *

Safely seated in a back booth, stein of draft in hand, Curtiss regained his color. It was a favorite bar—just off the Strip section of the University area. When Stryker had first come to the area years back, it had been a traditional Rathskeller college bar. Styles had changed, and so had students. Long hair had replaced crewcuts, Zen and revolution had shoved fraternities and football from conversational standards, and there was a faint hint of marijuana discernible through the beer smell. Someone had once suggested changing the name of the Yardarm to the Electric Foreskin or some such, and had been tossed out for his own good.

Stryker didn't care. He'd been coming here for years—sometimes having a round with his creative writing students. Now—well, if they wanted to talk football, he'd played some; if they wanted to talk revolution, he'd fought in some. The beer was good, and the atmosphere not too frantic for conversation.

His office was a block or two away—an upstairs room in a ramshackle office building only slightly less disreputable in appearance than the dilapidated Edwardian mansion turned community clinic where Russ worked. This was several blocks in the other direction, so the bar made a convenient meeting place for them. Afternoons often found the pair talking over a pitcher of beer (Knoxville bars could not serve liquor at the time), and the bartender—a huge red-bearded Viking named Blackie—knew them both by name.

"You were saying that your faith in the supernatural was fraught with skepticism," Mandarin reminded, wiping foam from his mustache.

"No. I said it was tempered with rationality," Stryker hedged. "That doesn't mean I don't believe in the supernatural. It means I examine facts with several of those famous grains of salt before I offer them to my readers."

"I take it then you're going to use this business today in your new book."

Stryker nodded enthusiastically. "It's worth a chapter, I'm certain."

"Well, that's your judgement, of course," commented Mandarin, glancing at his watch. "Personally, I didn't read any irrefutable evidence of the supernatural into all this."

"Science scoffing under the shadow of truths inadmissible to its system of logic." Stryker snorted. "You're as blind in your beliefs as the old-guard priesthood holding the bastions of disease-by-wrath-of-God against the germ-theory heretics."

"I suppose," Russ admitted around a belch.

"But then, I forgot that you were back in Libby's room while I was finishing up the interview with Gayle Corrington," Stryker said suddenly. "Hell, you missed out on what I considered the most significant and intriguing part of her story. Let me read this off to you." He fumbled for his notepad.

Mandarin had had enough of hauntings for the day. "Let me have you fill me in later," he begged off. "I've got an evening clinic tonight, and I'd like to run back to the house beforehand and get packed."

"Going out of town?"

"I need to see my high-priced lawyers in New York tomorrow."

"That's right. How's that look?"

Russ frowned, said with more confidence than he felt: "I think we'll make our case. Police just can't burglarize a physician's confidential files in order to get evidence for a drug bust."

"Well, I wish you luck," Stryker allowed. "There's a few angles I want to check out on this business first, anyway. I'll probably have the chapter roughed out by the time you're back in town. Why don't I give you a carbon then, and let you comment?"

"Fine." Russ stood up and downed his beer. "Can I give you a lift somewhere?"

"Thanks—but I've got my car parked just down the block. You take it easy driving back though."

Russ grinned. "Sure. Take it easy yourself."

Two nights later Mandarin's phone woke him up. Stryker hadn't taken it easy.

IV

Dishevelled and coatless in the misty rain, Mandarin stood glumly beside the broken guardrail. It was past 3 AM. His clothes looked slept in, which they were. He'd continued the cocktail hour that began on his evening flight from New York once he got home. Sometime toward the end of the network movie that he wasn't really watching he fell asleep on the couch. The set was blank and hissing when he stumbled awake to answer the phone.

"Hello, Russ," greeted Saunders, puffing up the steep bank from the black lakeshore. His face was grim. "Thought you ought to be called. You're about as close to him as anyone Stryker had here."

Mandarin swallowed and nodded thanks. With the back of his hand he wiped the beads of mist and sweat from his face. Below them the wrecker crew and police diver worked to secure cables to the big maroon Buick submerged there. Spotlights, red tail lights burning through the mist. Yellow beacon on the wrecker, blue flashers on the two patrol cars. It washed the brush-grown lakeshore with a flickering nightmarish glow. Contorted shadows wavered around objects made grotesque, unreal. It was like a Daliesque landscape.

"What happened, Ed?" he managed to say.

The police lieutenant wiped mud from his hands. "Nobody saw it. No houses along this stretch, not a lot of traffic this hour of night."

An ambulance drove up slowly, siren off. Static outbursts of the two-way radios echoed like sick thunder in the silence.

"Couple of kids parked on a side road down by the lake. Thought they heard brakes squeal, then a sort of crashing noise. Not loud enough to make them stop what they were doing, and they'd been hearing cars drive by fast off and on all night. But they remembered it a little later when they drove past here and saw the gap in the guard rail."

He indicated the snapped-off stumps of the old-style wood post and cable guard rail. "Saw where the brush was smashed down along the bank, and called it in. Investigating officer's flashlight picked out the rear end plain enough to make out the license number. I was on hand when owner's identification came in; had you called."

Russ muttered something. He'd met Saunders a few years before when the other was taking Stryker's evening class in creative writing. The detective had remained a casual friend despite Mandarin's recent confrontations with the department.

"Any chance Curtiss might have made it?"

Saunders shook his head. "Been better than a couple hours since it happened. If he'd gotten out, he'd've hiked it to a house down the road, flagged down a motorist. We'd have heard.''

Someone called out from the shore below, and the wrecker's winch began to rattle. Russ shivered.

"Rained a little earlier tonight," Saunders went on. "Enough to make this old blacktop slick as greased glass. Likely, Curtiss had been visiting some friends. Had maybe a few drinks more than he should have—you know how he liked gin in hot weather. Misjudged his speed on these slippery curves and piled on over into the lake.''

"Hell, Curtiss could hold his liquor,'' Mandarin mumbled. "And he hardly ever pushed that big Buick over 35.''

"Sometimes that's fast enough.''

The Buick's back end broke through the lake's black surface like a monster in a Japanese horror flick. With an obscene gurgle, the rest of the car followed. Lake water gushed from the car body and from the open door on the passenger side.

"OK! Hold it!'' someone yelled.

The maroon sedan halted, drowned and streaming, on the brush covered shore. Workers grouped around it. Two attendants unlimbered a stretcher from the ambulance. Russ wanted to vomit.

"Not inside!'' a patrolman called up to them.

The diver pushed back his facemask. "Didn't see him in there before we started hauling either.''

"Take another look around where he went in,'' Saunders advised. "Someone call in and have the Rescue Squad ready to start dragging at daylight.''

"He never would wear his seatbelt,'' Russ muttered.

Saunders' beefy frame shrugged heavily. "Don't guess it would have helped this time. Lake's deep here along the bluff. May have to wait till the body floats up somewhere.'' He set his jaw so tight his teeth grated. ''God-damn it to hell.''

''We don't know he's dead for sure.'' Russ's voice held faint hope.

Sloshing and clanking, the Buick floundered up the lakeshore and onto the narrow blacktop. The door was sprung open, evidently by the impact. The front end was badly mauled—grill smashed and hood buckled—from collision with the guard rail and underbrush. Several branches were jammed into the mangled wreckage. A spiderweb spread in ominous pattern across the windshield on the driver's side.

Russ glowered at the sodden wreck, silently damning it for murdering its driver. Curtiss had always sworn by Buicks—had driven them all his life. Trusted the car. And the wallowing juggernaut had plunged into Fort Loundon Lake like a chrome-trimmed coffin.

Saunders tried the door on the driver's side. It was jammed. Deep gouges scored the sheet metal on that side.

''What's the white paint?'' Mandarin pointed to the crumpled side panels.

''From the guard rail. He glanced along that post there at he tore through. Goddamn it! Why can't they put up modern guard rails along these back roads! This didn't have to happen!''

Death is like that, Russ thought. It never *had* to happen the way it did. You could always go back over the chain of circumstances leading up to an accident, find so many places where things could have turned out OK. Seemed like the odds were tremendous against everything falling in place for the worst.

''Maybe he got out,'' he whispered.

Saunders started to reply, looked at his face, kept silent.

V

It missed the morning papers, but the afternoon *News-Sentinel* carried Stryker's book-jacket portrait and a few paragraphs on page one, a photograph of the wreck and a short continuation of the story on the back page of the first section. And there was a long notice on the obituary page.

Russ grinned crookedly and swallowed the rest of his drink. Mechanically he groped for the Jack Daniels' bottle and poured another over the remains of his ice cubes. God. Half a dozen errors in the obituary. A man gives his whole life to writing, and the day of his death they can't even get their information straight on his major books.

The phone was ringing again. Expressionlessly Mandarin caught up the receiver. The first score or so times he'd still hoped he'd hear Curtiss's voice—probably growling something like: "The rumors of my death have been greatly exaggerated." Eventually he'd quit hoping.

"Yes. Dr. Mandarin speaking."

(Curtiss had always ribbed him. "Hell, don't tell them who you are until they tell you who's calling.")

"No. They haven't found him yet."

("Hot as it is, he'll bob up before long," one of the workers had commented. Saunders had had to keep Russ off the bastard.)

"Yeah. It's a damn dirty shame. I know how you feel, Mrs. Hollister."

(You always called him a hack behind his back, you bloated bitch.)

"No I can't say what funeral arrangements will be made."

(Got to have a body for a funeral, you stupid bitch.)

"I'm sure someone will decide something."

(Don't want to be left out of the social event of the season, do you?)

"Well, we all have to bear up somehow, I'm sure."

(Try cutting your wrists.)

"Uh-huh. Goodby, Mrs. Hollister."

Jesus! Mandarin pushed the phone aside and downed his drink with a shudder. No more of this!

He groped his way out of his office. That morning he'd cancelled all his appointments; his section of the makeshift clinic was deserted. Faces from the downstairs rooms glanced at him uneasily as he swept down the stairs. Yes, he must look pretty bad.

Summer twilight was cooling the grey pavement furnace of the University section. Russ tugged off his wrinkled necktie, stuffed it into his hip pocket. With the determined stride of someone in a hurry to get someplace, he plodded down the cracked sidewalk. Sweat quickly sheened his blue-black stubbled jaw, beaded his forehead and eyebrows. Damp hair clung to his neck and ears. Dimly he regretted that the crewcut of his college days was no longer fashionable.

Despite his unswerving stride, he had no destination in mind. The ramshackle front of the Yardarm suddenly loomed before him, made him aware of his surroundings. Mandarin paused a moment by the doorway. Subconsciously he'd been thinking how good a cold beer would taste, and his feet had carried him over the familiar route. With a grimace, he turned away. Too many memories haunted the Yardarm.

He walked on. He was on the strip now. Student bars, bookshops, drugstores, clothing shops and other student-

oriented businesses. Garish head shops and boutiques poured
out echoes of incense and rock music. Gayle Corrington
owned a boutique along here, he recalled—he dully wondered which one.

Summer students and others of the University crowd
passed along the sidewalks, lounged in doorways. Occasionally someone recognized him and called a greeting.
Russ returned a dumb nod, not wavering in his mechanical
stride. He didn't see their faces.

Then someone had hold of his arm.

"Russ! Russ, for God's sake! Hold up!"

Scowling, he spun around. The smooth-skinned hand
anchored to his elbow belonged to Royce Blaine. Mandarin made his face polite as he recognized him. Dr. Blaine
had been on the medicine house staff during Mandarin's
psychiatric residency. Their acquaintance had not died out
completely since those days.

"Hello, Royce."

The internist's solemn eyes searched his face. "Sorry to
bother you at a time like now, Russ," he apologized.
"Just wanted to tell you we were sad to hear about your
friend Stryker. Know how good a friend of yours he was."

Mandarin mumbled something appropriate.

"Funeral arrangements made yet, or are they still
looking?"

"Haven't found him yet."

His face must have slipped its polite mask. Blaine winced.

"Yeah? Well, just wanted to let you know we were all
sorry. He was working on a new one, wasn't he?"

"Right. Another book on the occult."

"Always thought it was tragic when an author left his
last book unfinished. Was it as good as his others?"

"I hadn't seen any of it. I believe all he had were notes
and a few chapters rough."

"Really a damn shame. Say, Russ—Tina says for me to ask you how about dropping out our way for dinner some night. We don't see much of you these days—not since you and Alicia used to come out for fish fries."

"I'll take you up on that some night," Russ temporized.

"This week maybe?" Blaine persisted. "How about Friday?"

"Sure. That'd be fine."

"Friday, then. 6:30, say. Time for a happy hour."

Mandarin nodded and smiled thinly. Blaine squeezed his shoulder, gave him a sympathetic face, and scurried off down the sidewalk. Mandarin resumed his walk.

The hot afternoon sun was in decline, throwing long shadows past the mismatched storefronts and deteriorating houses. Russ was dimly aware that his feet were carrying him along the familiar path to Stryker's office. Did he want to walk past there? Probably not—but he felt too apathetic to redirect his course.

The sun was behind the old drugstore whose second floor housed a number of small businesses, and the dirty windows of Stryker's office lay in shadow. Behind their uncurtained panes, a light was burning.

Mandarin frowned uncertainly. Curtiss never left his lights on. He had an obsession about wasting electricity.

Leaning heavily on the weathered railing, Russ climbed the outside stairway that gave access to the second floor. Above, a dusty hallway led down the center of the building. Several doorways opened off either side. A tailor, a leathershop, several student-owned businesses—which might or might not reopen with the fall term. Only Frank the Tailor was open for the summer, and he took Mondays off.

Dust and silence and the stale smell of disused rooms.

Stryker's office was one of the two which fronted the
street. It was silent as the rest of the hallway of locked
doors, but light leaked through the not-quite-closed doorway.

Mandarin started to knock, then noticed the scars on the
door jamb where the lock had been forced. His descending
fist shoved the door open.

Curtiss's chair was empty. No one sat behind the scarred
desk with its battered typewiter.

Russ glanced around the barren room with its cracked
plaster and book-laden, mismatched furniture. Anger drove
a curse to his lips.

Stryker's office had always been in total disorder; now it
looked like it had been stirred with a stick. Whoever had
ransacked the office had done a thorough job.

VI

Through the Yardarm jukebox Johnny Cash was singing
"Ring of Fire" for maybe the tenth time that evening.
Some of those patrons who had hung around since night-
fall were beginning to notice.

Ed Saunders hauled his hairy arms out of the sleeves of
his ill-fitting suitcoat, slung the damp garment over the
vacant chair beside him. He leaned over the beer-smeared
table, truculently intent, like a linebacker in a defensive
huddle.

"It still looks completely routine to me, Russ," he
concluded.

Mandarin poked a finger through the pile of cold, greasy
pizza crusts, singing an almost inaudible chorus of "down,
down, down, in a burnin' ring of far . . . " A belch broke
off his monotone, and he mechanically fumbled through

the litter of green Rolling Rock bottles for one that had a swallow left. Blackie the bartender was off tonight, and his stand-in had no conception of how to heat a frozen pizza. Mandarin's throat still tasted sour, and he felt certain a bad case of heartburn was building up.

The bottles all seemed empty. He waved for two more, still not replying to Saunder's assertion. A wavy-haired girl, braless in a tanktop, carried the beers over to them—glanced suspiciously at Saunders while she made change. Mandarin slid the coins across the rough boards and eyed the jukebox speculatively.

The city detective sighed. "Look, Russ—why don't you let Johnny Cash catch his breath, what do you say?"

Russ grinned crookedly and turned to his beer. "But it wasn't routine," he pronounced, tipping back the bottle. His eyes were suddenly clear.

Saunders made an exasperated gesture. "You know, Russ, we got God knows how many break-ins a week in this neighborhood. I talked to the investigating officer before I came down. He handled it OK."

"Handled it like a routine break-in—which it wasn't," Mandarin doggedly pointed out.

The lieutenant pursed his lips and reached for the other beer—his second against Mandarin's tenth. Maybe, he mused, it was pointless to trot down here in response to Mandarin's insistent phone call. But he liked the psychiatrist, understood the hell of his mood. Both of them had known Curtiss Stryker as a friend.

He began again. "By our records, two of the other shops on that floor have been broken into since spring. It goes on all the time around here—I don't have to tell you about this neighborhood. You got a black slum just a few blocks away, winos and bums squatting in all these empty houses here that ought to be torn down. Then there's all these other old dumps, rented out full of hippies and junkies and God knows what. Hell, Russ—you know how bad it is. That clinic of yours—we have to just about keep a patrol car parked in front all night to keep the junkies from busting in—and then the men have to watch sharp or they'll lose their hubcaps just sitting there.''

Mandarin reflected that the cessation of break-ins was more likely due to the all-night talking point now run by university volunteers at the community clinic—and that the patrol car seemed more interested in observing callers for potential dope busts than in discouraging prowlers. Instead, he said: "That's my point, Ed. Routine break-ins follow a routine pattern. Rip off a tv, stereo, small stuff that can easily be converted into cash. Maybe booze or drugs, if any's around. Petty theft.

"Doesn't hold for whoever hit Stryker's office. Hell, he never kept anything around there to attract a burglar.''

"So the burglar made a mistake. After all, he couldn't know what was there until he looked."

Russ shook his head. "Then he would have taken the typewriter—beat up as it is—or finished the half bottle of Gallo sherry Curtiss had on the shelf. Doubt if he would have recognized any of his books as worth stealing, but at least he would have taken something for his trouble.''

"Probably knew the stuff wasn't worth the risk of carrying off,'' the detective pointed out. "Left it to try somewhere else. Looked like the door on the leathershop was jimmied, though we haven't contacted the guy who leases it. It's a standard pattern, Russ. Thief works down a hallway room by room until he gets enough or someone scares him off. Probably started at Stryker's office, gave it up and was working on another door when he got scared off.''

"Ed, I know Curtiss's office as well as I know my own.

Every book in that place had been picked up and set down again. Someone must have spent an hour at it. Everything had been gone through.''

"Well, I've been up in his office before, too," Saunders recalled, "and I'd be surprised if anyone could remember what kind of order he kept his stuff in—if there *was* any order. I don't know—maybe the thief was up on his rare books. Say he was scanning title pages for first editions or something."

"Then he passed up a nice copy of Lovecraft's *The Outsider* that would have brought him a couple hundred bucks."

"Did he? I never heard of it. I meant stuff like Hemingway and all—things you'd likely know were valuable. Or maybe he was just checking for money. Lot of people keep maybe ten twenty dollars lying around the office for emergencies—stuck back in a drawer, behind a picture, inside a book or something."

Mandarin snorted and finished his beer. He signaled for two more despite the other's protest.

"Look, Russ," Saunders argued gently, "why are you making such a big thing out of this? So far as we can tell, nothing was taken. Just a simple case of break and enter—thief looks the place over a bit, then gives up and moves on. It's routine."

"No, it isn't." Mandarin's thin face was stubborn. "And something *was* missing. The place was *too* neat, that's the conclusion. Usually Curtiss had the place littered with notes, pieces of clippings, pages of manuscript, wadded-up rough drafts—you've seen how it is. Now his desk is clean, stuff's been picked up off the floor and shelves. All of it gone—even his wastebaskets!"

"Do you want to report a stolen wastebasket, Russ?" Saunders asked tiredly.

"Goddamn it all, can't you put it together? Somebody broke into Curtiss's office, spent a good deal of time gathering up all of his notes and pages of manuscript—*all* of it, even the scrap paper—then piled it into the wastebasket and walked out. Who'd stop a man who was walking down the alley with a wastebasket full of paper?"

Saunders decided he'd have that third beer—if for no better reason than to keep the psychiatrist from downing it. "Russ, it seems to me you're ignoring the obvious. Look, you've been gone for a few days, right? Now isn't it pretty likely that Curtiss just decided to tidy the place up. So he goes through all his stuff, reorganizes things, dumps all his scrap paper and old notes into the wastebasket, sets the wastebasket out to be picked up, and takes the stuff he's working on for the moment on home with him."

"That place hasn't been straightened out in years—since the fire inspectors got on his ass."

"So he figured it was high time. Then later some punk breaks in, sees there's nothing there for him, moves on. Why not, Russ?"

Mandarin seemed to subside. "Just doesn't feel right to me, is all," he muttered.

"So why would somebody steal Curtiss's scrap paper, can you tell me?"

Mandarin scowled at his beer.

"Morbid souvenir hunters? Spies trying to intercept secret information? Maybe it was ghosts trying to recover forbidden secrets? Hell, Russ—you've been reading too many of Stryker's old thrillers."

"Look, I don't know the motives or the logic involved," Russ admitted grandiosely. "That's why I say it *isn't* routine."

The detective rolled his eyes and gave it up. "All right,

Russ. I can't go along with your half-assed logic, but I'll make sure the department checks into this to the best of our ability. Good enough?"

"Good enough."

Saunders grunted and glanced at his watch. "Look, Russ. I got to make a phone call before I forget. What do you say you wait around and after I get through I'll run you on back to your place?"

"My car's just over at the clinic."

"Are you sure . . . ?"

"Hell, I can drive. Few beers don't amount to anything."

"Well, wait here a minute for me," urged Saunders, deciding to argue it later. He lifted his sweaty bulk from the chair's sticky vinyl and made for the payphone in the rear of the bar.

Mandarin swore sourly and began to stuff the rinds of pizza crust into one of the empty bottles. Heartburn, for sure. He supposed he ought to get headed home.

"Well, well, well. Dr. Mandarin, I presume. This is a coincidence. Holding office hours here now, Doctor?"

Russ glowered upward. A grinning face leaned over the table. Russ continued to glower.

Natty in double-knit slacks and sportshirt, Brooke Hamilton dropped onto Saunders' vacated chair. "Rather thought I'd find you here, actually," he confided. "Believe you and the old man used to drop by here regularly, right?"

Hamilton was drinking beer in a frosted mug. It made an icy puddle on the cigarette-scarred tabletop. Mandarin had a private opinion of people who drank beer in frosted mugs.

"Really a shock hearing about old Stryker," Hamilton went on. "Really too bad—though I'm sure a man like Stryker never would have wanted to die in bed. A man of action, old Curtiss. A living legend now passed on to the

realm of legends. Yes, we're all going to miss the old
man. Not many of the old pulp greats left around. Well,
sic transit.'' He made a toast.

Mandarin did not join him. He had met Hamilton at
various cocktail parties and writers' symposiums around
the University. He was quite popular in some circles—
taught creative writing, edited several "little magazines"
and writers' projects, was prominent at gatherings of re-
gional writers and camp followers. His own writing consisted of several startlingly bad novels published by various
local presses—often after Hamilton had cornered their editors at some cocktail affair.

Stryker had loathed him—calling him at one such gathering an ingratiating, self-serving conceited phoney. Hamilton had been within earshot, but chose not to hear. Their
admiration was mutual. Since Hamilton was in the habit of
referring to Stryker as an over-the-hill pulp hack, Mandarin was not moved by the man's show of grief.

"Where's the funeral, Dr. Mandarin—or do you know?"

Mandarin shook his head, measuring the distance to the
other man's Kirk Douglas chin. "No body found yet," he
said.

"Well, I suppose they'll have some sort of memorial
service before long, whatever. Give the writers' community opportunity to pay our last respects to the old man.
Professor Kettering has asked me to act as spokesman for
the University. A little tribute for the school paper, and I
suppose I'll say a few words at the memorial service. Old
Stryker is going to be missed by those of us who carry
on."

"I'm sure."

"Thought I might get you to fill me in on a few details
of his career, if you don't mind. After all, you saw a lot of

the old man here in his last years." Hamilton glanced pointedly at the litter of beer bottles. "But I can catch you another time."

Mandarin grunted noncommittally.

"One thing I did want to ask though. Has old Stryker finished that last book he was working on?"

"No, he was still working on it last time I saw him."

"Oh, you don't think he did. Christ, isn't it tragic to think of all the unfinished work his pen will never take up again. And just when Stryker was as popular with readers as he ever was in the golden age of the pulps."

"Damn shame."

Hamilton nodded gravely. "Yes, it is a shame. You know, I was over at the Frostfire Press this morning, talking with Morris Sheldon about it. Christ, they're all so down about it over there. But we got to talking, and Morris suddenly came out and said: 'Brooke, how'd you like to edit a memorial volume for old Stryker?' You know, sort of an anthology of his best stuff, and I'd write the introduction—a short biography and criticism of his work. Well, I told him I'd be honored to do it for old Stryker, maybe even edit a few of his last, unfinished works for publication.

"Well, this started Morris thinking still further, and all of a sudden he came out and said: 'Brooke, there's no reason Stryker's public has to be deprived of these last few masterworks. He always made extensive notes, and you were always close to him as a writer and friend . . .' "

"You son of a bitch."

"How's that?"

"You ass-kissing, cock-sucking son of a bitch." Mandarin's voice was thick with rage.

Hamilton drew himself up. "Now hold it there, Mandarin.'' In his egotism it had not occurred to him that Mandarin might resent his assumption of role as Stryker's literary heir. But he was confident of his ability to destroy the other man in any verbal duel—his wit, termed variously ''acid'' or ''rapier,'' had dazzled his fans at many a social function.

Heads were turning, as both men came to their feet in an angry crouch.

''You ass-licking fake! You couldn't write your name and phone number on a shithouse wall! And after all the snotty condescension you had for Stryker, you're stealing his name and his work before his grave's even been spaded!''

''I don't have to take that—even from a drunk!'' Hamilton snarled. ''Although I understand I'm not likely to ever find you sober.''

The distance to his movie-star chin had already been noted. Mandarin reached across the table, put a fist there.

Hamiton sat down, hard. The rickety chair cracked under him. Arms flailing, he hit the floor in a tangle of splintered wood. The beer stein smashed against the dirty concrete.

Anger burned the dazed look from his eyes. Accustomed to urbane exchanges of insults at cocktail parties and catfights, Hamilton had not expected the manners of a barroom brawl. ''You goddamn drunk!'' he spat, struggling to rise.

Mandarin, who before medical school had spent a lot of Saturday nights in Montana saloons, was not a gentleman. He waited until Hamilton had risen halfway from the wreckage of his chair, then put another straight right to his chin. Hamilton went down again.

The writer shook the stars from his head and came up frothing mad. He was only five years or so older that Mandarin and of approximate physical size. Regular workouts at the faculty health club had hardened his body into the finely tuned fighting machine of the heroes of his novels. Now he discarded his initial intent of dispatching his drunken opponent with a few precisely devastating karate blows.

The beer stein had shattered with a jagged chunk still attached to its handle. Hamilton rolled to his feet, gripping the handle in his fist like a pair of brass knucks.

Mandarin, unhappy that he had not had more on his punches, cleared the end of the table with no apparent intention of helping the other man to his feet. Hamilton's fist with its jagged knuckleduster slashed at his face.

Rolling under the punch, Russ blocked Hamilton's arm aside and threw a shoulder into his chest. They smashed to the floor, Mandarin on top with a knee planted in the other man's belly.

Breath whooshed from the writer's lips as his head cracked against the floor. Mandarin took the broken stein away from him, grinned down at his pinned opponent. Hamilton gave a hoarse bleat of fear.

"Jesus H. Christ! Russ, stop it!"

Saunders shouldered through the crowd, caught Russ's arm in a shovel fist, hauled the two men apart. His interference was booed.

Groggily, Hamilton came to his feet, his face astonishingly pale. He glared at Mandarin, struggling to break away from the burly detective, decided not to risk a punch against him.

"Call the police!" he said shakily. "This man attacked me!"

"I'm a policeman, buddy!" Saunders growled. "What I saw was this man disarming you after you tried to jam a busted bottle in his face! Want to take out a warrant?"

The writer composed himself, massaging his bruised chin. "A policeman? Yes, I believe I recognize you now. One of the late Curtiss Stryker's night school proteges, I recall. No doubt you learned more effective ways of writing parking tickets, officer—although it's always encouraging to see one of your sort trying to improve his mind."

"Ask him if he's stolen any good wastebaskets lately," Mandarin suggested, wriggling out of the detective's grasp.

"Very clever, aren't we," Hamilton sneered. "I wonder what the state medical association will say about an alcoholic psychiatrist who gets into barroom brawls?"

"I wonder what the English department will say about faggot faculty members who try to chop a man's face up with a busted beer stein?" Saunders wondered.

Hamilton brushed himself off, his smile supercilious. "Well, I can see there's no point taking out a warrant when the arresting officer is a personal friend of the guilty party."

He turned to the onlookers. "You see the kind of police protection our community enjoys. I leave you to judge!"

"Hit him again, Doc!" Someone yelled from across the bar. "We'll keep the pig from pulling you off before you're finished!"

Hamilton's face turned pale again.

"I think you'd better get going," Saunders warned. "Russ, get back here!"

"We shall, of course, take this up again when we aren't immersed in the rabble," Hamilton promised, moving for the door.

"Oh, to be sure!" Mandarin mimicked.

The writer swept out the door to a chorus of catcalls.

"OK, what started that!" Saunders demanded, picking up his coat.

The wavy-haired barmaid had brought Mandarin another beer. He was toasting her with a pleased expression on his stubbled face. Despite his annoyance, Saunders reflected that it was the first smile he'd seen from the psychiatrist since the accident.

"That son of a bitch Hamilton," Mandarin informed him, "that piece of shit—he's talked Stryker's publisher here into letting him edit Curtiss's last work—do a memorial volume and shit like that! Hell, you know how he and Curtiss felt about each other. Ed, get your fingerprint men up to Stryker's office. You'll find Hamilton's sticky little fingers were all over the place."

"Let's not get started on that one again," Saunders told him wearily.

"Bet you dollars to dogshit, and you can hold the stakes in your mouth."

"Come on, Russ. I'll drop you off."

Protesting, Mandarin let himself be led away.

VII

"What's the matter?"

Mandarin had paused with his hand on the door of Saunders' Ford. He stared out across the parking lot. "Somebody's following us. Just saw his shadow duck behind that old VW van. If it's that son of a bitch Hamilton looking for more trouble . . ."

Saunders followed Mandarin's gaze, saw nothing. "Oh hell, get in, Russ! Jesus, you're starting to sound paranoid!"

"There's somebody there," Russ insisted. "Followed us from the Yardarm."

"Some damn hippy afraid of a bust," Saunders scoffed. "Will you just get in!"

His expression wounded, Mandarin complied.

Backing the Ford out of the parking place, Saunders turned down Forest Avenue. Mandarin took a last swig from the Rolling Rock he had carried with him from the bar, then stuck his arm out and fired the green bottle in the general direction of his imagined skulker. From the darkness came the rattle of breaking glass.

"Ka-pow!" echoed Russ.

Saunders winced and drove on in silence.

"Hey, you went past the clinic," Russ protested several blocks later.

"Look, I'll run you back down in the morning."

"I can drive OK."

"Will you let me do this as a favor?" Saunders asked, not making it clear whose favor he meant it to be.

Mandarin sighed and shrugged. "Home, James."

Pressing his lips tightly, the detective turned onto Kingston Pike. After a while he said: "You know, Russ, there's several on the force who'd really like to put your ass in a sling. Drunken driving is a really tough charge."

When Mandarin started to argue, Saunders shouted him down. "Look, Russ. I know this is rough on you. It is on all of us who knew Curtiss. But damn it, this isn't going to make it any better for you. I thought you finally learned that for yourself after Alicia . . ."

"Goddamn it, Ed! Don't *you* start lecturing me now!"

"OK, Russ," his friend subsided, remembering the hell Mandarin had gone through three years before. "Just wanted to remind you that you'd tried this blind alley once before."

"Ed, I drink only socially these days." He waited for the other to say something, finally added: "Except for an occasional binge, maybe."

"Just trying to make a friendly suggestion."

"Well, I can do without friendly suggestions."

"OK, Russ."

They drove the rest of the way in silence. Saunders expected the psychiatrist to drop off, but the other sat rigidly upright all the way. Too much adrenalin, Saunders decided.

He pulled into the long driveway of Mandarin's Cherokee Hills estate. It was a rambling Tudor style house of the 1920s, constructed when this had been the snob residential section of Knoxville. Although most of the new money had now moved into the suburbs, Cherokee Hills had resisted urban decay with stately aloofness.

"I'll give you a ring in the morning," Saunders promised.

"It's all right; I'll call a cab," muttered Russ.

Saunders shrugged. "Good night, Russ."

He climbed out of the car. "Sure."

Saunders waited until he was in the front door before driving off.

The phone started to ring while Russ was dropping Alka-Seltzers into a highball glass. Holding the frothing glass carefully, he picked up the receiver.

"Hello." He wondered if he could finish the conversation before the tablets finished their dancing disintegration.

"Dr. Mandarin?"

"Speaking." He didn't recognize the voice.

"This is Morris Sheldon from the Frostfire Press. Been trying to get in touch with you this evening."

"Yeah? Well, what can I do for you, Morris old buddy?"

"Well, I know you were close to poor Curtiss Stryker. I believe he mentioned to me that you were giving him some medical opinions relative to the research he was doing on this last book."

"I was," Russ acknowledged, taking time for a swallow of Alka-Seltzer.

"Do you know how far along he'd gotten . . . before the accident?"

"Well now, you probably know better than I. All I'd seen were several of the early chapters."

"I'd wondered if you perhaps had seen the rough draft of the chapters you were involved in."

"The poltergeist house? No, didn't know he'd had time to put that in rough draft yet."

"Yes, he had. At least he said so in our last conversation."

"Well, that's news to me. I was out of town the last couple days." Mandarin downed the last of the seltzer. "Why do you ask?"

Sheldon paused. "Well, frankly I'd hoped Curtiss might have passed a carbon of it on to you. He didn't send me the typescript. And we're rather afraid it was with his papers when the accident occurred. If so, I'm afraid his last chapter has been lost forever."

"Probably so," Russ agreed, his voice carefully civil. "But why are you concerned?"

"Well, as a friend of Curtiss's you'll be glad to know that Frostfire Press had decided not to let his last book go unfinished. We've approached his close friend and colleague. Brooke Hamilton . . ."

"Oh," said Mandarin, revelation dawning in his voice. "Hey, you mean his confidant and bosom pal, Brooke Hamilton, hopes to use Stryker's notes and all for a posthumous collaboration?"

"That's right," Sheldon agreed. "And naturally we want to locate as much of Stryker's material as we can."

"Well, then you're in luck, Morris old buddy. Stryker's dear friend, that critically acclaimed writer and all around *bon vivant,* Brooke Hamilton, was so overcome with grief at his mentor's death that he wasted no time in breaking into Stryker's office and stealing every shred of Stryker's unpublished writing. Just give him time to sort through the wastebasket, and dear old Brooke will keep you in posthumous collaborations for the next ten years.''

"Now wait, Dr. Mandarin! You mean you're accusing Brooke Hamilton of . . .''

"Of following his natural talents. And may the pair of you be buggered in hell by ghouls! Good night, Morris old buddy.''

He slammed the receiver over Sheldon's rejoinder, and swore for a while.

Returning to the sink, he carefully rinsed his glass, then added a few ice cubes. There was bourbon in the decanter.

Sipping his drink, he collapsed on the den couch and glared at the silent television screen. He didn't feel like watching the idiot tube tonight. Nor did he care to go to bed, despite extended lack of sleep. His belly felt sour, his head ached. He was too damn mad and disgusted to relax.

Ghouls. All of them. Gathering for the feast. *More Haunted Houses of the South,* by Curtiss Stryker and Brooke Hamilton. Probably they'd already approached Stryker's agent, set up a contract. Stryker would spin in his grave. If he ever reached his grave.

Mandarin wondered if he ought to phone Stryker's agent and protest—then remembered that he had no idea who his agent had been. No, make that *was,* not *had been.* As a literary property, Curtiss Stryker was suddenly more alive than before.

Sheldon would know who the agent was. Maybe he should phone and ask. Russ discarded the idea. Who was he to protest, anyway? Just another obnoxious "friend of the deceased.''

His thoughts turned to Stryker's unfinished book, to the missing last chapter. Curtiss had promised to give him the carbon. Probably Hamilton had made off with that along with his other tomb spoils.

Maybe not.

Stryker kept a file of all his more recent manuscripts. A big filing cabinet in his study at home. Sometimes he worked there at night—when he was pushed by a deadline, or really caught up in something.

Russ hauled himself to his feet. A picture was taking shape. Stryker due at a friend's home for dinner, knowing he wouldn't be back until late. But too interested in his new chapter to leave the material in his office. Instead he brings his notes home and works on the manuscript until time to leave. Had anyone thought to check his study?

Someone would soon—if they hadn't already. Climbing the stairs to his bedroom, Russ fumbled through his dresser. There it was—in a box crammed mostly with cuff-links, tie-tacs and spare keys. The key to his house that Stryker had given him once when the author left for several months knocking about Mexico.

A look of angry resolve on his black-stubbled jaw, Mandarin snatched up the key and stalked to the garage. The battery was low in the old GTO that he'd kept because it had been Alicia's favorite car, but the engine caught at the last moment. With an echo of throaty exhausts, he backed out of the garage.

His plans were only half formulated, as he carefully steered the rumbling Pontiac through the downtown streets. He meant to check Stryker's study immediately, however. If the chapter manuscripts were there, he'd take it to read, and Brooke Hamilton could go to hell. And if he didn't find the manuscript—maybe that would be because somebody had already broken into the house. A horrid grin twisted Mandarin's face. He'd like for that to be the case. Like to show the evidence to Saunders, place charges against Brooke Hamilton for stealing from a dead man.

It was past 11, and traffic was thinning out—for which Russ was grateful. With far more caution than was his custom, he overcame his impatience and made the short drive out Lyons View Pike without mishap.

He turned into the empty drive and cut his lights. Stryker's house, an old brick farmhouse laid out in a *T*, hunched dark beneath huge white pines. The windows were black against the brick from the front; the remainder of the house was shadowed by the looming pines from what little moonlight the clouds hadn't kept.

Mandarin remembered a flashlight in the glove compartment and dug it out. The beam was yellow and weak, but enough to see by. Suspiciously he played the light across the front of the house. Seeing nothing untoward, he started around back.

The front of the house was two storeys and contained living quarters. Like the stem of a *T*, the rear section came out perpendicularly from the rest—a single storey wing that housed kitchen and storage. A side porch came off from one side of the kitchen wing, where Stryker and Russ had spent many a summer evening, slouched in wooden rockers and with something cold to drink.

Having seen nothing out of the ordinary, Russ crossed the unscreened porch to the kitchen door, jabbed his key at the lock. As he fumbled for the knob, the door nudged open.

Mandarin brought up his flashlight. The old-fashioned latch had been forced.

He breathed a silent curse. Stealthily he pushed open the door, stepped inside.

Thunder spat flame from across the room. Russ pitched backward onto the porch, and the flame burst across his skull.

VIII

She was the most beautiful, and at the same time the most frightening, woman Mandarin had ever seen. She danced in a whirl of blue, how could his heart forget? Blue were the skies, and blue were her eyes, just like the blue skirt she wore . . .

And she whispered to him as she waltzed, and the things she whispered to him were beautiful, and Mandarin wanted to hear more, even though her whispers terrified him.

And the more she danced and whispered and sang, the worse his vertigo became, and he was dizzy and falling, and he was clutching at her blue skirt to keep from falling, and she kept dancing away from him, and he cried out to her to come back . . .

He didn't understand . . .

But he *had* to understand . . .

"Come back!" he screamed. His voice was a tortured rasp.

The blue light became a lance of blue flame, searing his brain. And her hands of coldest ice pierced through him and seized upon his soul, and the blue lady was drawing him away, pulling him through the darkness . . .

Dimly, through the haze of throbbing pain, Mandarin became aware of the man bending over him.

Gritting his teeth, he forced his eyes to focus. It was hard. A bright beam of light bored into his face.

"Christ! He's coming around, Sid!"

The light swept away.

Mandarin struggled to rise—groaned and fell back. Bright flashes of pain rippled from the numbing ache of his skull.

"Just stay put, buddy. Jesus! We thought you were . . ."

Russ's vision was clearing. Blotchy green afterimages swam across his eyes. But he saw the patrolman's uniform, and the rising wave of panic subsided.

"Neighbor says she knows who he is, Hardin." The other voice drifted from farther away. "He's a friend of the guy who owned this place. Drops by every week or so."

Russ dully recognized the floor of Stryker's side porch spread out around him. It was damp and sticky. He could hear a woman's voice speaking from the kitchen, though he couldn't follow her words.

"I think the bullet must've just grazed the top of his forehead," the first man called out. "There's blood all over the back of his head, but it looks like he just busted his scalp open falling back against the post here. You're one lucky hard-headed bastard, buddy."

His partner was examining Russ's billfold. "Name's Dr. Russell Mandarin. He's that shrink friend of Lieutenant Saunders, I think. Hope that's the ambulance I hear coming. He's been out a damn long time."

"I'm all right," protested Mandarin without conviction. He tried again to rise, made it to his knees. The porch seemed to whirl and pitch. He shut his eyes hard and waited.

An arm steadied his shoulder. "Maybe you better stay down, buddy. You got blood leaking all across the back of your head."

Doggedly Mandarin got his feet under him, lurched onto

a porch rocker. The chair almost tipped, then steadied.
With careful fingers he touched his forehead, found pain
there. His hair was clotted with blood. Squinting across
the narrow porch, Russ saw the support post opposite the
back door. He remembered a gunshot, and falling backward. He must have bashed his head against the oak pillar.

"Dr. Mandarin? Are you all right?"

Russ recognized Mrs. Lieberman, Stryker's closest neighbor. Russ had often kidded Stryker that the widow had
designs on him, and Stryker would always reply that only
a cad tells.

"I heard that loud old car of yours turn into Mr. Stryker's
driveway," she was saying. "And then I heard a shot. I
thought it must be a gang of burglars, and so I called the
police."

"And it's good you did, ma'am. They might have
finished the job on your friend here otherwise."

The one called Hardin looked down the driveway. "Here's
the ambulance—and our back-up, now that we don't need it."

"I think I heard them miss the turn-off twice," his
partner replied.

"What's happening?" Mandarin asked, recovering enough
to become aware of his situation.

"You been shot, Doc, but you're going to be all right
now."

"Shot?"

"Reckon you busted in on whoever it was that'd broke
into the house. Can't see that anything's taken, but the
place is sure a mess."

IX

Saunders was waiting for him when Mandarin got out of x-ray. Russ had insisted on viewing the films himself, after making enough of a scene that the radiologist seemed a little disappointed to find no evidence of fracture or subdural. Russ let them wheel him back down to the ER, where a nervous resident began to patch him up.

"I am goddamn glad to see you here," was Saunders' first comment.

"Same to you, sideways," Russ said. "Did you know those two clowns of yours had radioed me in as DOA? Damn lucky I didn't bleed out waiting."

"Damn lucky you got a thick skull and a hippy haircut. Somebody bounced a bullet off your head, and if they'd aimed an inch or so lower, it'd've gone between your eyes instead of parting your hair. I hear you busted loose a porch rail banging it with your head afterward."

"Nothing much hurt but my good looks," Russ allowed. "They want to keep me overnight for observation, but I'm heading home from here. I can damn well observe myself—no point in being a doctor if you can't change your own oil. And don't tell me the one about '. . . has a fool for a physician.' "

Saunders was serious now. Too serious.

"Russ, I'm going to tell you that the only reason you're not headed from here to the station is because you were lying there DOA on Stryker's porch at the same time Brooke Hamilton was being murdered."

Mandarin decided he was still suffering the effects of his concussion. "What's that about Hamilton?"

Saunders was looking for a cigarette, then remembered he couldn't smoke there. "Just came from his place. A boyfriend let himself in around midnight, found Hamilton tied to a chair, throat had just been cut. And he'd been cut up pretty good elsewhere before he got his second smile. After that business this afternoon, I was afraid it was you I'd be bringing in. I was at your house when word came in that you were dead at the time of the murder. Reckon we'll hold his boyfriend now instead."

"Jesus!" Russ muttered. It was all coming too fast for him.

"These queers do some weird shit when they have their love spats," Saunders informed him. "Likely high on pot and LSD."

"I didn't know Hamilton was gay."

"No? Well, he *looked* queer. I can spot them. Anyway, if you hadn't been busy getting shot in the head at Curtiss's house at the time Hamilton was last seen alive, you'd be in worse trouble now."

"I think I want to go home."

"I'll see that you get there," Saunders said. "Only this time you stay put."

"Scout's honor." Russ held up three fingers.

Saunders watched him without amusement. "And when you get there, you can help fill out a report. Tell us if anything's missing."

"Missing?"

"Somebody'd broke into your house right before we got there."

X

Mandarin had a bottle of Percodan tablets for pain—
contraindicated, of course, in the presence of recent head
injury—and he prescribed himself a couple and washed
them down with a medicinal glass of Jack Daniels. He
supposed he should sue himself for malpractice. After all,
he'd only been permitted to leave the hospital after signing
an "against medical advice" form. A fool for a physician.

Was it possible for a head to ache any worse than his
did? He had a gash above his forehead where the bullet
had grazed his scalp, a lump across the back of his skull
from his fall, and a terminal hangover. Russ almost wished
his assailant had aimed lower. Saunders' people hadn't
turned up any brass, and Saunders was of the opinion that
Russ's attacker had got off a lucky shot with a junk .22
revolver—probably one of his hippy dopefiend patients.
Typical of the times, Saunders judged, and with our boys
dying in Viet Nam while scum like this dodged the draft.

Three break-ins in one night—not to mention the bur-
glary of Stryker's office the day before—hardly seemed
random, Mandarin had argued. Saunders had pointed out
that these were only a few of the dozens of break-ins that
took place each night, and that it was all due to drugs, and
that if certain psychiatrists would stick to shrinking heads
and let the police go about their business, a lot of this sort
of thing would be stopped.

Russ promised to go to bed.

But neither the Percodan nor the bourbon could ease the
pain in his skull. And the thoughts kept running through

his brain. And every time he closed his eyes, she was
there.

I dream of that night with you,
Darling, when first we met . . .

Mandarin realized that his eyes weren't closed. She was
there. In his room. And she whispered to him . . .

Mandarin screamed and sat up. His drink, balanced on
the back of the couch, fell over and spilled melted ice
cubes onto his lap.

The dancing image faded.

Never, thought Mandarin, *never* mix Percodan and alcohol. He was shaking badly, and his feet seemed to float
above the floor as he stumbled into the kitchen for another
drink. Maybe he ought to take a couple Valiums. Christ,
he was in worse shape now than when Alicia died.

Could a poltergeist direct a bullet?

Russ noticed that he was pouring bourbon over the top
of his glass. He gulped down a mouthful, not tasting it.
His hands were steadier.

Could a poltergeist direct a bullet?

Either he was succumbing to paranoid fantasies and
alcoholic hallucinations, or maybe he should have stayed
in the hospital for observation. Was he going over the
edge? What the hell—he hadn't been worth shooting since
Alicia died.

Someone thought he was worth shooting.

Could a poltergeist direct a bullet?

Was *he* haunted?

It wasn't random; Saunders was wrong. There *was* a
pattern, and it had all started that afternoon when Gayle
Corrington told them about her poltergeist. A ghostly les-
bian who dabbled in the occult and who liked blue. The
stuff of one of Stryker's pulp thrillers, but now there were

two people dead, and someone—or something—had broken into the homes of everyone involved and scattered things about like a vengeful whirlwind.

Mandarin decided that a walk in the early dawn would do him good. He just might be sober by the time he reached the clinic and his car.

Could a poltergeist *deflect* a bullet?

XI

This one ends on a bright summer morning, and a fresh dew on the roses that perfume the dawn.

Russ Mandarin eased his Jensen Interceptor into the driveway and killed the engine. All at once it seemed absurdly dramatic to him. He really should have phoned Gayle Corrington before driving over to her house at this hour.

Or maybe he shouldn't have.

He closed the door quietly and walked up to the carport. The white Corvette was parked there as before, only before there hadn't been a scraping of maroon paint along its scored right front fender. Fiberglass is a bitch to touch up.

Russ tried the doorbell long enough to decide that Gayle Corrington wasn't going to answer. Either not at home (her car was still there) or a sound sleeper. Russ pounded loudly against the door. After a time his knuckles began to hurt. He stopped and thought about it.

Nothing made sense. Mandarin wished he had a drink—what was always a good answer to any crisis.

He ought to call Saunders, tell him about the maroon paint on Gayle Corrington's white Corvette. Maybe just a fender-bender, but it might match up with the crease on

the left side of Stryker's Buick. And so what if it did?
Curtiss was a terrible driver—he might well have paid
Gayle a second visit, scraped up against her car in parking.

Nothing made sense.

Just this: Gayle Corrington had told Stryker *something*
in the course of the interview—while Mandarin had been
out of the room. Stryker had been excited about it, had
written it into his account of the haunting. And someone
had gone to a lot of trouble to make certain that whatever
Stryker had discovered would never be published.

Only Gayle Corrington had freely asked Stryker to investigate her haunted house.

Nothing made sense.

Mandarin thought he heard a television set going. Maybe
Gayle was around back, catching some early morning sun,
and couldn't hear his knock. Worth trying.

Russ headed toward the rear of the house. As he reached
the patio, he saw Prissy lying beside a holly bush. At first
he thought the little border collie was asleep.

Not random. A pattern.

The sliding glass door from the patio was curtained and
at first glance appeared to be closed. Russ saw that the
catch had been forced, and he cautiously slid the glass
panel open, stepped inside.

Gayle Corrington was wearing dark slacks and a black
sweatshirt. She was hog-tied with her wrists bound back to
her ankles, her body arched like a bow upon the couch.
Her lips were taped with adhesive, but the cord knotted
tightly into her neck would assure that she would never cry
out.

Russ stared at her dumbly. He knew there was no point
in searching for a pulse.

"Hello, Russ," said Stryker. "Come on in."

Russ did as he was told.

Curtiss Stryker was straightening out from where he worked over the brick hearth. The hearth had been lifted away, revealing an opening beneath the floor.

"Used brick hearth on a mountain stone fireplace. Should have tipped me off from the first—an obvious lapse in taste." Stryker was holding a Colt Woodsman. It was pointed at Mandarin's heart.

"Rumors of my death have been greatly exaggerated," said Stryker.

"You son of a bitch," said Mandarin.

"Probably. But you just stand still where you are."

Russ nodded toward Gayle's body. "Your work?"

"Yes. While you were ringing. Just not quite in the nick of time, Doctor. But don't waste any tears on our Mrs. Corrington. She tried to kill both of us, after all—and I gather she was certain that you, at least, were most decidedly dead. This is her gun, and she would be disappointed to learn that her aim was not as infallible as she imagined."

"I don't get it," Russ said. "What are you doing?"

Stryker glanced toward the opened hearth. "Just getting a little social security. Maybe you can understand."

"I don't understand a goddamned thing! I came here to ask Gayle what it was that she told you while I was out of the room that day. Seems that a lot of people are interested."

"You might as well know," Stryker decided. "She wanted me to perform an exorcism."

"An exorcism?"

"Or something to that effect. She'd read my books on the occult, decided I was a better ghostchaser than a priest would be. Maybe she'd already tried a priest."

"I don't follow."

"Then I'll make it short and snappy."

"Is this the point in your story there the villain always explains everything to the hero before he shoots him?"

"It is. I'm afraid this story won't have a happy ending, though. After all, an author has his privileges."

"I wept for you."

"I know. I'll weep for you."

Stryker kept the Colt Woodsman steady in the direction of Mandarin's chest. Russ recalled that Curtiss had always bragged about his marksmanship.

"Our Mrs. Corrington changed a few details, and she changed a few names. She played the part of Cass in the highly revised account she gave us of this house. She and her Libby were medical secretaries. They had access to patients' records, and they knew various prominent citizens who had certain sexual quirks. Knowing their particular weaknesses, it was simple enough to lure them out here for an odd orgy of two—black magic, S&M, any sort of kink their secret selves desired. Then there were the hidden mikes and camera, the two-way mirrors. Made for some lovely footage. Here's a respected publisher who likes to dress up in women's clothing and be whipped, here's a noted doctor who prefers to give enemas to submissive girls. Maybe just a Baptist preacher who can't get a blow job from his wife. They knew about them, and preyed on them.

"But they needed another girl—another feminine one for their fantasies-delivered orgies. So they brought in a third girl—and that was a crowd. Cass—Gayle—liked her better than Libby, and Libby got jealous. She was going to blow the whistle on the entire operation, unless the other girl was sent away. But that was too dangerous, and Gayle was growing tired of Libby. They had a special black sabbath orgy that night, and when it was over they gave Libby an injection of insulin. Your friend, Dr. Royce Blaine, didn't give any trouble over signing the death certificate; after all, he was in the photos. Later, when

Gayle grew tired of Tina, she married Dr. Blaine—probably saved her life, his too, maybe.''

"But why did Mrs. Corrington call you in on this?" Russ wondered if he could jump the older man.

"Because she really did think she was being haunted. Nothing more than a nuisance, but it preyed on her nerves. So she made up this plausible story, and she reckoned I'd perform some magical miracle, just like the heroes in my stories. But she didn't reckon on how good a researcher I was. I got suspicious—you know: 'Doctor, I have this friend . . .' and it didn't take long to dig out the facts. It happened while you were off in New York."

"So then?"

"Well, I wrote down my findings, made a carbon for you, then set out for another talk with Gayle Corrington. Of course, then I didn't know about the blackmail angle—I just wanted to confront Gayle with the fact that I knew her part in the story was more than just an innocent bystander.

"She followed me after I left her house, ran me off the road into the lake. By then I knew about the blackmail— she was too upset with me to lie convincingly that night—so I thought I'd just lie doggo for a few days and see what happened. I destroyed my notes, but that little bastard Brooke Hamilton beat me to my office and stole your carbon of the chapter rough. I caught up with him last night, made him tell me where he'd hidden everything, then destroyed it all—and that little shit. In the meantime, Gayle knew of my carbons, so she was checking out my house and afterwards yours. You walked in on her at my house, and she thought she'd killed you. That's two mistakes. You should have seen her expression when she walked in here afterward. Thought she'd seen a real ghost this time."

"Just Uncle Dudley in a monster suit."

"Just like one of my old thrillers. No ghosts. Just greed. And a guilty conscience that made ghosts out of chance phenomena."

"Now what?"

"I take over the racket, that's all. After a little persuasion, Gayle told me what I already knew—that the films and tapes were all hidden in a little safe here beneath the raised hearth. I've got enough on some of our city's finest and wealthiest to retire in style. I'll just make an appearance later on today, say I was knocked for a loop by my accident, took a day or two wandering around the lakeside to remember who I was."

"What about me?"

"Now that does bother me, Russ. I hadn't counted on your dropping in like this. I think you'll be the drugged-out killer in the story—the one who conveniently takes his life when he realizes what he's done."

"Saunders won't buy that."

"Sure he will. You've been walking around town with a screw loose ever since your wife died—before that maybe. You were the one who blew her diagnosis when she complained of chronic headaches."

"I was your friend, Curtiss."

"Writers don't have friends. Only deadlines. And cheating publishers. And meddling editors. And carping reviewers. And checks that never come when they're supposed to come, and are always short when they do come. I've scraped along for a living at this damn trade for over forty years, and I'm still living hand to mouth, and I'm just an old hack to my fellow writers. This is my chance to make someone else pay—pay big."

Stryker steadied the pistol. "Sorry, Russ. I'll miss you. Hope you can understand."

The Victrola behind them made a rattle and whir. There was an audible *clunk* as the heavy tone arm descended.

Stryker looked toward it for an instant. Russ started to go for him. Stryker nailed him through the upper left shoulder with his first shot. Russ collapsed.

I dream of that night with you . . .

"Going to be a tough job of suicide now," Mandarin whispered.

"I'll figure something," Stryker assured him.

Blue were the skies
And blue were your eyes

Stryker leveled his pistol again. "Very interesting."

Come back, blue lady, come back

"There are too many dead!" Russ managed. "She's grown too strong."

"I never really believed in ghosts," said Stryker, lining up on Russ's heart.

Don't be blue anymore.

There was a sudden scraping at the fireplace behind them.

From its brackets, the Parker shotgun swung away from the stone wall. It seemed to hesitate an instant, then slowly fell to the hearth, stock downward.

Stryker turned to stare at it, open-mouthed in wonder. He was still gaping into its double barrels, looking down into the blackness within, when both shells fired at once.